Ensnaring the
Dove

Jayne Castel

All characters and situations in this publication are fictitious, and any resemblance to living persons is purely coincidental.

Ensnaring the Dove, by Jayne Castel

Published by Winter Mist Press

ISBN: 978-1-99-117477-2 (Paperback)

Edited by Tim Burton
Cover design by Winter Mist Press
Cover photography courtesy of www.depositphotos.com

Map of Briton tribes, Ptolemy Cosmographia, courtesy of Wikipedia Commons.

Visit Jayne's website: www.jaynecastel.com

He's her protector. But will he end up her ruin? A Roman noblewoman, a Brigante warrior, and forbidden love across cultures in Ancient Britain.

Colombia Juventus is promised to a Roman officer posted upon Hadrian's Wall. Determined to be with her betrothed, she sets off across the seas to Britannia to join him. But when Brigante rebels attack the supply convoy she's traveling in, Colombia's privileged, sheltered life shatters.

Aedan is a Brigante chieftain's son, yet his fate has always been entwined with the Romans. He fought them, lost, and was taken as a slave. He then gained his freedom only to discover he no longer belonged in his old life. Now he's part of a band of outlaws that preys on travelers to the northern frontier.

But when an attack on a Roman convoy turns savage, and Aedan steps in to stop a noblewoman from being raped, his destiny is again tied to those he once served.

Colombia finds herself on the run with a man who will change her life forever.

Set in 2nd Century AD, during the Roman occupation of what is now Britain and Scotland, ENSNARING THE DOVE is a powerful, steamy standalone romance about finding true love in the unlikeliest of places.

***

For Timbo.

***

MAP

NOVANTAE
SELGOVAE
Hadrian's
Wall
BRIGANTES
PARISI
BRIGANTES
Humber
Estuary
CORNOVII
The Wash
Vnys Môn
(Anglesey)
ORDOVICES
CORIELTAUVI
ICENI
CATUVELLAUNI
DOBUNNI
TRINO-
VANTES
DEMETAE
DOBUNNI
SILURES
ATREBATES
CANTIACI
Severn
Estuary
DUROTRIGES
BELGAE
REGNI
DAMNONII
Isle of
Wight
Peoples of
Southern Britain
c. 150
Based on Ptolemy's map
0   km   100
0   mi   50

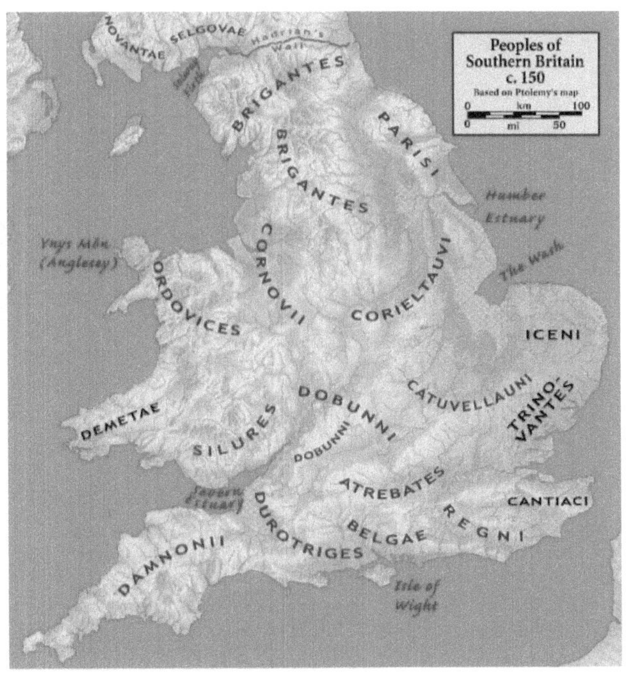

"Look not mournfully into the past,
it comes not back again."
—Henry Wadsworth Longfellow

I. GHOSTS

Moedin Fort,
The River Wear, Brigantia
Northern Britannia

Late summer, 122 AD

GOING HOME WAS a mistake.

Even as Aedan approached the fort, his gut clenched in foreboding.

Many years had passed since he'd last seen Moedin—although, at first glance, it appeared unchanged. Birds chattered in the oakwood that surrounded the wide river valley, and his father's fort still perched high and proud, crowning a spur of land above the lazy curve of the Wear. High walls of turf and wood encircled a cluster of sod roof dwellings, and wisps of pale smoke drifted lazily into the robin's-egg-blue sky.

Leaving the track that hugged the southern bank of the river, Aedan took the path leading up to the fort. It was a steep climb, and he was sweating by the time he reached the top.

A deep ditch, spanned by a narrow wooden bridge, encircled the landward approach. Aedan's forebears had chosen this site well, for the Wear enclosed the fort on three sides. His grandfather had strengthened Moedin's defenses to protect it from neighboring tribes. However, in the last years, the fort had been forced to defend itself against a far worse foe: the Caesars who'd marched over this isle, claiming it as their own.

Inside the walls, Aedan inhaled the aromas of stewing mutton and baking bread. The late afternoon sun gilded the fawn-colored stone of the squat huts, outlining the bulk of the largest of them—his father's roundhouse.

Aedan's pulse quickened.

He'd thought of his father often over the years. Colmus, son of Bel, was a stern man who'd been hard on all his children. He'd demanded much from them. Had he spared his eldest son a care over the past years?

Was Aedan dead to him now?

The knot in Aedan's belly tightened further, although he attempted to push aside the worry. Aye, he'd been nervous about returning to his people—but, like a beacon burning bright upon a faraway hill, Moedin had drawn him back.

This was his home, after all. He belonged here; once his father died, he would rule this fort. His mouth tightened then, his step quickening. The Romans had stripped much away from him, yet he wouldn't let them take his birthright as well.

He walked the narrow street between tightly packed clusters of dwellings, his gaze taking in achingly familiar sights. Children ran barefoot across the hard-packed earth, fowl pecked in the dust, and women with red or brown hair gathered washing hanging on lines outside their cottages. Many of them had bright blue eyes, like his own, and they watched him curiously, their gazes taking in the blue swirls etched into the skin of his upper arms—markings of their people.

Aedan's pulse quickened. The sight of the women reminded him of the red-haired lass he'd left behind. A lass he'd never forgotten.

There were few men about at this hour—although Aedan knew where to find them.

It was the end of a long working day. The warriors would have downed tools and retired to the chieftain's roundhouse. They'd be seated around the fire, hands clasped around cups of ale.

Aedan's step quickened as he approached his father's home, his gaze taking in the conical, newly-thatched roof. The wide wattle door was open, and the rumble of male voices, punctuated by barks of laughter, drifted out into the still air.

A smile curved Aedan's lips. Despite his uneasiness at his return, he longed to be part of this again—to sit with his father, brother, and their warriors and converse in his own tongue.

To belong somewhere again.

He could have hesitated before entering the roundhouse, could have waited outside for a few moments until someone inside noticed they had a visitor.

But this was Aedan's birthplace. He wasn't a guest here.

And so, he ducked through the doorway, careful not to catch the crown of his head on the low stone lintel, and stepped inside.

Conversation died at his entrance.

Gazes swiveled in his direction, faces hardening at the sight of a stranger in their midst.

Aedan straightened up to his full height, waiting for someone to recognize him. The interior of the house was as dark and smoky as he recalled. Two hearths dominated the space, and shadowy alcoves, screened by sheepskins, lined the walls. A group of men sat on the floor around the largest of the hearths, served by a red-haired woman, while two slaves, their iron collars gleaming in the dull glow of the fire, cooked rounds of bread upon a griddle at the second hearth at the back of the space.

Everyone stared blatantly for a moment or two before the woman who'd been refilling the warriors' cups from a ewer gasped. "Aedan? Is that you?"

Aedan's heart kicked against his ribs at the voice he hadn't heard in years—soft and sweet like a lark's song.

Tall and slender, her russet hair piled high on her head and a golden torc around her throat, Bronwen had matured from a gangly lass to a lovely woman. Even in the dim light inside the roundhouse, she glowed. Her pale skin was lustrous, and her green eyes gleamed.

An instant later, he noticed the swell of her belly under the long, sleeveless tunic she wore.

The warmth that had suffused him at seeing Bronwen again seeped away, leaving a chill in its wake.

Aedan's attention shifted right to the man who sat at the head of the great hearth. Unlike his warriors, he reclined upon a low chair carved out of oak.

It wasn't Colmus, son of Bel.

Instead, the man was young, with a thick head of light auburn hair and a well-groomed mustache as yet unmarked by strands of grey. Sharp blue eyes watched Aedan—a familiar gaze indeed.

Aedan smiled, even as his chest constricted. If his younger brother sat upon the High Seat, then his father was no longer with them. "Deaglan."

The chieftain stared back at him for a few moments more before speaking. "Greetings, brother."

It wasn't the warmest welcome Aedan had ever received. Likewise, the gazes around the fire pit were wary rather than joyful.

It was as if an unwelcome spirit had just ventured into their midst.

Aedan shouldn't have been surprised. He was a reminder of a bitter defeat they all likely wished to forget. Once again, misgiving tickled his nape.

Maybe the Romans had stolen more from him than he'd realized.

"Back from the dead, eh?" Deaglan took a swig from his horn of ale, his gaze never leaving Aedan's face.

Aedan nodded. "As you can see, I'm very much alive. I was taken that day ... and have been a slave for the past seven years." He paused then, his pulse quickening. "But no longer ... I've just been given my freedom."

This admission caused tension to ripple around the fireside. Warriors exchanged glances, and some of them even murmured oaths under their breaths.

"That'll account for your strange look," Deaglan said finally, raking his gaze over his elder brother, from the crown of his head to his feet.

Aedan shrugged. He knew his short hair, clean-shaven jaw, and lack of mustache made him stand out. However, his clothing, at least, was no longer Roman. Before departing from Vindolanda, he'd cast aside the tunica and sandals he'd worn as a slave, for woolen bracae—trousers—and a sleeveless tunic of bright ochre fastened with a narrow leather belt. Light leather boots shod his feet.

"I'm still me, brother," he murmured, holding Deaglan's eye.

The pair of them locked gazes for a few moments, the tension inside the roundhouse drawing tighter still.

"Why did those shit-eaters let you go then?" his brother asked finally.

"I was slave to the general, Justinian Aquila," Aedan replied. The name of the dreaded 'Eagle' made the faces inside the shadowy space harden. "And spent much time in Caledonia ... mostly at the fort of Ardoch." He paused then, aware of the aggression that now glinted in the eyes of the men he'd once named as friends. "When the north fell, Aquila moved to Vindolanda. The emperor wasn't pleased with his failure and stripped him of rank. The Eagle now commands the garrison there ... and he took one of the Cruthini as a wife ... a woman who'd once been his slave. After that, he gave all the slaves in his household their freedom."

Deaglan inclined his head, gaze glinting. Aedan knew how strange his tale sounded; indeed, the love that had blossomed between Aquila and his willful slave Fenella had shocked everyone.

He'd expected a response from his brother, yet none was forthcoming. Eventually, Aedan cleared his throat and broke the heavy silence. "When did father die?"

"Four winters past," Deaglan replied, no emotion in his voice. "A fever carried him off."

Aedan nodded, even as something deep inside his chest clenched. Colmus had died thinking his firstborn son was lost forever. He wished he could have said goodbye to him. It was just another regret that Aedan would have to add to a growing list.

Deaglan motioned to Bronwen then. She moved close to the chieftain, taking the hand he outstretched.

No words were needed. With just one gesture, Deaglan had told him that the comely Bronwen—the woman Aedan had once loved—was his wife.

Aedan's pulse quickened further, a sickly sensation washing over him.

Bronwen watched him steadily, her lovely face veiled. Likewise, Deaglan's gaze was shuttered.

Everyone, even the slaves, was watching him now, with rapt fascination. As if they were all wondering what he'd do next.

"Congratulations," he ground out. The words were difficult. He had to force them up his throat and between his teeth. There was a part of him that wanted to fly across the hearth and smash his fist into his brother's smug face.

Aedan and Bronwen had grown up knowing they would wed one day—knowing that they were meant for each other. They'd been close, two halves of one whole. They'd been lovers too, unable to wait for their wedding day, which had been just five days away when he'd ridden off to fight the Caesars.

Memories of the pair of them lying naked together in a woodland glade, in the aftermath of their loving, had sustained Aedan over the long years of his slavery.

But no longer.

That fateful battle had changed everything, and Aedan had been a fool to think he could return here and step back into his old life.

Seven years was a long while. Had he really expected his lover to wait for him?

Bitterness flooded his mouth as he realized that he had.

"Thank you," Bronwen murmured.

Deaglan's mouth stretched into a smile. However, his gaze narrowed. "Bronwen has borne me two strapping sons." He patted her belly with a possessive air that made Aedan itch to kill him. "And now carries another."

"Congratulations," Aedan repeated, even as his pulse roared in his ears. Dizziness swept over him then.

"Why did you come back, Aedan?" Deaglan asked finally. His tone was bland, yet there was no mistaking the iron just beneath. "Are you here to challenge my rule? To claim your *birthright*?"

Aedan's hands curled into fists at his sides. Once he might have answered 'aye'—but looking around this smoky roundhouse, at the warriors who had sworn blood oaths to his brother, he knew he was an interloper. None of these men would follow him.

"We thought you'd fallen in battle," Bronwen said then, her voice barely above a whisper.

"He should have done," Deaglan replied, his tone sharpening. "A chieftain's son who has lived as a Roman slave has forfeited all honor."

The chieftain's words fell like axe blows inside the roundhouse, each one cleaving deep into Aedan's chest. Whatever frail hope he'd been clinging to that he'd find peace in this place dissipated like morning mist on a hot summer's day.

The memories that had sustained him, the hopes that had kept him going over the years, crumbled. Aquila had freed him, yet his former master couldn't erase the dishonor that now followed Aedan like a foul stench. A Brigante warrior couldn't live as a Roman slave and expect to be welcomed home again.

Aye, it had been a grave mistake to return here.

He was a ghost—and ghosts had no place amongst the living.

II. A WOMAN OF THE WORLD

A year later ...

"LOOK AT THEM ... arrogant turds."

"Aye ... yet their conceit will be their undoing. Look at all those carts. This will be our richest haul yet."

Lying on his belly, on the edge of a scrubby hill, Aedan listened to his companions' whispered conversation, while his own attention remained focused on the long shadow that traveled the valley below.

The first warrior, Lucon, was right.

The Romans marched across this territory—Brigantia—as if they held dominion over not just Britannia, but the sun and the moon as well. They made no attempt to conceal their passing or to blend in with their surroundings. Soldiers, both on foot and on horseback, led the supply convoy—crimson cloaks flashed as bright as blood, and silver armor gleamed despite the dull day. Their pilums bristled, making it look as if a giant, prickly caterpillar passed through the vale.

Aedan's mouth thinned as he caught snatches of their sharp-edged tongue—a language he was fluent in—and watched a standard rippling in the wind.

He understood these people, had lived amongst them, but a year since gaining his freedom, a deep resentment now soured his belly. Aquila had let him go, but the man had also destroyed his life.

This shouldn't have been his fate—to run with outlaws instead of ruling his people. Yet here he was, crouching in the undergrowth, unable to walk tall with his head high in his own lands.

Gut clenching, Aedan shifted his attention to the row of covered carts rumbling through the valley. A harsh smile tilted his lips then. The second of his companions, Sego, was also right. Judging by the heavy escort, this supply convoy was likely to be a rich one.

It was headed to the Wall: the vast stone fortification that now stretched from one coast to the other.

Just another symbol of Roman vanity, several forts studded the Wall—and this convoy could be going to any of them.

Those heavy carts would be laden with weapons, food, and coin. The Britons throughout this territory would welcome the supplies. Brigantia was vast; it stretched down from the Wall to the great boundary river of Afon Merswy far to the south. Of course, many of their people wouldn't personally benefit from this haul— but a few would.

"We'd better alert the others," Aedan said then, speaking for the first time since he'd joined Lucon and Sego on the edge of this valley. "The attack needs to be here ... once they reach the end of the vale, they'll be harder to corner. The trees will provide cover for our bowmen."

Sego grunted in agreement, even if his dark-blue gaze was cool when it settled on Aedan. "Come on then."

The three warriors, clad in leather and wool, slithered backward on their bellies and crept through the press of alders to the rest of their band.

The others were waiting for them, their faces tense, their gazes sharp with anticipation.

Their leader, Maccus, stepped forward, large hands clenching at his sides. The outlaw was heavily tattooed and lanky, with a thick brown mustache and long hair tied back at the nape of his neck. "Well?"

Aedan nodded to him. "The convoy is passing through the valley now."

"It's bigger than we thought," Lucon added, his gravelly voice catching with excitement.

Maccus's hazel eyes glinted. "How many supply carts."

"Over a dozen," Aedan replied without hesitation.

"And soldiers?"

"A full century."

Maccus nodded, although he frowned. A century was eighty men, a band of legionaries led by a centurion. It was nearly double their number.

"Those whoresons are definitely carrying riches with them," Sego muttered. "They wouldn't have such a heavy escort otherwise."

Maccus's gaze narrowed further, an expression that emphasized his hawkish features. "Aye, but we have the element of surprise." His attention then snapped back to Aedan. "Anything else I should know?"

Aedan shook his head. There was a challenge in Maccus's voice—as there always was when he addressed Aedan. The outlaws' attitude to him had been ambivalent from the very beginning.

After leaving his brother, and walking away from his old life forever, Aedan had been rudderless, lost. For a few days, he'd wandered without purpose, brooding over the fate the Gods had dealt him, and cursing the Caesars for ever setting foot in Britannia.

When he'd set Aedan free, Justinian Aquila had offered him a position in his household, as a paid servant rather than a slave—but he wouldn't return to Vindolanda and take him up on it.

Aedan was too embittered for that. Too proud.

Nor would he live in any of the townships outside the forts on the Wall. To do so would be like pouring salt on the wound.

Instead, he wanted to leave his old life behind, to strike out afresh. He needed a purpose. And he thought he'd found it when he encountered Maccus and his warriors.

But a year on, he was as restless and resentful as ever. He didn't belong to these people either. They appreciated his knowledge of the Caesars and their ways, and had used it to their advantage many times, but they saw him as tainted. It didn't matter that Aedan hadn't lived amongst the Romans willingly. The other warriors viewed him as if he were a half-breed. A man who didn't belong in either world.

Satisfied that Aedan wasn't holding anything back—and he wasn't—Maccus whirled on his heel. He then gave a high, piercing whistle, causing the rumble of conversation farther back to die. "We move," he barked, his gaze sweeping their faces. "Leave no Roman alive."

The carpentum bounced high before crashing down upon its axles. The traveling cart's wooden sides shuddered and gave an ominous creak.

Wincing, Colombia shifted from her seat and moved close to the small window. Peering out, she spied tall grass framed by a press of trees: the sides of a long valley that seemed to stretch on for eternity. The journey up from Londinium had been a long and tiring one so far, yet today's road felt as if it were paved with boulders.

Outside the large, covered wooden cart, the light had developed a golden hue. The day was waning; the convoy would halt soon.

Colombia gnawed at her bottom lip, impatience thrumming through her. She then turned to her companion. "Surely, we can't be far from Onnum now?"

Flavia glanced up from where she was nibbling from a dish of dried fruit, nuts, and cheese. "Atticus told me we should reach the fort tomorrow afternoon, at the latest," her maid replied. Flavia's mouth curved in a sly smile as she spoke the name of the bodyguard they'd brought with them from Asculum in northeastern Italia.

Colombia knew what that smile meant. When they'd set out, her maid and bodyguard had barely tolerated each other, yet during the long weeks that followed, Colombia had marked the thawing of their relationship.

In the past days, she'd also noticed how her maid disappeared sometimes in the early evenings after they'd made camp for the night. She wouldn't be gone for long, but when she returned, the neat braid wrapped around the crown of her head was slightly askew and flecks of grass and straw covered her tunic.

Her bodyguard and maid were now lovers.

Flavia's behavior was reckless, yet Colombia had so far refrained from making any comment about it. She hoped that Atticus would do the noble thing and propose to Flavia when they reached Onnum.

"One more night on the road then," Colombia murmured, settling back into her pillows. The interior of their carpentum was richly decorated with brightly colored cushions and soft furs, as befitted Colombia's rank. She was a garrison commander's daughter and traveled in relative comfort. Excitement fluttered under her ribcage. "And then I shall finally see Linus again."

Her gaze met Flavia's, and her maid's dark eyes glinted. Flavia knew just how much her mistress longed to see her betrothed once more. Five years had passed since Linus Calix Aurelius had proposed to her at her father's villa.

"It's been a long while," Flavia pointed out, unnecessarily. "Do you think he will have changed?"

Colombia's brow furrowed. "I'm sure we *both* have," she replied, glancing down at the gleaming gold band she wore upon the Venus finger of her left hand. Indeed, she'd been nineteen years old when he'd given her this ring, and was now four and twenty. "But our union cannot be delayed any longer."

Flavia gave another, knowing, smirk, and Colombia tensed. Travel put even the strongest relationships to the test, and over the past weeks, she'd grown weary of her maid. Ever since Flavia's relationship with Atticus had taken a turn, she'd developed a supercilious attitude, as if she was a woman of the world now and Colombia wasn't.

"I look forward to seeing the Wall finally," Colombia said crisply, shifting the focus from her drawn-out betrothal. "Linus tells me it is a truly magnificent feat of engineering … stretching from one coast to the other."

Flavia nodded, her expression turning thoughtful. "I wonder if the natives put up much opposition to it," she murmured. "The building of such a fortification must have shocked them."

Colombia's brow furrowed. "Linus assures me that the locals have welcomed our rule," she replied. "In his last missive, he—"

She didn't get the chance to finish her sentence, for the carpentum lurched abruptly. Flavia's dish of dried fruit and cheese flew in one direction and she in the other. She hit the wooden side of the cart and muttered an unladylike oath.

"What was that?" Colombia gasped.

"These cursed backwater roads," Flavia muttered, picking herself up from the fur-covered floor of the cart. "Surely, we must make camp soon … I shall ask Atticus."

Their bodyguard rode up front with the carpentum driver.

"We've stopped," Colombia noted. After that great lurch, the cart had stilled. Outside, she could hear raised male voices. Her skin prickled then as if the air inside the carpentum had just grown chill. "Wait … Flavia. Something might be amiss. Best you let Atticus be for the moment."

Flavia snorted. "Nonsense ... he'll tell us what's happening."

With that, her maid moved to the window and stuck her head out. "Atticus!" she called. "Why have we—"

The maid's query cut off, and she reeled backward, collapsing on her back upon the furs.

A silent scream clawed its way up Colombia's throat when her gaze alighted upon the arrow embedded in Flavia's left eye.

III. THE GREATEST OF PRIZES

AEDAN NOTCHED A fresh arrow and sighted his target: a big man wearing a flowing red cloak, who marched at the head of the column. The centurion had drawn his gladius with one hand and raised his shield with the other, his dark gaze flicking around as he tried to catch sight of their attackers.

Aedan's bow sang as the arrow flew, embedding in the centurion's throat. An instant later, the soldier sagged to his knees, mouth gaping.

Watching the man fall, Aedan's mouth flattened into a thin line.

He'd long since ceased to feel vindicated by killing Romans. It no longer set his blood alight. Slaughtering the men that escorted the convoy wasn't a pleasant task—but it had to be done.

Hidden by the shadowed boughs of alders, Aedan had a clear sight of the front of the supply convoy. They'd prepared well for this moment, and their best archers had hidden themselves on the opposite side of the valley, before the Romans approached, awaiting Maccus's signal. When a crow cawed three times, the harsh sound echoing over the vale—the archers loosed their arrows.

The attack was sudden, and from both sides, and it caught the leaders of the convoy—four men on horseback—by surprise.

A hail of dark arrows flew across the valley, peppering the column.

Heartbeats later, a familiar cry echoed toward the tree line. "Testudo!"

Aedan had seen the Romans form the shield wall a number of times over the years. Nonetheless, it never failed to impress.

The fine hair on the back of his arms prickled as he watched the soldiers move as one. They interlocked their shields overhead and along the sides, dropping down on one knee to create a tortoise-like, protective covering.

Aedan's gaze narrowed. The testudo was strong, but not invincible. It was slow, unwieldy, and prevented the soldiers from fighting in hand-to-hand combat. However, his arrows would do no more good now—it was time to move closer.

Slinging his bow over his shoulder, Aedan drew his sword.

"Charge!" The order tore from his throat as he erupted from the trees and raced toward the shield wall. The thunder of footfalls behind him let him know that his companions were right there.

In the past, when he'd led his father's warriors into battle, they'd fought with chariots—sleek carts drawn by fast ponies. However, this band of Brigante outlaws, men who rebelled against the rule of the Caesars, relied on secrecy and stealth. Only a fool faced the might of Rome in open warfare. Better to attack them in a valley like this, where they could use the cover of the woods to pick off their adversaries.

Reaching the testudo, Aedan hacked at the ankles of the soldier nearest. A howl of pain followed, mingling with the feral yells of the outlaws as they swarmed around the tortoise.

Maccus was among them, slashing his sword, his blood-spattered face alive with wild joy. The outlaw leader lived for these moments. Hate burned in him like a smoldering lump of peat, bursting into flames when he got to spill Roman blood. Years earlier, his wife had been brutally beaten and raped by a group of Roman soldiers; she'd later died from her injuries. Maccus's need for reckoning had never been sated since.

Instead, he'd made it his life's mission to bring down the Caesars.

The battle turned in the outlaws' favor fast, and a group of warriors broke off from the band who were attacking the testudo, to deal with the drivers of the line of plaustrums—supply carts.

Leaving Maccus and the most savage of his men to deliver death to the last of the legionaries, Aedan jogged down the line, his gaze traveling over the first of the heavy, covered, two-wheeled wagons, drawn by pairs of oxen. The beasts bellowed, distressed by the chaos reigning around them.

There were other ways, besides dealing out death, to hit the Caesars where it hurt. Unlike Maccus, spilling Roman blood didn't excite Aedan half as much as gathering the riches they were bringing north.

The first of the plaustrums Aedan opened up was laden with sacks of grain, and clay amphoras of honey and olive oil. A grim smile split his face as he surveyed the packed interior. This food would sustain many Britons over the coming winter. It had been a wet summer and a poor harvest, and with the numbers of soldiers growing on the Wall, the Romans had taken most of the grain and vegetables that would prevent the locals from starving over the bitter months.

Now, it was the legionaries manning the Wall who'd have empty bellies.

They won't like that much.

Aedan moved on to the next wagon, discovering it laden with weaponry. This too would come in useful. However, when he continued down the line—stepping over the corpse of a burly driver, and pulling back the covering on the third plaustrum—his breathing caught.

Heavy sacks of coin filled the shadowy space. Digging his hand into the nearest one, Aedan gazed down at the gold aureus, silver denarius, and brass sestertius coins that glinted upon his palm.

Another smile curved his lips. He'd hoped to find coin here, but this was a gift indeed.

The Warrior be praised, he'd just discovered a pay wagon. The Caesars were careful not to draw too much attention to these carts; the pay wagon looked exactly like those hauling food supplies.

Of course, the soldiers defending the Wall received a salary. When he'd lived in Caledonia, he remembered pay wagons arriving at Ardoch three times a year. The carts would be wheeled right into the principia, at the heart of the fort, and the sacks deposited inside a strongroom. The soldiers would then eagerly queue up outside the pay office to pick up their wages. Out on the frontier, you'd have thought the men had little use for coin—yet many of them gambled it away or spent it on drink and women in the vicus outside the walls of the fort.

Aedan's belly tightened as he deposited the handful of coins back in the sack.

Just one of these bags would set him up for life. He'd be able to walk away from Maccus and his mob and strike out on his own somewhere. He could build himself a cottage, purchase livestock and seeds, and live as a farmer.

But, instead, the outlaw leader would take possession of these riches and dole them out where he pleased.

Aedan would be lucky if he received a handful of sestertii from the stingy bastard.

Muttering a curse under his breath, he dropped the leather flap that covered the back of the wagon and strode to the next one. This one was full of amphoras of wine. The yeasty odor of fermented fruit filled the interior of the cart.

It looked like they'd all be getting rolling drunk when this was over.

Shouting from farther down the convoy drew Aedan's attention then. Leaving off his exploration of the plaustrums, Aedan walked toward it, sword at the ready.

A tussle was taking place up ahead.

In amongst the cumbersome supply carts was a wooden carpentum. Taller than the plaustrums, with four wheels, an arched roof, and small windows, the traveling cart was made of oak and had elegant lines. It was the type of cart the wealthy traveled in.

Rough laughter drifted toward Aedan as he approached.

Two Romans, one of them big and heavily muscled, lay sprawled on the ground in front of the cart, their blood pooling into the dust. Meanwhile, four outlaws, Lucon and Sego among them, prowled around the carpentum like circling wolves.

Lucon then knelt and made a grab for something under the cart.

A woman's outraged squeal followed, and a foot, clad in a leather slipper, kicked out, catching the warrior in the chin.

Cursing, Lucon reeled back. The blow had made him bite his tongue, for he spat out blood and wiped his mouth with the back of his hand.

"You shall pay for that, Caesar slut."

"You're too slow," Sego sneered at his friend. "Catch her by the ankle, and drag her out here."

"You do it," Lucon replied sourly. "I don't want to lose my front teeth."

"Coward," Sego muttered, getting down on all fours. "I'll show you how it's done." He moved under the cart, while the two remaining warriors encouraged him with coarse comments.

Sego was much wirier than Lucon, and quicker too. The woman screamed when he grabbed hold of her ankle, the panicked sound carrying down the line while he dragged her out from under the carpentum.

Aedan's gait slowed as he approached.

None of the warriors had seen him. They were enjoying the view of the woman's naked, shapely legs now, for the long tunic and stola she wore had both ridden up as she struggled. Her skin was pale, untouched by the sun.

"We've got a pretty one here," the youngest of the outlaws noted, his voice tight with lust. "Can I have her first?"

Indeed, even from a few yards distant, Aedan could see the unfortunate woman was lovely. She was slender and long-limbed, with dark-flaxen hair—an unusual shade for one of the Romans.

"Wait your turn," Sego growled. "I snared the bitch … and I'm humping her before any of you."

Pinning the struggling woman to the ground with one hand, he started to undo the laces of his bracae with the other.

"*Caenum!*" the woman shrieked as she clawed at his arm. "*Vah apage te a me!*"

The warriors merely laughed at her insults. None of them understood her, yet Aedan did. His fluency in Latin was another skill that Maccus had found useful over the last year.

Filth. Get away from me!

"Don't you know who I am?" the woman's voice cracked. "You're attacking the daughter of Commander Severus Juventus. He will have your guts for laying a finger on me!"

Aedan's breathing caught, and he drew to a halt.

Severus Juventus.

The Reaper take her, the foolish woman shouldn't be shouting that name here.

Luckily for her, the other outlaws hadn't picked it out amongst the string of panicked words. Even so, they knew the name of the man who commanded Onnum fort—and if she continued to shriek it, they'd soon realize what a prize they'd stumbled upon.

A prize just as great, if not greater, than a pay wagon.

Catching Severus Juventus's daughter would please Maccus greatly. The outlaw leader despised all Romans, yet he nursed a special hatred for the Second Legion.

Gods only knew what he'd do to her.

Gaze remaining upon the still struggling woman, Aedan slowly exhaled.

Curse it.

Warriors did all manner of brutal things when battle fever was upon them. Like the four men about to rape their captive, he was now spattered in Roman blood and gore.

Yet could he stand by and watch while they brutalized this woman?

IV. ON MY MOTHER'S MEMORY

"STILL YOUR STRUGGLING," Sego snarled, slapping the woman hard across the face. The crack of his palm against her cheek made her gasp. Yet she fought him even harder, twisting and writhing under his grip.

"She'll be a wild mare to ride," Lucon observed, a wide grin on his face now.

"She will," Sego grunted, still struggling to untie the laces to his bracae. "Although if she keeps struggling, I'm going to knock her out."

Aedan cleared his throat then, drawing their attention.

Sego's gaze cut his way, his brows knitting together. "Piss off, Aedan," he growled. "This is our prize ... not yours."

Feigning nonchalance, Aedan shrugged. He still held his sword, loosely at his side now, although his left hand hovered near the hilt of the knife he'd strapped to his thigh. "That's a bit selfish, Sego," he replied, careful to keep his tone bland. "If it wasn't for me, you'd have been gutted on a Roman blade moons ago." He flashed Sego a smile. "You should let me climb on first ... to show your gratitude."

Lucon growled a curse. "Go find yourself a horse to hump, shit-weasel," he snarled.

Aedan kept walking, a smile curving his lips. "I don't think so."

He'd never liked Sego or Lucon. They were excellent scouts, as was he, and so the three of them often worked together, but both men had the manners of a goat, and they'd barely tolerated his company over the past year. As such, Aedan felt no remorse as he drew his dagger and flew for Sego's throat.

The warrior fell, clutching at his severed windpipe, but Aedan was already turning, his sword slicing through the air.

He'd have taken off Lucon's head with it, if the warrior hadn't ducked, staggering back out of reach.

Aedan followed, grim resolve filtering through him.

Now he'd set out on this path, there could be no hesitation. All these four had to fall.

With howls of fury, the two others set upon him, but Aedan brought them both down within moments. He then whirled to face Lucon's wrath.

The outlaw's heavy-featured face was twisted, his dark-blue eyes glinting as he circled Aedan with his own sword at the ready. "I knew you'd turn on us one day," he growled. "Maccus shouldn't have taken you in ... you lived too long amongst the Roman filth. You've been tainted by them."

The insults washed off Aedan. He'd heard them frequently already since earning his freedom. It didn't matter how many times he told his companions that he bore the Caesars no love. In the eyes of the other outlaws, he'd indeed been soiled.

That no longer mattered now though. After this, he'd be hunted by both Romans and his own people.

The clash of iron rang across the valley, blending with the grunts and shouts of the fighting that continued at either end of the convoy.

Urgency tugged at Aedan then. Time was running out. Soon the fighting would end, and outlaws would swarm around them. He couldn't linger here.

Yet Lucon was hard to beat. Heavyset and broad-shouldered, he looked as if he'd lumber in a fight, yet he was surprisingly light on his feet, and each cut of his sword was savage.

Eventually though, Aedan ducked under his guard and cut his blade deep into his opponent's thigh.

Lucon roared in agony, although the sound abruptly cut off when Aedan head-butted him, knocking him out. Lucon sprawled onto the ground and lay still.

Whirling, his heart now pounding like a battle drum, and his forehead throbbing, Aedan glanced around for the woman.

He caught sight of a flash of blue under the carpentum and realized she'd taken refuge there once more.

"Come on," he gasped in Latin, approaching the traveling cart and lowering himself onto his haunches. "You can't stay here."

Wide, frightened grey eyes stared out at him on a pale, heart-shaped face. Understandably, the woman was terrified. However, he couldn't treat her gently. Any moment now, they'd have company, and he wouldn't be able to save her.

"We need to run," he said, holding out his hand to her. "If we wait much longer, it'll be too late ... for *both* of us."

She gaped at him, her breast rising and falling sharply. The woman was terrified, frozen in place.

Aedan held her gaze, his hand stretching out farther still. "We have to go." He paused then. He didn't want to scare her further, yet he needed her to listen to him. "If we don't leave now, more men will come. They'll rape you, torture you ... and I won't be able to stop them."

The woman gasped, the whites of her eyes glittering. An instant later, a small yet surprisingly strong hand grasped his. Gently, so as not to send her into full-blown panic, Aedan drew the woman out from under the carpentum and pulled her to her feet.

She was wearing a long tunic and a flowing sky-blue stola—the voluminous overdress donned by Roman noblewomen—not practical attire at all, but at least her leather slippers looked sturdy enough.

Still grasping her hand, Aedan broke away from the convoy and made for the woods. The woman stumbled along behind him, barely able to keep up.

"Faster," he grunted.

She choked out a protest and tried to pull free from his hold, yet Aedan didn't let her go. He wouldn't until they were safely away from the valley.

They were fortunate, for the line of densely packed alders was close at that point of the valley. Aedan crashed into the trees, towing the woman behind him. He dove into their midst, heedless of the thick undergrowth of brambles.

Thorns clutched at their clothing and any exposed skin, yet Aedan didn't slacken his pace, nor did he relax his grip on the woman's hand.

His lungs started to burn, and sweat trickled down his back and chest, causing his clothing to chafe. Aedan pushed on regardless.

The woman tired much faster than he did, and soon he was dragging her after him. She'd ceased her struggles, although when he glanced her way, her flushed face was stricken and her smoky eyes glittered with fear.

Aedan was about to reassure her he wasn't stealing her away so that he could ravage her, when the splintering sound of branches and rough shouts echoed through the woods.

The woman let out a low whimper.

A chill swept over Aedan as he realized his mistake.

Lucon. Why hadn't he killed him?

Aedan had been so intent on getting the woman to safety that he hadn't ensured no one was left alive to betray him.

On and on they ran, weaving through the press of trees into the heart of the woods. The woman clung desperately to his hand now, for he was towing her through the woods. The going gradually become slower, for the tangle of trees and undergrowth became almost impenetrable.

Eventually, his companion gasped out a stuttered question. "D... do they have dogs?"

"No," he panted in reply, "but some of them are expert trackers nonetheless ... and we're leaving a clear path to follow."

"How w... will we escape then?"

"I don't know."

That wasn't exactly true, for Aedan was already thinking ahead, recalling the layout of this swathe of woodland. If his memory served him, there was a stream farther east. If they could reach it, they might be able to get away.

The woman didn't question him further. The rasp of their breathing, the rustle of leaves, and the creak of branches surrounded them as they pressed on—and a short while later, they found the stream.

It was deep enough to reach mid-calf as they waded into it.

Halting in the midst of the flow, the icy water swirling about him, Aedan glanced around. He could still hear shouting, yet it was farther behind now. Even so, they had to keep moving. If he was correct, this burn flowed from a larger water course to the north.

Still gripping the woman's hand, for the river stones were slippery and the current strong enough to make the progress hard going, Aedan waded upstream.

It wasn't easy for the woman, as, despite that she did her best to hold her skirts above the water, they still got wet. Stubbing her toe on a rock, she then hissed a curse.

Aedan glanced her way, once or twice, to check she was all right. He noted the deep flush on her cheeks now, the sweat glistening on her forehead, and the jerky rise and fall of her chest. She was nearing the limits of her endurance.

He needed to get her to safety before she collapsed.

The stream gradually deepened, until the water reached mid-thigh. At that point, they clambered up onto the mossy bank and continued upward. And as they traveled, the sounds of pursuit faded further. The outlaws wouldn't have given up though—not yet. The land grew steeper and rockier, and then eventually, they reached the fork where this stream departed from a gushing river.

Halting on the western bank, Aedan took a few moments to recover his breath. He finally released his companion's hand, allowing her to sink down onto a wide, flat rock. "Rest a little," he panted. "While I make us a raft."

She nodded, her wide grey eyes—the same color as the surrounding river stones—surveying him warily. Sweat trickled down her flushed face.

He flashed her a tight smile. "I'm Aedan, by the way."

Her throat bobbed before the tip of a pink tongue darted out, wetting her lips. The gesture was unconsciously sensual, and Aedan found himself staring at her mouth—which was both small and lush. "My name's Colombia," she replied huskily.

"Dove," he murmured, his smile widening. "That's a pretty name."

Alarm ignited in those smoky eyes, and she took a smart step back, nostrils flaring, ready to bolt.

"Whoa." Aedan lifted his hands in a placating gesture before lowering his voice. "I'm not going to hurt you."

She stared back at him. Her slight frame trembled now as the shock of what she'd just narrowly escaped hit her. "Do you swear it?"

"I do." He reached up and placed a hand over his heart. "On my mother's memory."

Moments passed before Colombia slowly nodded. However, when she spoke, her voice held a quaver. "Who were those men?"

"Outlaws."

The flush upon her cheeks deepened, her jaw tightening. "Were you with them?"

"I was." He held her gaze steadily. "But not any longer."

They stared at each other for a long moment before Colombia asked, "How is it you speak my tongue?"

"I was a Roman slave for a time." Satisfied she wasn't going to flee back down the hill toward their pursuers, Aedan turned away and hurriedly started collecting long, thin pieces of driftwood from along the riverbank. "My former owner taught me your language."

"You speak it well."

Aedan gave a soft snort. "I had plenty of practice."

He turned his attention from her then, continuing his collection. Luckily, there was plenty of driftwood strewn by the river. He had to work fast; when he had enough branches, he would weave them together in a lattice to form a raft. It wouldn't be a sturdy craft, but it just needed to get them out of the woods and far enough away from Maccus and his band.

They'd outdistanced them for a short while, but the outlaws would be gaining on them again now they'd stopped.

They weren't safe yet.

V. AN UNLIKELY SAVIOR

COLOMBIA CONCENTRATED ON taking deep, even breaths as her pulse gradually slowed and the terror that had given her feet wings subsided to a fluttering anxiety in her belly.

Seated upon a sun-warmed rock, she noted the light was fading. The sky above was the color of old bone, the air cool, and a wind, laced with the scent of moss and damp earth, whispered through the trees surrounding the river. It was a lonely, wild spot. Sharp rocks peeked up through the foaming water, and branches and twigs littered the stony riverbanks.

However, Colombia's attention didn't remain on her environs for long.

Her gaze returned to her unlikely savior.

Aedan.

The warrior had collected a pile of branches and now knelt before them, deftly weaving the wood in a crisscross pattern. The sculpted muscles of his bare, lightly freckled arms flexed as he worked—and Colombia noted the blue swirls that had been etched into the skin of his upper arms. Tribal markings.

Aedan's bright-blue eyes narrowed in concentration as he worked with impressive speed. A couple of years her elder, he had shaggy light-auburn hair that kept falling in his eyes. Unlike the men he'd saved her from— who'd all sported thick, drooping mustaches—he was clean-shaven. His hands, which worked the branches into a raft, were long-fingered and nimble.

Colombia continued to survey him, her pulse quickening once more. Fear tightened her throat.

Could she trust him?

He'd come to her rescue back there, and had sworn he meant her no harm, but what if his kindness was a ruse? He'd been one of the mob that had attacked the convoy. He was an *outlaw*.

Their pursuers were closing in, and Aedan was eager to put some distance between them. But what would happen when they were safe?

Colombia clasped her fingers together on her lap as trembling assailed her again.

Her gaze flicked to the bow and quiver he carried on his back, the sword sheathed at his hip, and the wickedly sharp, long-bladed dagger strapped to one thigh.

If he meant her harm, she wouldn't be able to defend herself against him.

Wrapping her arms about herself, Colombia tried to calm her shaking—but memories of the attack rushed in then.

Her maid's frozen face. The arrow embedded in Flavia's eye. The blood-chilling howls of the warriors encircling her as she crouched under the carpentum. The iron grip of the man who'd grabbed her by the ankle and yanked her out from under the wagon.

She'd fought him yet had known she was done for— until Aedan intervened.

"Have we outrun them?" she asked finally.

The warrior shook his head. "Not yet … that's why I'm building us a raft. They'll be here shortly. We can't relax until we put some real distance between us."

Pulse quickening, Colombia glanced over her shoulder at the shadowy woodland behind them. A moment later, she heard the faint rumble of men's voices echoing up the hillside. They were still distant, but the sound frightened her, nonetheless.

Jumping to her feet, she edged toward the river. "You're doing an impressive job of weaving those branches together," she muttered, "but can you work faster?"

"No," he grunted, shooting her an irritated look. "Don't worry though ... it'll be ready soon."

He turned back to his work, and Colombia watched him jam the lengths of wood together to form a mat. Moments later, she asked, "Why did you save me?"

"I agreed to attack Roman supply lines ... to take their riches for our people," he said gruffly, not looking up from his weaving. "But I'm not a defiler of women."

"I don't understand," she replied, cursing the wobble in her voice. "Why would you attack us?"

Aedan arched an eyebrow. "We're Brigante ... and you're Roman. Isn't that enough?"

She frowned, now genuinely confused. "But we brought you civilization ... aren't you grateful?"

Aedan shot her a startled look before he started to laugh.

Chagrined, Colombia drew herself up. "What's so funny?"

Aedan shook his head, turning back to his work. "Gods, I thought you were serious for a moment there."

Colombia's frown deepened as heat ignited in the pit of her belly. "I am," she ground out.

Aedan didn't look her way, for he was focused on his task. However, his expression sobered, his own gaze narrowing with incredulity. "You believe we're *grateful* to you?"

Heat rose to Colombia's chest. "Yes ... my father told me so. He said the Britons welcomed our ways, our knowledge and culture."

"Ah yes, your father. Severus Juventus."

Colombia stiffened. She didn't like the inflection in his voice. "You know him?"

"I know *of* him ... as do most Brigante this close to the Wall. I wondered why you foolishly told those outlaws you were his daughter ... but now I understand. You thought we were your allies." He cast her another, quick, glance. "Fortunately for you, only I grasped your words ... but your father lied to you. The Romans and the

Britons aren't friends. We've *never* been friends, and while the sun rises in the east and sets in the west, we won't be."

The warmth in Colombia's chest spread up her throat to her cheeks. Humiliation roasted her, and she fell silent.

Surely, pater didn't lie to me?

If he had, then Linus had also misled her. Not once in all the missives he'd sent her from the frontier had he mentioned strife between her people and the Britons.

Colombia's jaw tightened.

She'd take her father and Linus's word over this man's.

He was arrogant and clearly full of resentment. That rabble he'd been running with would be punished for attacking the convoy. As soon as word reached the Wall, soldiers would be sent out to hunt them down like dogs.

Drawing in a deep breath, Colombia swallowed the urge to argue with him. This man was the only lifeline she had; it was wise to speak carefully.

Aedan rose swiftly to his feet then, bringing the large rectangular raft with him. "It's done," he announced.

Nodding, Colombia stepped close. "I'm ready."

"How much longer?"

"Not much ... we've almost reached the bottom of the hill."

Clutching onto the branches of the rickety raft, Colombia whispered yet another prayer to Fortuna. The Goddess had shone upon her so far today, sparing her a terrible fate at the hands of those outlaws.

However, she didn't want to escape rape and a blade to the throat, only to drown in this wild river.

The raft bobbed and twirled in the swift current, thrown around like a child's toy.

Her lower legs and feet, which hung off the raft, had turned numb from the icy water, yet she didn't care about that—she was too focused on holding on. Colombia couldn't swim, and the current was so fast that if she lost her grip on the raft, she'd be dragged under within moments.

Panic clawed up her throat. Trying not to think about the possibility of a watery death, she chanced a look around.

It was difficult to get any sense of where they were, for a canopy of trees stretched overhead, and the light was so dim now the world appeared leached of color. For a spell, they'd hurtled downriver on a slope, and now the river had flattened out and widened.

"When I tell you, start kicking," Aedan ordered then. "We need to get toward the bank."

"Yes," Colombia replied through clenched teeth. It was just as well this wild ride was nearly over, for her fingers were gradually weakening from cold and gripping on so tightly. She'd soon lose her hold.

"Right ... kick!"

She did as bid, flailing around like a landed fish.

Aedan had been holding on to the opposite side of the raft, yet he lowered himself into the water now and moved around so they were shoulder-to-shoulder.

Together, they kicked the raft out of the swirling current, angling it toward the far bank—and when they finally reached it, a sob of relief rose in Colombia's breast.

Aedan made it to the bank first before hauling her up after him.

They then crawled over wet stones, the gasps of their ragged breathing mingling with the rush of the river.

Colombia flopped onto her back, her chest heaving as she dragged in gulps of air. Her feet throbbed from the cold, yet by some miracle, she hadn't lost either of her slippers. Above, the sky, framed by dark trees, had turned grey-purple, and the first of the stars twinkled down at her.

"So ..." she finally wheezed. "We're safe *now*?"

"I think so ... yes," he panted. "They should be far behind us now. This river has taken us southeast ... far from Dere Street."

Relief barreled into Colombia, flattening her against the stony riverbank.

Now that the immediate danger had passed, she could think to the future, to reaching Onnum—and Linus.

Moments passed, and then she glanced over at her savior. He was still lying on his back, his profile shadowed in the half-light.

Nerves clenched at her belly as she studied him. He appeared deep in thought, as if considering something.

This was the moment of truth. Would he keep his word or reveal his true motives? Swallowing, Colombia wrapped her fingers around a large, smooth river stone at her side. If he attacked her, she'd be ready. She wouldn't let him rape her.

Silence swelled between them before she asked, "What do we do now?"

Aedan glanced her way, his eyes glinting. "Now we dry off."

VI. I SHALL NOT FORGET IT

THE CRACKLING OF burning driftwood filled the small glade.

Moving close, Aedan fed the fire another stick or two. He'd deliberated a little before deciding it was safe to light one. Maccus and his friends wouldn't be hunting them tonight, and thanks to the river, they were a considerable distance south now.

The outlaws wouldn't chase them indefinitely, especially since they needed to cart away the spoils of their attack. Nonetheless, Maccus *was* vengeful enough to hunt him afterward.

The reminder made Aedan's gut tighten. He'd seen the outlaw leader's wrath firsthand many times— including when he'd dealt with insubordination amongst his men.

It was best their paths never crossed again.

Sitting back on his haunches, he glanced over at the woman he'd saved.

Colombia had stripped off her stola and hung the garment up to dry on a nearby tree. She sat in a light-blue tunic that clung damply to her slender body. The garment reached her ankles and was girded under her breasts with a thin, jeweled belt. Her hair, which had initially been pinned up in a half-bun, had come loose and fell in messy dark-flaxen waves around her face.

Just one look at her—the woman's pale skin, soft hands, and the expensive cloth of her dress—and it was obvious she was of noble blood. Of course, the carpentum she'd been traveling in also indicated her status, and she spoke a crisp, refined Latin.

The firelight bathed her like honey, emphasizing her pretty features and soft mouth.

Colombia Juventus was far from home. She didn't belong here in these damp, wild woods of northern Britannia.

Even though it was just after the harvest, and there were still a few moons until the weather turned bitter, the evening air was cool—and this summer, like many, had been grey and damp. Aedan's former master, Justin Aquila, had told him about Italia—of its wide blue skies, long hot summers, and rolling hills terraced in grape vines and olive groves.

Aedan wagered Colombia was new to these shores— for she'd made her innocence regarding the politics of this land painfully clear—but that hadn't prevented the haughty tilt of her chin earlier. Her superiority galled him.

Just like the rest of the Caesars, she was entitled.

She thought she commanded the very earth she walked upon.

A low growl filled the glade. However, it wasn't the noise of a woodland creature, but of his companion's belly.

Aedan's own stomach rumbled then, reminding him he'd eaten little save some hard bread and cheese at noon. His mouth lifted at the edges. "I'm hungry too," he admitted. "I will see about catching us something to eat tomorrow."

He'd been so intent on distancing themselves from their pursuers that there had been no time for him to fish for a trout or hunt a grouse for their supper.

They'd have to sleep with empty bellies.

Colombia nodded before picking up a leaf and smoothing it against her thigh. "I'm just grateful we got away." She paused then, glancing up, her gaze spearing him. He was relieved to see no fear in their pewter depths, just a lingering wariness. "I don't think I've thanked you yet."

Aedan didn't reply. She hadn't.

She cleared her throat. "Well, I must remedy that … you were brave to take on those warriors as you did … to escort me to safety while making enemies of your own people. I shall not forget it."

Their gazes held for a moment, a sudden tension rippling through the glade.

Eventually, Aedan looked away, focusing his attention on the dancing flames in the small fire he'd built. Aye, she was haughty, yet something about this woman threw him off-balance, and he didn't like it. He glanced back at his companion, and when he finally answered her, his tone was terse. "No offense, Colombia, but this is no land for a sheltered, pampered woman … why did your father send for you?"

Her small, full mouth pursed, heat flaring in her eyes, before she replied, "He didn't."

Aedan arched his eyebrows. "You traveled here without his knowledge?"

She nodded before dropping her gaze to where she was still smoothing the leaf against her thigh. "It's not *pater* I'm journeying to see … but my betrothed."

Betrothed?

Aedan inclined his head. Just when he believed this woman couldn't surprise him any further, she did. "He's at Onnum?"

"His name is Linus Calix Aurelius," she said softly, still not meeting his eye. "He's the *primus pilus* of the Second Legion."

Tension rippled down Aedan's spine at this news. Her husband-to-be was the highest-ranking centurion of the legion. "And does *he* know you're on your way?"

Colombia's cheeks flushed slightly. Clearing her throat, she tossed the leaf aside. "No ... I wanted to surprise him."

Astonishment stole over Aedan then. "You made the trip on your own?"

"Of course not. I traveled with a maid and a bodyguard." A nerve ticked under one eye as her expression shadowed. "But your *friends* killed them both during the attack on our convoy."

Silence fell in the glade while Aedan digested her words. He still didn't understand why a woman would make such a journey, especially if her betrothed hadn't sent for her. "You must be eager to see him ... if you'd put yourself in such danger," he said after a lengthy pause. His mouth pursed before he added. "He's a lucky man."

His belly hardened then. Centurion Aurelius *was* a fortunate man, indeed. What would it be like to have a woman love him enough to leave her home behind and trek to the far edge of the frontier? It wasn't likely Bronwen would have ever done the same—she'd wed his brother, after all.

"I *am* keen to see him," Colombia admitted, although there was a subdued edge to her voice now. The mention of her maid and bodyguard's violent deaths had caused a veil to lower over her eyes. "I didn't expect our convoy to be attacked though ... just a day out from our destination."

Silence fell between them once more, and a breeze fluttered through the trees. Moths danced around the flames while the gurgle of the nearby river formed a soothing backdrop.

Aedan glanced once more at Colombia. Her gaze still had a haunted, faraway look. No doubt she was reliving the horror of the attack, the death of her companions, and her near rape.

And despite that he felt uneasy in her presence tonight, despite that she chafed at him, Aedan had the urge to soothe her worries, to erase the shadow from her face.

"When did you last see your betrothed?" he asked finally. Since she'd traveled so far to see the man, he imagined she'd be happy to talk about him.

"Five years ago," she replied, meeting his gaze once more. "Just days after our engagement, he was given a posting to Britannia ... but he hasn't been home since."

Aedan's mouth quirked. "So, you thought you'd go to him?"

Colombia raised her chin in that supercilious gesture that had riled him earlier. Yet, this time, it intrigued him. This woman was soft and pampered, yet there was iron just beneath the surface. He found himself wanting to see more of it.

"We have corresponded regularly ever since his posting," she replied. "But Linus insists he hasn't had time to return home ... even for a short visit." Her voice trailed off, her pale cheeks flushing pink as if realizing she was being too candid.

"I'm sure he's very busy and important," Aedan replied, his tone dry.

Actually, he thought Linus Calix Aurelius sounded like a caudex—a blockhead.

Haughty or not, if he had a beauty like Colombia Juventus waiting at home for him, he'd have put in for a transfer—or at least ensured she joined him at the first opportunity.

Colombia sighed. "He is."

"I imagine he's *handsome* too," Aedan taunted. He knew he was being rude, but he couldn't help himself. Something about this woman made him want to provoke her—that and a bitterness that festered deep in his chest. Even when they'd been sweethearts, he'd never seen Bronwen's face light up like that at the mention of his name.

"Linus is devastatingly attractive," she countered, her eyes narrowing.

"And I suppose he has the bravery of ten men?"

"He's a fine soldier," she snapped. "Respected by those he serves and commands."

Unable to help himself, Aedan snorted. "And what of his character?"

She drew herself up, her jaw tightening. "What of it?"

Aedan arched an eyebrow. "Well, you have gone on about his external merits ... his military prowess and his looks ... but what of the thing that really matters? The man beneath it all."

VII. YOU OWE ME NOTHING

COLOMBIA'S FROWN DEEPENED.

The Briton was openly goading her.

Aedan had saved her life—and she hadn't lied when she'd told him she'd never forget it—but it was fast becoming clear he resented her and everything she stood for. His questions were pointed, insolent, and she was rapidly losing patience.

She didn't need to explain herself to this man—and she certainly wasn't going to let him best her.

The firelight played across the proud lines of his face, turning his eyes a darker shade of blue. There was no mistaking the challenge in their depths.

Leaning forward, she held his gaze. "Linus is noble-hearted, strong, and courageous," she replied, enunciating each word deliberately. "Why else do you think I've traveled all this way to see him?"

Aedan flashed her a goading smile. "And he'll be pleased to see you?"

"Of course!"

His gaze glinted. "You seem very sure of that, Colombia."

Anger ignited in Colombia's belly. She wished she hadn't been so candid with this man, for he was using everything she told him as weapons against her. Folding her arms across her chest, she gave him a withering look—one her aunt back in Asculum used with impertinent servants.

"You know a great deal about me, Aedan of the Brigante," she said, her tone clipped now. "But I'm not that interesting. *You*, on the other hand" —her gaze narrowed— "are no common warrior."

Aedan snorted at this, picked up some twigs, and threw them on the fire.

"Whom did you belong to ... when you were a slave?" she pressed.

Her companion scowled, making it clear he didn't welcome her question. Nonetheless, Colombia didn't care. Now it was *his* turn to squirm.

Silence drew out before he gave her his terse answer, "General Justinian Aquila."

Her gaze widened.

Aedan regarded her coolly. "You've heard of him?"

Her mouth kicked up into a half-smile. "Of course. Linus wrote me of General Aquila ... and how he'd held Ardoch against the Picti." She paused then, her expression sobering. "I heard that the emperor was displeased that he lost the north."

"He was ... which is why he was stripped of the rank of general and demoted to garrison commander at Vindolanda."

"Sounds like you two were firm friends."

Aedan's brows crashed together. "No, we weren't."

"Come," Colombia replied with a disbelieving snort. "No general just sets his slave free."

"Well, he did ... he gave all three of his slaves their freedom."

This admission caught her off-guard. "He did?"

"One of his slaves was a Picti woman ... he took her as his wife."

Colombia's eyes sprang wide. "Minerva," she gasped. "How irregular."

Aedan pulled a face. "The local magistrates thought so too ... he had to go before the emperor to gain permission to wed her."

"Really?" Like most people, Colombia had never met the emperor, although she'd glimpsed him once from a distance during a rare visit to Rome. "He had an audience with Hadrian?"

Aedan nodded.

Colombia shifted position, pulling her knees up to her chest and wrapping her arms around them. It was growing cool; she could feel the chill through her tunic. She wished there had been time to grab her palla—her long shawl—before running, but it had been impossible. Her stola was still wet from the river ride and needed to dry out a little more before she could wear it.

She drew in a deep breath then, her arms tightening around her legs.

Strangely, her verbal duel with Aedan had energized her. All her senses were alert, and her earlier fatigue had lifted. But as invigorating as poking the viper with a stick was, it served nothing. Instead, she had to focus on where she needed to be.

The nightmarish attack on the convoy still haunted her—Flavia and Atticus had been with her for years—yet she had to reach the Wall.

Speaking about Linus earlier had renewed her sense of purpose.

"I need your help, Aedan," she said after a pause. "Will you escort me to Onnum?"

He tore his gaze from where he'd been staring moodily at the fire and scowled.

"I'll make it worth your while," she added, holding his eye. "I'll ensure you're paid well."

His mouth tightened. "I don't want your money."

He was lying—she could tell by the glint in his eye—yet he was too proud to admit it. Everyone needed coin; he and the outlaws hadn't attacked that supply convoy for entertainment, but for the riches it was transporting.

The reminder of who this man really was made her pulse quicken. Although she was reassured he wasn't going to rape her, he was still a brigand—and he'd killed Roman soldiers.

"No," she replied evenly, "but it might come in useful."

Aedan tossed another handful of twigs on the flames. "Did you think I'd abandon you out here?" he asked roughly.

Colombia suppressed a shiver. If he did, she was done for. "I don't know what to think," she admitted softly. "Fortuna threw us together today, Aedan. You owe me nothing."

Their gazes locked, and silence settled over the glade. Long moments passed, and then Aedan huffed a sigh. "You're right, I'm not in your debt … but I didn't make myself an enemy of my own people only to throw you to the wolves." His mouth quirked. "And I could do with some coin too. Fear not … I shall take you to the Wall."

"Time to go," Aedan's voice shattered the morning's stillness.

Colombia jolted awake. Groggy and disoriented, she pushed herself up into a sitting position, rubbing at her eyes to clear her foggy head. Curse him, did he have to wake her so rudely?

She could have slept for a while longer. The ground, which was covered in knobbly roots that stuck into her back and side, hadn't been a comfortable mattress. Nonetheless, the exhaustion that had claimed Colombia had been so heavy she'd fallen asleep shortly after stretching out, placing her stola over her as a blanket.

Glancing around, she saw that, indeed, dawn had risen. Pale light filtered through the surrounding trees.

Aedan was kicking earth over the smoking embers. "It's still early," he announced. "But we need to move. We've got quite a distance to travel."

Colombia stiffened, alarm rippling down her spine. "I thought we were only a day from Onnum?"

"You *were* yesterday," he answered, glancing her way. "However, we traveled some way south to escape our pursuers. The safest route north is a roundabout one … it'll take us three and a half to four days to get to the Wall."

Colombia's stomach clenched. She then struggled to her feet and pulled on her crumpled stola. The garment was still slightly damp, yet she would have to wear it. "That long?"

He nodded. "Unless you want to meet trouble. It's not just the outlaws you have to worry about either … a Roman woman traveling with a Brigante won't impress any Roman patrols we encounter."

The knots in Colombia's stomach tightened. She hadn't considered that. Of course, without her escort, she was no longer a respectable lady. If they encountered soldiers, she could tell them she was Severus Juventus's daughter—but what if they didn't believe her?

Until yesterday, she'd felt supremely confident in the world she inhabited and her role within it. But this morning, she wasn't quite so sure of herself. She still didn't believe that his people truly resented hers, yet she decided to let the matter lie.

Aedan's expression was unreadable this morning. His voice was polite, yet a little off-hand. She wouldn't have been surprised if their barbed exchange the evening before had made him wary of her.

That suited Colombia. At least he wasn't mocking her this morning.

For her part, she wasn't interested in locking horns with him any longer. She just wanted to focus on getting safely to Onnum.

"I don't want any trouble," she admitted after a pause.

"Good," he replied. "Neither do I."

VIII. BAD BLOOD

THEY WALKED SOUTH for a spell, through woodland
that grew increasingly sparse, before Aedan turned left,
and they trekked over rolling hills. Traveling a couple of
yards behind the Brigante, Colombia struggled to keep
up with his long stride. The day before, he'd towed her
after him during their flight from the outlaws—and that
run had left her muscles aching, her body stiff. She
wasn't used to journeying long distances, and her
clothing and footwear weren't suited to it either.

She wanted to ask him to slow his pace a little, yet
every time she opened her mouth to do so, she recalled
the leering face of the outlaw who'd tried to rape her, and
the sight of her dead companions.

Those memories made Colombia grit her teeth and
quicken her step. Pride also kept her going. Aedan
already thought her a pampered, spoiled—and foolish—
Roman noblewoman. She didn't wish to give him more
reasons to look down his nose at her.

Even so, her leather slippers were starting to chafe
badly now.

Mid-morning, she could endure the burning pain in
her feet no longer. She called out to Aedan to halt, while
she lowered herself onto the grass and yanked off her
footwear.

She was examining the bloody, weeping blisters that had burst on her toes and heels when a shadow fell over her.

Colombia glanced up to see Aedan standing there, his brow furrowed. "Why didn't you tell me your feet were paining you?"

Colombia frowned back at him. "I didn't want to slow us down."

He huffed a sigh before hunkering down to take a closer look. "Well … you're not much good to us if you can't walk."

Colombia was about to shoot back a clipped retort when he reached out.

The feel of his fingers, strong and warm, yet gentle, wrapping around her ankle, made her catch her breath. His move was unexpected, yet he didn't seem to notice her surprise. Instead, he raised her foot so he could examine the burst blisters on her heel.

His mouth compressed. "Those slippers are coming off," he muttered. "They'll cut your feet to ribbons if you continue wearing them."

Colombia stiffened. "I'll have to travel barefoot?"

He nodded, gently setting her foot back down and releasing her ankle.

A frisson of disappointment arrowed through Colombia—a discomforting reaction indeed—at the severed touch. She should have been indignant that he'd taken hold of her ankle without asking permission first, but instead, once the initial surprise had passed, she'd found the feel of his long fingers circling her ankle reassuring.

"But won't I get prickles and thorns in my soles?"

"You will." He rose to his feet, his mouth curving. "Although your feet will toughen up soon enough." He paused there, the glint in his blue eyes telling her that he was enjoying her indignation. "Fear not … there's a village we should reach by nightfall where we can get you leather foot wrappings and some more suitable clothes."

He'd drawled those last few words; however, Colombia wasn't going to rise to the bait. She wasn't going to live up to his poor opinion of her. Biting back a tart comment, she rose to her feet and picked up her battered-looking slippers. She might as well carry them, just in case she needed them to cross boggy or muddy ground.

She then favored Aedan with a level look. "Come on, we'd better get moving."

They set off again, and Colombia had to admit that it was a relief not to have burning pain lance through her heels and toes with every stride. They walked over grassy hills, and she kept a look out for thistles or anything that might hurt her tender soles.

She was fortunate, for she walked across soft grass at present; even so, fatigue pulled down at her limbs, and her thigh muscles burned. Her body wasn't used to such rude treatment. She'd sleep like a stone tonight.

Despite her exhaustion, Colombia found herself glancing over her shoulder as they traveled. After yesterday, her nerves were stretched taut. Aedan had assured her they were far from the outlaws now, yet she kept expecting to see figures appear on the horizon behind her in pursuit.

Nonetheless, it was impossible to ignore that it was beautiful out here, surrounded by a wide pale-blue sky and endless emerald hills. From the moment she'd disembarked from the boat that had brought her to Britannia, she'd been fascinated by just how green this land was.

Within days, she realized why. It rained a lot here, and despite that it was summer, the sun lacked force. It was no wonder the grass grew so thick and lush. She was certainly grateful for it now, for she wore no head covering to protect her pale skin.

Aedan strode out in front of her, his gait determined, his head moving left and then right as he surveyed their surroundings.

Unease tickled the back of her neck once more.

It seemed that, despite his assurances, he too was on the lookout for trouble.

Eventually, Colombia asked, "Won't the outlaws eventually give up on us?"

Aedan glanced over his shoulder, pushing a lock of light-auburn hair out of his eyes. He wore his hair longer than the men of her own people did; it was wild and reached just above his shoulders.

"Unfortunately not." Perhaps seeing the alarm on her face, Aedan flashed her an apologetic half-smile. "It's not just you they want … it'll be reckoning against me. That's why we need to get to Onnum."

Colombia quickened her stride, and cast another quick glance about her, before drawing level with his shoulder. She didn't want to think about what would happen if those outlaws caught up with them. Her memory of the Brigante warriors—their feral cries as they cut down the supply convoy's escort, the glint in their eyes as they prepared to rape her—warned her that Aedan wasn't exaggerating.

"Well then," she said crisply. "We can't dawdle."

She cut Aedan a sidelong glance to see he was watching her. His expression was still enigmatic, although there was a warmth in his eyes. "How are your feet?" he asked after a pause.

"They're bearing up."

"Good."

He sighed then, his gaze shifting out into the distance once more as he resumed his surveillance. "I wanted to hunt for food … but we'll have to wait until we reach the village to eat."

Colombia nodded, even as her belly rumbled loudly in protest. It was starting to ache from emptiness, and she was feeling a little light-headed. They'd drunk from the river before setting off this morning but hadn't passed a stream since. Her mouth and throat were now parched.

It was water more than food she craved right now.

She'd never known thirst like this in her life. Aedan hadn't complained once about such things, although that didn't surprise her. He was clearly much tougher than she was.

"I *am* very thirsty," she admitted after a brief pause.

Aedan nodded and gestured ahead. "There's a burn not far from here ... we'll be able to slake our thirst there."

Colombia nodded. "You know this land well," she observed, impressed.

"I've hunted in these lands since I was old enough to leave my mother's skirts," he replied. "My father would take me and my brother away for weeks at a time to search for boar and deer. He taught us the contours of the land." He gestured right. "The coast lies a day's travel that way ... but I'm taking us north now."

"Where do your kin live?" she asked, curiosity wreathing up like woodsmoke. He'd been cagey the evening before about his past, and she'd sensed his reluctance to speak of it. Nonetheless, she wondered at how he'd come to join a band of outlaws. What of his family? A man of his age should be wed with sons of his own by now.

"Northeast of here, at a fort called Moedin, above the banks of the River Wear." He paused then, his jaw tightening. "The river your people call the River Vedra."

Colombia inclined her head, wondering at the name, which meant 'clear' in Latin. "Is it a beautiful river then?"

He shrugged. "Pretty enough, although the name in my own tongue means 'river of blood'."

"Why is that?"

"I'm not sure ... my grandfather told me that the local tribes have always fought over it. Maybe there was a battle there once."

"And why don't you live with your kin?"

Silence fell between them as they crested yet another hill. A light breeze wafted up from the south, warm and sweet with the smell of grass, feathering across their faces. The quiet drew out, and Colombia was beginning to think Aedan wouldn't respond to her bold question, when he spoke.

"After I was captured, they believed me dead." He didn't look her way, and Colombia found herself observing the clean, strong lines of his profile. "They didn't know I survived … but even if they had, I'd still have been dead in their eyes." His jaw tightened. "A warrior taken prisoner by the enemy forfeits all honor."

Colombia nodded. It was harsh, yet she understood the sentiment. "So, you can never go home?"

He glanced her way then, and his gaze shadowed. "I tried … after Aquila gave me my freedom. It was a mistake."

"What happened?"

His mouth twisted, and he glanced away once more. "I was my father's heir and promised to a woman … one I loved. Our wedding day was just days away when I was taken by the Caesars. I never forgot her though … even with the passing of the years. Part of me knew she'd have married another, would have a family of her own by now, but that didn't stop me from hoping she'd waited." He cleared his throat then. "But when I went home, I discovered she'd married my younger brother … he's chieftain now."

Colombia noted the way his voice changed when he mentioned his brother, the edge that crept in. It dawned on her then, why he'd been so scathing the eve before when she'd talked about Linus. He'd been burned by a woman and was bitter as a result. Empathy tightened her chest; that must have been hard for him.

"Is there bad blood between you?"

Aedan rubbed at his jaw, flashing her a rueful look.

Colombia braced herself to be told to mind her own business; growing up, her father had always told her she was too direct in her speech, and her aunt and uncle hadn't appreciated her frankness either.

And now she'd likely vexed Aedan too.

"You don't have to answer that," she murmured after a brief pause. "I know I'm too curious."

"You are."

"My father used to despair of my boldness … he told me it was 'unfeminine' to ask so many questions."

"And what of your betrothed?"

Colombia tensed, casting her mind back to the few interactions she'd shared with Linus before his posting.

In truth, she'd been on her best behavior. "I've always been demure around him," she admitted.

Aedan barked a laugh. "Demure?"

"Yes," Colombia replied, indignant now. "He's so handsome that I was in awe of him … and a little tongue-tied."

Aedan's eyes glinted, although his mouth twitched as if he wished to say something else yet was trying to stop himself. "You certainly have no such reticence around me," he murmured. "I must have a face like a horse's arse."

Colombia snorted, even as her cheeks warmed at his crudeness. "No, you don't," she muttered. "You just don't intimidate me, that's all."

And it was true—he didn't. Yes, he angered her at times, yet, oddly, she felt safe with this man.

Aedan's blue eyes narrowed a little, his expression turning thoughtful. Silence fell between them once more while they approached the bottom of the hill, where a small stream meandered its way through a scattering of rocks.

They'd almost reached the watercourse when Aedan released a deep sigh. "To answer your question … no, there isn't bad blood between Deaglan and me. It was just difficult to stomach seeing my brother sitting in the chair that should have been mine, wed to the woman I'd once loved … and her belly swollen with his child." He huffed a humorless laugh then. "Of course, deep down, I *knew* I wouldn't get a warm welcome … but I went back anyway."

IX. THE MAGPIE

"THAT'S A PRETTY belt." The elderly woman squinted at Colombia, her shrewd gaze raking over her. "If I can have it … and the clothes she's wearing, I'll give you shelter for the night, supper … and food to take with you."

"That's not enough," Aedan replied. "Colombia can't walk around naked. She'll need to be clothed … a tunic, shawl, and foot coverings will be sufficient."

The woman pulled a face, casting him an irritated look. "Do I look wealthy to you?" she griped.

No, she didn't. However, the crone who lived on the edge of Achwig, the village they'd reached as dusk settled, was the only local who'd been prepared to take them in overnight.

Aedan wasn't the problem, but the villagers had taken one look at the Roman woman standing at his side, and their welcome had cooled. Many of them had shut their wattle doors in Aedan and Colombia's faces.

But Enid hadn't.

She'd ushered them into her dark, damp roundhouse and sat them down by the fire. A pot of mutton stew bubbled over the embers of the hearth, and the aroma made Aedan's mouth fill with saliva. His gut ached with hunger now, demanding food.

It made it difficult to focus on negotiating with Enid, yet he had to.

Colombia drew too much attention dressed in her expensive tunic and stola. If they were to reach the Wall, she needed to blend in better. It was fortunate that she didn't have the tanned skin and black hair typical of many of the Roman nobility; her paler looks would be an advantage once she was dressed like a Brigante woman.

Enid considered his words for a few moments, her lined face changing into a look of veiled calculation before she eventually nodded. "I'll have those shoes too then," she said, motioning to the slippers that Colombia carried. "Since she won't be wearing them."

"Agreed," Aedan said curtly. Then, remembering his manners, he dipped his head. "Many thanks, Mother. We appreciate your hospitality."

Enid snorted. She moved over to the fire and stirred the mutton stew. "You're paying for it."

Aedan didn't reply. He cast a glance over at where Colombia had been watching their conversation. A groove had etched between her brows as she tried to understand what had transpired.

"She's agreed to help us," he murmured. Her expression was subdued, her gaze wary, and Aedan wondered if the poor welcome they'd received so far at Achwig had humbled her. When he'd told her his people didn't welcome hers making this land their own, he sensed she hadn't believed him—but after today, perhaps she would.

Enid glanced over her shoulder at him, her sharp gaze glinting. "Do you speak their tongue?"

Aedan nodded. "I was a Roman slave for a time."

The old woman screwed her face up before muttering something under her breath.

Ignoring the insult, Aedan motioned to Colombia. "Go on ... take a seat. She's going to give you clothes, but she wants the ones you're wearing ... and your belt and shoes ... as payment."

He expected Colombia to stiffen at this news, or to protest, but she merely nodded. She then moved over to one of the low stools by the hearth and lowered herself down upon it.

A sigh gusted out of her.

"Have you traveled far?" Enid asked then, her shrewd gaze sweeping from Aedan back to Colombia.

"Far enough," Aedan replied, deliberately cagey.

"And where are you headed?"

"To the mouth of the River Tin."

It was a deliberate lie, for it was probable Maccus and his men would travel this way in the next day or two. Enid would likely be only too happy to tell him what she could about the man and woman she'd given shelter to overnight.

This was a chance to send them in the wrong direction, for the River Tin opened into the sea, to the northeast—and after tonight, Aedan and Colombia were traveling northwest.

"Are your people from there?" Enid asked, not yet finished with her questions.

"Aye."

The old woman's gaze flicked to Colombia then, naked curiosity upon her face. "And why are you traveling with a *Roman* woman?"

Aedan favored her with a thin smile. He'd been waiting for this question. "Colombia is my woman," he said simply, deciding it was easier not to tell the truth. Even so, as he spoke the words, his pulse quickened, warmth spreading through his chest. The sensation was unsettling. It wasn't the lie that made him uneasy, but the fact he *liked* the crone thinking Colombia belonged to him.

Quickly, he shut that line of thought down.

Enid's mouth pursed as if she'd just sucked upon a sour plum. "Why would you take up with the enemy?"

Aedan shrugged. "She's beautiful ... and her husband didn't treat her well. I wanted her ... so I killed him and took her."

It was an arrogant statement, but not an uncommon one for a warrior.

Enid continued to observe him, and Aedan wondered if she believed him.

However, after a few moments, she turned to the simmering pot over the hearth.

A short while later, she dished them out clay bowls of stew, accompanied by hunks of coarse bread. It was simple fare, yet as he fell upon the meal, Aedan decided he'd never tasted anything so good. His hollow belly cried out for food.

He could have easily devoured four bowls, yet there was only enough for them to have two helpings each.

"I will make fresh bread for you to take with you tomorrow," Enid announced, taking away their empty bowls. "Along with a few boiled eggs and some cheese." She cast them an irritated look then. "I suppose you want a skin of ale too?"

"Yes, please, Mother," Aedan replied, smiling warmly this time. He'd guessed she was the wise woman of Achwig, and as such addressed her with the respectful title her position owed. Like the druids, wise women—who also possessed healing skills—were both respected and feared, for they could communicate with the Gods.

Muttering under her breath, Enid shuffled outside with the dirty bowls. There was a well in her garden, where she would wash up.

As soon as they were alone, Aedan glanced over at Colombia. In the golden glow of the fire, she looked tired. They'd walked since daybreak, with only short rests along the way. They'd crossed two burns, where they'd been able to slake their thirst—and they'd found a growth of brambles heavy with fruit at the second burn, which had taken the edge off their hunger.

However, she looked ready to collapse.

Their gazes met before Colombia's mouth curved into a half-smile. "I'm grateful this woman took us in."

Aedan smiled. "Enid believes we're lovers … so you might want to favor me with a dreamy look or two this eve."

Colombia stiffened, a crease forming between her eyebrows. "Why did you tell her that?"

Aedan's expression sobered. "It's what everyone here believes anyway," he pointed out, irritated at her response. "Don't worry, I'll keep my hands to myself."

A tense silence fell between them then, stretching out until Aedan finally broke it. "Enid is a magpie," he said tersely, "and she coveted that jeweled belt of yours, from the moment she set eyes on you."

Colombia glanced down and ran a finger along the delicately wrought belt. It was indeed beautiful, threaded with gold and semi-precious gems. "This was a gift from *pater*," she murmured, "for my sixteenth birthday."

Aedan frowned. He hadn't realized the belt had sentimental value. "I'm sorry you have to give it up," he said, his tone softening.

Colombia looked up, her lips curving. "*Pater* will understand," she replied. "I'd like to think he'd care more about my safety than a belt."

Aedan marked the way her voice flattened then. He wondered at her relationship with her father; he imagined they hadn't seen each other often over the past years, since he was a garrison commander on the frontier.

And he didn't know his daughter was nearby either.

He wouldn't be surprised if she was worried how he'd react when she turned up unannounced at Onnum.

Colombia adjusted the ankle-length tunic and knotted a length of string under the bodice. The material was a faded pale blue, and it smelled musty. It was also coarse and scratchy against her skin. Nonetheless, Colombia pushed aside the discomfort and wrapped the woolen shawl Enid had given her about her shoulders. It was surprisingly warm and soft, reminding Colombia of a smaller version of the voluminous palla she'd left behind.

Stepping out from behind the goatskin hanging, which divided a tiny sleeping alcove from the rest of the dwelling, Colombia found Aedan and Enid sitting together before the hearth, talking in low voices.

Listening to the lilt of their conversation, she reflected on how musical their language was compared to her own. She wished she could understand what passed between them—especially when Aedan said something that made Enid cackle.

Not being able to understand put her on edge and made her feel like an outsider, even more than she did already.

Nonetheless, Enid fascinated her.

The wise woman had a face like a wrinkled walnut, and when she laughed, she revealed more gum than tooth. However, her dark-blue eyes glinted with sharpness and vibrancy.

Enid was indeed a magpie, and from what Aedan had told her, insufferably nosey, but she had taken them in while others had turned them away. The villagers' lack of hospitality had surprised her, although pride meant she was careful not to admit so to Aedan.

This settlement was isolated. Nearer the forts, folk would be more open-minded.

Glancing up, Aedan's gaze settled on Colombia.

He scrutinized her for a moment, and she found herself growing warm under his stare.

"Do I look presentable?" she asked hesitantly.

He cleared his throat, blinked, and shifted his gaze to the glowing embers of the hearth before him. "Yes."

Enid rattled off a long sentence then, flashing Colombia a wry, gummy smile.

"What did she say?" Colombia asked.

Aedan glanced up, his mouth quirking. "Enid says you look like one of us ... that if you were wearing a torc and bracelets, you'd pass for a chieftain's wife."

Colombia's cheeks warmed. "*Tapadh leat*," she murmured, using the phrase that Aedan had taught her earlier. She then cast him a sidelong glance, hoping she'd pronounced that correctly.

She clearly had, for her thanks earned a nod from Enid.

Aedan rose to his feet then, stretching out his back, and yawning. "It's been a long day … Enid says we can sleep in the alcove."

Colombia's pulse quickened. She hadn't reacted well earlier when she'd learned Enid thought they were lovers. Her response had been instinctive, yet when she'd seen Aedan's gaze shutter, she realized she'd offended him.

Even so, she wasn't sure about spending the night in the same bed as him. She'd just come from the alcove and had noted that the pile of furs they were to sleep upon wasn't that wide.

"And where will she retire for the night?" she asked, trying to ignore the warmth rising to her cheeks.

Aedan turned to Enid and asked her something.

The crone motioned to the floor in front of the hearth, and then to a sheepskin that hung from one wall, making it clear that she'd be wrapping herself up in that before the fire.

Colombia nodded, even as guilt constricted her chest. She didn't like the idea of turfing an elderly woman from her bed. Nonetheless, she was too tired to argue about it.

She reminded herself then that she'd handed over her jeweled belt and clothing in exchange for a night's accommodation and a meal. Enid was simply giving them what they'd paid for.

Colombia retreated behind the hanging. Usually in the evening, she had quite a ritual—one that involved bathing, before her maid brushed out her hair, applying a little scented oil. Colombia would then don a sleeping tunic and slip between clean, scented sheets.

Those luxuries seemed a distant memory now though. Poor Flavia was dead, and *she* was wearing Briton clothing. She would have to tease out the knots in her hair with her fingers—and bathing would have to wait until she reached Onnum.

Her breathing grew shallow then as she imagined arriving at the fort—and seeing Linus, and her father, again. Yet, a lingering dread shadowed her anticipation.

When Aedan had queried whether she'd get a warm reception from her betrothed, she'd been sure she would.

Now, she wasn't so confident. *What if neither of them is happy to see me?*

Dismissing her worries, Colombia moved over to the musty-smelling furs. She was clearly overtired if she was letting doubt creep in. Of course, Linus would welcome her, as would her father. It was ridiculous to think otherwise.

She looked forward to retreating to the sanctuary of her father's residence, to soaking up to her chin in a hot bath.

Sinking down onto the bed, Colombia wriggled over, trying to get as close as possible to the stacked stone wall. And when Aedan joined her shortly after, she was relieved that, although he pulled off his boots, he lay down, like her, fully clothed. She wasn't used to being in such proximity to a man.

"Sorry," he muttered, as he accidentally jostled her with his elbow when he pulled a fur over them. "It's a bit cramped."

"It is," Colombia murmured.

This journey was starting to feel increasingly surreal. And she was no closer to understanding her traveling companion either. Bitterness, at the hand life had dealt him, cast a long shadow over Aedan. He was a hard man to pin down: arrogant and dismissive one moment and considerate the next. He could treat her like an unwelcome traveling companion, and then take pains to ensure she was taken care of. She still wasn't sure he had any respect or liking for her, but she had warmed to him—and the realization unnerved her.

"Goodnight, Colombia," Aedan said, intruding on her thoughts. He then rolled onto his side so that his back faced her. "Sleep well."

X. IN THE MOONLIGHT

COLOMBIA AWOKE TO the sound of shouting.

Groggy and disoriented, she pushed herself up into a sitting position and tried to make sense of the rough voices filtering through the dwelling.

"What's happening?" she croaked, blinking as she peered into the gloom.

"Trouble has found us." Aedan's voice was sharp, wide-awake. "Get up, Colombia ... quickly, and put on your foot coverings and shawl. We're leaving."

Heart pounding, Colombia did as bid. She scrambled to the edge of the furs, grabbed the crude leather foot coverings Enid had given her, and jammed them onto her feet, securing them with twine. She then fumbled for her shawl and stood up.

Aedan had already left the alcove, and she found him moving toward the door. The interior of Enid's roundhouse was dimly lit, as the glowing embers were slowly dying, but there was enough light for Colombia to make out the glint of his unsheathed dagger.

Colombia's mouth went dry, and her legs wobbled beneath her.

Minerva, had the outlaws caught up with them so soon?

But when she followed Aedan to the door of the dwelling and peeked out, she spied the hostile faces of the villagers who'd turned them away the evening before.

An angry mob bearing flaming torches had gathered in Enid's garden.

Colombia couldn't understand what they were saying, although the rough voices of the burly men at the front of the group, all of them carrying farming tools—hoes, rakes, and vicious-looking scythes—needed no translation.

And to Colombia's shock, Enid was facing off against them.

Hands on hips, her spine straight, the old woman seemed to be giving the men a tongue-lashing.

However, when Aedan appeared, the villagers turned their attention from Enid to him.

One of them shouted out something, and a chorus of jeers followed.

Colombia moved up behind Aedan. "What are they saying?"

"Best you don't know," he murmured. His voice was soft, yet flat. He then glanced over his shoulder at her, his gaze gleaming in the semi-darkness. "Stay back ... and get ready to run."

Their gazes fused for an instant, and she nodded.

Nonetheless, Colombia's heart started to kick hard against her breastbone. A sickly sensation washed over her.

Aedan had warned her that her people weren't universally loved, but there had been a part of her that refused to believe it. Yes, there were pockets of outlaws, of rebels, but most of the Britons lived peacefully under their Roman overlords.

She saw now that wasn't the case.

Aedan then turned away and answered the villagers.

His voice, hard-edged now, carried across the crowd, quietening the heckling. Once again, Colombia had no idea what had been said, yet since the expressions of the villagers hadn't warmed—she guessed he wasn't trying to placate them.

Indeed, she saw some of them tighten their grip on their tools, and a big man wielding a huge scythe stepped forward. The farmer growled something before spitting on the ground.

Enid muttered an answer, only to get snarled at, and when Aedan replied, Colombia caught the warning in his voice.

He was vastly outnumbered here, yet he'd also been so when he'd saved her from those outlaws. She'd seen him fight too and knew he could hold his own. Nonetheless, these villagers were riled. Danger shivered through the still night air.

Colombia's belly twisted.

Some of the men weren't glaring at Aedan now, but at her—resentment glinting in their eyes. It didn't matter that she'd done none of them any wrong; she symbolized the people they saw as their oppressors. And they despised Aedan too for helping a Roman woman.

Just like Enid, they believed she and Aedan were lovers.

The scythe-wielding villager lunged then. He was a huge man with great, muscular arms, yet he was slow, and Aedan dodged him easily.

Snarling curses, the farmer came at him again, swinging that scythe in a deadly arc.

Aedan ducked under his guard and stabbed him in the lower arm.

With a howl, the farmer dropped his scythe, clutching at his forearm, where blood now flowed.

Aedan backed up a few steps, his gaze sweeping the crowd. He then shouted something. It sounded like a taunt, and Colombia's already racing heart started to thunder in her ears.

Jupiter, he wasn't goading them, was he?

Enid spoke to Aedan then, her voice sharp. Unlike earlier, her gaze wasn't full of cunning and curiosity, but alarm. Like Colombia, she knew what would happen if this confrontation continued.

The injured farmer started to berate him again, his harsh voice echoing through the night.

Backing up farther, Aedan took Colombia by the arm with his left hand, while he kept his knife raised in his right. "Time to depart," he murmured.

"But what about Enid?" she gasped.

"She's going to threaten to curse the lot of them," he replied. "That should give us time to get away."

He guided her back, into the shadows that flanked Enid's tiny roundhouse.

Colombia swallowed hard. There was no time to thank Enid, or to worry about what might happen to the woman who'd sheltered them.

They melted into the darkness, skirting the edge of the circular garden that surrounded the dwelling, before pushing through the wattle fence.

Rough male voices followed them, interspersed by Enid's higher-pitched, vexed voice. Silence followed her words, and Colombia's throat constricted.

The woman owed them nothing; her gesture was a brave one.

"Why is she helping us?" she whispered to Aedan as they hurried away from Achwig, up a grassy hill. A waxing moon sailed high above them, casting a silvery veil over the world. Although Enid had taken them in, Colombia had believed it was for purely mercenary reasons.

"She's guardian of this village," Aedan answered, his tone grim. "And doesn't want to see any of her menfolk die on my blade. Helping us get away without more bloodshed is in everyone's interest."

"Will they come after us?"

"Yes ... the wise woman won't keep them at bay for much longer."

Aedan's words were prophetic, for moments later, the roar of the mob, which had started to fade, grew closer once more. Colombia glanced over her shoulder to see the glow of torches approaching from the bottom of the hill, like a cluster of huge, angry fireflies in pursuit.

Her breathing caught. "What are we going to do now?"

"Don't worry," Aedan replied. "If we run fast, they'll give up soon enough."

Turning, they sprinted away from the village, cresting the hill, and stumbling down the other side.

Just like when they'd fled the outlaws, Colombia was grateful Aedan gripped her hand. Despite the moonlight, it was difficult to see in the darkness, although fear gave her a burst of speed. The leather foot coverings were surprisingly comfortable—far more than her slippers had been—and her tunic and shawl, although of far poorer cloth than the garments she'd given Enid, were much less restrictive. It made it easier to keep up with Aedan.

They ran over shadowed hills—and soon left the mob behind. As Aedan had predicted, the men quickly gave up, once they'd chased them from the village.

Colombia was tiring now, sweat pouring down her face, chest, and back. Her heart pounded against her ribs, and the muscles in her legs burned.

To her relief, Aedan slowed to a brisk walk as the hills gave way to woodland. Finally, he released her hand, and they strode amongst moonlit trees, twigs snapping underfoot. The hoot of an owl filtered through the woods, followed by the far-off howl of a wolf.

And despite that she was overheated from running, Colombia shivered. She'd been in a deep, dreamless sleep when Aedan woke her earlier, her body relaxed and warm. But now she was fleeing again.

"I don't understand," she panted, still struggling to catch her breath. "They could have run us out of the village when we arrived earlier ... why wait until halfway through the night?"

"Did you notice how slow that man who attacked me was?" Aedan replied. "I'd say they'd been downing ales all evening, working each other up until their aggression spilled over like boiled milk."

"Will they harm Enid?"

Aedan glanced her way, his face all shadows and angles in the moonlight streaming through the trees. "I think not ... as I said, she's the village wise woman. Most of the men fear her wrath."

A relieved sigh escaped Colombia. She didn't want anyone else hurt because of her. She couldn't help but blame herself for Flavia and Atticus's deaths. No, she hadn't wielded the arrow or blade that killed them—yet they'd only been in Britannia because of her.

Her belly clenched. She was beginning to wish she'd never set foot on this cursed isle. This land was brutal, and piece by piece it was tearing away the beliefs that had cocooned her over the years.

She couldn't believe her father had lied to her about the Britons—but he had. The realization was as bitter as wormwood on her tongue, and it also made her nervous.

What else wasn't real?

Aedan quickened his stride, and Colombia followed, falling in behind him. They moved softly through the woodland, and despite that she was still frightened, despite that her heart still hammered in her chest, and dread clenched her gut, Colombia noted the beauty of her surroundings. She'd never been in the woods in the middle of the night like this. The air was cool and rich, and the silvery light of the moon made the woods seem otherworldly.

"I almost expect to see nymphs out here," she admitted finally, grateful to focus on something other than the gnawing worry deep in her chest, "cavorting in the moonlight."

Aedan gave a soft snort. "This is Britannia ... you won't see any such creatures here."

"What do you have instead then?"

"The Sidhe."

He pronounced the word 'Shee', and Colombia was intrigued. "What are they then?"

"Fairies ... little people. They live in the hidden places of this world, and no two are the same in temperament. Some are friendly, while others will unleash their wrath if you offend them." He paused then. "But if you are kind to one of the Sidhe, they will bless you with luck."

Colombia managed a half-smile. "And have you ever helped a fairy?"

"No ... does my life seem blessed with good fortune to you?"

Colombia pulled a face. "I suppose not," she admitted. "Although despite everything that's befallen you, you're still alive ... Fortuna must be smiling upon you a little."

"I don't worship the same gods as you, Colombia."

His tone was sharp, and heat rose in Colombia's cheeks. *Goose.* Of course, he wouldn't believe in Fortuna. She'd heard that, like her own people, the Britons worshipped a few deities. "And what God would you pray to for good luck then?"

"The Hag," he replied. "Goddess of the dark, winter, and the earth."

"The Hag?" Colombia's mouth quirked. "It's just as well our paths crossed with Enid's then."

He snorted a laugh then before casting her a glance over his shoulder, his gaze glinting in the silvery light of the moon. "So, you believe me now ... about the relations between your people and mine?"

Colombia frowned. Pluto take him, of course he'd bring that up. The man wouldn't let her suffer her humiliation with dignity. Instead, he'd rub her face in it.

"I've little choice, do I?" she replied, her tone brittle. "After what just happened."

Silence fell then, broken only by the soft pad of their feet across the bed of leaves and moss. When Aedan eventually spoke, his voice was subdued. "The truth is sometimes difficult to take, Colombia ... but better that than to go through life believing a lie."

XI. SHE ISN'T YOUR WOMAN

STOPPING ON THE edge of the woods, Aedan pushed wet hair out of his eyes and glanced around. He then peered through the sheets of driving rain.

The night had been clear when they'd set out from Achwig, but—in typical fashion—the weather suddenly changed. As they marched toward dawn, a cold wind sprang up from the north, and shortly after, he'd felt spits of rain on his face.

The rain had started slowly, increasing in force until it poured down.

By daybreak, they were both soaked to the skin, despite the canopy of leaves above them.

Aedan wouldn't have minded so much if it had been a warm summer rain. However, now that they were out in the open, with the chill north wind buffeting them, he was starting to feel uncomfortably cold. And when he turned his attention from his surroundings and glanced back at where Colombia had halted on the tree line, he frowned.

She'd pulled her wet woolen shawl close, yet she was shivering. Her hair was plastered against her skull, her heart-shaped face pale.

"Do you know where we are?" she asked, moving closer.

Aedan nodded. "We're still heading in the right direction." He gestured into the distance. "We just have to keep walking northwest, and we'll get to Onnum in the next couple of days."

"Good," Colombia murmured, her voice oddly flat. "The sooner I get there the better."

Aedan studied her face, his gaze narrowing further. His companion didn't look happy this morning. Her gaze had turned inward, and her mouth was pinched. Nonetheless, she couldn't deny what had happened in Achwig.

As they'd approached the village the evening before, viewing the huddle of sod cottages with smoke drifting from their thatched roofs, he'd felt a pang of misgiving. If he'd been traveling alone, the locals would have taken him in without issue, but folk in out-of-the-way places like this were wary of outsiders and wouldn't take well to a Roman woman striding into their village.

He hadn't been surprised when a few of them slammed their doors in his face, but he'd thought they'd leave things there. He should have realized that when the men had downed a few skinfuls of ale, their courage, and aggression, would rise.

The one who'd attacked Aedan had been the mouthiest, calling her his whore, and naming him a filthy, lice-ridden bitch-humper, among other things.

The words had washed off Aedan—he'd been called worse over the years—but he'd been glad that Colombia hadn't understood their coarse insults.

Watch yourself, a warning whispered to him then, *you're getting too protective of her. She isn't your woman.*

Aedan's mouth thinned. No, she wasn't.

Colombia was promised to a high-ranking Roman officer—a man who'd let five years pass without sending for her or making a trip home to see his bride-to-be.

Still, that wasn't his problem. He needed only to focus on getting Colombia safely to Onnum. After that, he'd have to think about what *his* future held.

Aedan fought the urge to scowl then. He was like a boat cast off to sea without oars or anchor. Lost. His chest tightened, yet he pushed the discomforting sensation aside. Enough. He'd think about himself later.

Instead, his gaze returned to Colombia's determined, yet exhausted, rain-slicked face. Aye, she was weary, but she swallowed any complaints. Her grit impressed him. If he was honest, there were many things he liked about Colombia—although it was wise not to dwell on them.

"Can you keep walking for a bit longer?" he asked, his tone more brusque than he'd intended.

She nodded, her slender shoulders straightening.

"There's a rocky valley up ahead, where I'll find us shelter and build a fire," he continued. "We should reach there by noon. I'll see about hunting us some food then."

"We'll stop there."

Colombia heaved a deep sigh at Aedan's announcement. *Finally.*

They'd traveled deep into the stone-strewn vale before he motioned right to where a rock overhand peeked out from a growth of spiky bushes. Leaden clouds hung overhead, while the rain continued to patter down.

Her body was aching now, and it felt as if she had rocks tied to her ankles. She desperately needed to sit down. Wearily, she followed Aedan up the side of the valley. Scree slid underfoot, and she stumbled.

Instantly, her companion was there, placing a hand under her elbow to steady her. "I know you're tired," he murmured. "I'm sorry if I pushed you too hard."

"You didn't," she said quickly. "We could hardly make camp on those hills, could we?"

His mouth kicked up into a smile, and Colombia's belly dived.

Her swift reaction startled her. She wasn't blind. She'd noticed that Aedan was handsome, yet the rain gleaming on his face, and the way his light-auburn hair was slicked back against his skull, highlighted his proud bone structure.

And when he smiled, a deep dimple appeared on his right cheek.

Colombia tensed then, alarm fluttering up. Finding herself attracted to Aedan, when she had her fiancé waiting for her at the Wall, wasn't wise at all.

Linus is handsome too, she reminded herself, *and he has a charming smile.*

Juno, she needed to focus on what she'd traveled this way for.

"We've made good time," Aedan assured her, oblivious to her inner struggle. "So, we should be able to rest here until tomorrow morning."

Colombia nodded. However, her relief at this news now warred with stabbing guilt.

I must reach Linus.

Yet, as desperate as she was to get to Onnum, exhaustion now clawed at her. She didn't understand why her limbs ached so; however, her body was unused to such harsh treatment. She'd never walked so far.

Reaching the overhang, she spied a circle of blackened stones underneath. "Someone else has camped here," she noted dully.

"Hunters most likely," Aedan replied. "Deer roam this valley ... I used to hunt here years ago with my father." He paused then, his gaze surveying the overhang. "I need to get a fire started."

Colombia bent low and stumbled over to the wall behind the remnants of the hearth. She then sank down, bracing her back against the cool stone. "Won't you have trouble finding dry wood?"

"It'll be a challenge," Aedan admitted, pulling a face. "But I've got a flint ... and there will be some dry twigs and branches tucked away in the valley." Their gazes met then. "Wait here ... I will go foraging."

Colombia nodded once more. He didn't need to worry. Now that she'd seated herself under this overhang, she didn't intend to move. Even so, unease feathered through her. *There are still a couple of hours of daylight left*, she reminded herself. *I should keep going.*

However, her body rebelled at the thought of traveling any farther today. As eager as she was to reach him, Linus would have to wait.

Watching Aedan disappear into the gloom, she sank back against the wall, her eyes fluttering shut.

Colombia awoke a while later to the feel of a hand upon her brow.

Opening her eyes, she looked up into Aedan's penetrating gaze. Concern shadowed their sea-blue depths. His face was slicked with rain.

"Did I fall asleep," she murmured.

He nodded. "Your cheeks are flushed ... and your forehead is warm ... I think you've caught a chill."

Colombia grimaced. That would account for why she felt so exhausted. Her sleep hadn't refreshed her. If anything, she was even more tired than earlier. Pushing herself up, for she'd fallen on her side while she slumbered, Colombia pulled her damp woolen shawl around her as a paroxysm of shivering seized her.

"Curse it," she muttered. "You could be right."

Expression grim, he nodded before pushing wet hair out of his eyes. "I need to get a fire going."

Colombia watched as he placed a handful of dry twigs and bark into the hearth and produced a flint from a pouch on his belt. Behind him was a messy pile of firewood. "Your hunt for wood was successful then?"

"It was," he murmured, crouching down and striking the flint against a dark-grey stone amongst the nest he'd created in the hearth. "However, it took me longer than I hoped ... the rain's gotten even heavier since we arrived here."

Colombia peered out into the valley beyond their overhang. Indeed, the clouds seemed to have lowered even farther, and the patter of the rain against the stony ground was louder now.

Thunder rumbled overhead.

Leaning back and trying to quell the shivers that rippled through her, Colombia watched Aedan strike the flint against stone repeatedly. Sparks flew, and the tinder started to smoke. Gently, he blew on the smoking wood, coaxing it into flame.

She couldn't take her gaze off him. And as she observed him start the fire, attraction tugged at her once more—a sensation that made her breathing quicken and belly flutter.

Gods, she had to do something about this. She had to remind herself of the nature of their relationship before she did something foolish.

The man is an outlaw, she told herself sternly, *and I'm paying him to take me to the Wall.*

"Thank you for agreeing to take me to Onnum," she said eventually, inwardly cringing at how stilted and formal her voice sounded. "I really am appreciative."

Aedan sat back on his haunches and glanced her way once more. His gaze was veiled as he nodded. "You're welcome ... although I still haven't found us any food," he replied. "As soon as I get this fire going properly, I shall go hunting."

"You should rest too," she murmured. In truth, Colombia wasn't that hungry at present. Perhaps her belly had gotten used to half-rations over the last couple of days. Or, maybe, the fever she was fighting had robbed her of an appetite.

"You must eat something," Aedan replied coolly. "You can't walk to Onnum on an empty stomach ... and neither can I."

He turned his attention back to the fire then, and a short while later, he had gorse branches crackling upon it. His expression had completely shuttered now, and Colombia fought a creeping sense of guilt. Despite that she'd thanked him, she'd treated him like a servant. He likely thought her cold and haughty—and suddenly it mattered greatly that he didn't.

Silence stretched between them before Colombia cleared her throat. "I feel safe with you, Aedan," she admitted softly. "I know you resent everything I stand for ... but I trust you."

His chin kicked up, surprise flickering across his face.

Colombia had taken herself aback too. That had come out a little too raw. One moment she was painfully formal, the next she was being overly familiar. Perhaps the fever was robbing her of good sense. Maybe it was best if she didn't speak at all.

"I don't resent you," he replied. "Do you really think I'm that petty?"

Colombia swallowed. "My people have done you wrong. I must be a constant reminder of it."

He snorted. "*Fate* has done me wrong ... but I don't blame you for it."

Their gazes fused across the fire, and Colombia's mouth lifted at the corners. "I'm glad," she murmured. Warmth spread across her chest then, dousing the last of her reserve and good sense. "I'd like to be your friend."

Their stare drew out before Aedan cleared his throat and eventually looked away. Moving toward the edge of the overhang, he collected the bow and quiver he'd laid down. He'd carried them with him ever since they'd fled the outlaws and had been careful not to leave them behind in Enid's cottage. Nonetheless, Colombia wasn't sure what he'd manage to hunt in the pouring rain.

"Keep the fire burning," he instructed, still avoiding her gaze. "And dry yourself off. I'll get back as soon as I can."

XII. BELONGING

I'D LIKE TO be your friend.

Aedan clenched his jaw, blinking the rain out of his eyes as walked. He was tracking his way down the meandering burn that cut through the high-sided vale, gaze flicking left and right as he went.

However, it was difficult to keep his thoughts on hunting.

He didn't understand Colombia. One moment she was thanking him with cool formality, as if he were her hired lackey, and the next she spoke with genuine trust and warmth.

He almost preferred it when she was aloof though; for when she let her guard down, when those smoky eyes held his, he lost his train of thought.

Colombia Juventus was a dangerous distraction. They couldn't be friends. They came from different worlds, and after he dropped her off at the Wall, their paths would diverge forever.

"Enough of this," Aedan muttered, shaking his head to clear it. "Focus."

Indeed, he had to keep his senses sharp, or he'd never catch them any supper. He'd hoped to stumble upon a hind in the valley, yet the foul weather had driven them away to seek shelter elsewhere.

The afternoon had drawn out, and the light started to fade. And all the while, the rain drummed down—

relentless. Aedan's wet clothes chafed his skin, while cold and fatigue dragged at his limbs. He was starting to lose heart and didn't want to catch a chill as Colombia likely had. Maybe they would go to sleep with empty bellies tonight.

Worry tightened his gut then. *Colombia needs to eat something*. He hadn't liked the heat he'd felt on her brow earlier, or the flush on her cheeks. If she got sick, they'd be in trouble.

Irritation speared him once more at just how easily his thoughts returned to the woman he was escorting—at how easy it was to worry about her.

He needed to get ahold of himself, to concentrate on keeping her safe and well until they reached the Wall. After that, she'd be her father's responsibility. He and her betrothed could take care of her.

Halting, Aedan growled a curse under his breath. There was no point in continuing. He wasn't going to catch anything this afternoon.

However, he'd just turned for home when he spied a grouse moving amongst a patch of heather only a few yards distant. Drawing to a sharp halt, he quickly unslung his bow and notched an arrow. The bird, with its distinctive dark-brown feathers, was plump.

Moments later, the grouse was dead, and Aedan strode to the clump of heather, grasping the bird by the feet.

He then set off at a jog up the valley.

A wry smile tugged at his lips. He wouldn't return to the overhang empty-handed, after all.

When Aedan finally ducked under the ledge, he was relieved to see Colombia was awake. She'd also kept the fire going, and he stifled a sigh as he lowered himself down, cross-legged before the hearth.

"You caught something," she greeted him, managing a wan smile. "Although you're soaking wet."

Aedan pushed his dripping hair off his face and grinned. "I am, but it was worth it ... a nice fat grouse." He began to pluck the hapless bird, in short, deft movements, glancing up at his companion periodically as he did so. "How are you feeling?"

"Much the same as earlier."

"Your fever's not worse?"

"I don't think so."

Aedan wasn't convinced. She had a tell-tale gleam to her eye, and the flush on her cheeks had deepened. It concerned him.

Once the bird was plucked, he used his knife to gut it—and then a short while later, the grouse was roasting over the embers upon a long stick.

The toothsome aroma of cooking meat wafted through the overhang, and Aedan's belly growled. He glanced Colombia's way once again. "You must be hungry too?"

She shrugged. "Not really."

Aedan's brow furrowed at this news. That wasn't a good sign.

Pushing his worry to one side, he focused on roasting the grouse. When it was done, they picked the rich meat off the carcass, eating their supper as the light beyond the overhang faded. The rain had slackened a little now though.

Despite her earlier comment, Colombia ate her share of the grouse without difficulty, and once they'd picked the bones clean, they washed their hands under a trickle of water that ran over the lip of the overhang and slaked their thirst with it too.

Aedan then put more fuel on the fire and shifted around so that he too sat with his back against the rock wall, shoulder-to-shoulder with Colombia. Noting that she was shivering, he shot her a sidelong glance. "Can I check your brow again?"

She nodded, and when he placed the back of his hand on her forehead, he noted it was hot and dry.

"Your fever is worsening," he murmured. "We're going to have to sleep close tonight."

Colombia jerked slightly at this, her glazed eyes widening. "Excuse me?"

"You must keep warm," he explained patiently, "and this fire isn't enough ... I'll use my body to prevent your chill from worsening. Your betrothed won't be happy if you turn up at Onnum sick, will he?"

Her throat bobbed, and she shook her head. "Very well," she said huskily. "That makes sense."

It did, although now that Aedan had suggested it, he wished he hadn't. He'd just spent the afternoon wrestling with himself. He'd already recognized he was strongly attracted to this woman. Was it wise to go to sleep with her in his arms?

Cursing himself, Aedan tore his gaze from hers. "Right then," he said, forcing briskness into his voice. "Let's try and make ourselves comfortable on this stony ground."

Aedan stretched out along the wall and drew Colombia against him so that the curve of her back molded into his chest and belly. He covered them both with her woolen shawl. It was still slightly damp, although the fire had done a good enough job of removing most of the moisture. Meanwhile, Aedan's wet clothing felt cold and clammy against his skin. He too needed to keep warm, or he'd sicken.

But the moment he pulled Colombia's supple body against his, Aedan knew for certain his protective gesture had been a mistake.

Unlike the thick, loose fabric of her old clothing, the tunic was much thinner. The furnace of her burning skin indeed soaked into his chilled body. Holding Colombia in his arms overnight would certainly keep the cold and damp at bay. However, he tensed at the feel of her gentle curves molded against his body. Her backside pressed against his groin.

It was distracting.

And to make matters worse, despite her earlier reluctance to sleep in his arms, Colombia gave a soft, shuddering sigh and sank against him. She then wriggled her bottom, as if trying to burrow deeper against his body.

Aedan went rigid, his groin hardening in response. He tried to pull away, to flatten himself up against the wall behind him—but there was nowhere to go.

Colombia's hair, which was drying in heavy waves, tickled his nose, and the sweet, musky smell of her skin enveloped him.

The Reaper take him, how was he supposed to sleep like this?

Colombia heaved another sigh and sank even deeper into Aedan's embrace. The moment he'd put his arms around her, all the tension seeped from her body. Even her shivering eased a little.

She shouldn't enjoy physical contact with him as much as she did—yet she didn't have the will this evening to fight the pull between them.

When Aedan had suggested they sleep like this earlier, she'd been shocked.

Despite that they'd shared a bed at Enid's, they hadn't actually touched.

She and Linus had kissed a couple of times before his departure—sweet, romantic moments she'd cherished— but he hadn't pulled her into his arms. She could feel the lean, hard length of Aedan's body pressed along hers— and despite that she was overly warm, the contact with him made her feel better.

However, when she wriggled her backside into him— an instinctive act—his body stiffened against hers. And then she felt something else—something hard and hot— pressing into the cleft between her buttocks.

Colombia's breathing grew shallow.

She was still a virgin and had lived in a cocoon of privilege until the past few days, but she knew what that hardness against her backside was.

She'd seen animals mate and had overheard the whispers of servants and slaves over the years. She hadn't grown up under a rock; she knew what a man did with the appendage between his legs.

If she was honest, she'd spent many a night lying abed, wondering what Linus would look like naked.

What would his manhood be like? Would it be large? Would it be straight or curved? One of the servants in her uncle's household had whispered to the cooks that her man's 'mentula' was shaped like a wheat scythe.

But now, treacherously, her betrothed and his shaft were far from her mind—instead, she found herself thinking about Aedan. Her movement had brought her hard against him and left no doubt in her imagination about the size and girth of his manhood.

Her mouth went dry, and her already fevered body grew hotter still. A moment later, a strange, needy ache started to pulse between her thighs.

Minerva, I must move away from him.

She shifted her hips—intending to slide forward—but Aedan's voice halted her.

"For the love of the Gods," he choked out. "Stop wriggling, will you?"

Colombia froze. There was a strangled edge to his voice. Of course, every time she moved, she caused more friction between their bodies.

His shaft was an iron brand now, burning into her.

Colombia's pulse quickened. Lying together like this wasn't a good idea. She wasn't sure she could sleep with *that* pressing into her.

Neither of them spoke, and after a few moments, the tension in Aedan's body eased—as did the hard press against her. He'd built the fire up before retiring for the night, and the heat washed over them both.

Colombia was still overly hot, yet her shivering slowly subsided.

Despite that she'd told herself she wouldn't be able to relax in Aedan's arms, her eyelids started to grow heavy. She melted into the safety of his embrace, giving herself up to exhaustion.

And as she drifted off to sleep, a sense of belonging—one that had eluded Colombia her whole life—stole upon her.

Colombia stirred awake to find sunlight streaming onto her face.

The embers of the previous night's fire smoked in the hearth, yet she no longer felt the warm strength of Aedan's body curled into her back.

Instead, her companion was already up.

Aedan was sitting on the other side of the fire, sharpening the blade of his dagger on a smooth stone.

He glanced her way as she struggled up into a sitting position, and Colombia noted the dark smudges under his eyes, the tension on his face. The man looked tired, and she wondered if he'd slept badly overnight.

"How are you feeling?" he asked.

Colombia took a moment to consider his question. Unlike the night before, her joints didn't ache, and a fever no longer bathed her skin. The chill had abated. "Much better," she murmured, favoring him with a shy smile. "Thanks to you."

He smiled back, although there was a brittleness to the expression. "I didn't do much."

"You kept me warm."

Colombia rose stiffly to her feet and moved out from under the ledge, peering out at the morning. Thankfully, the foul weather had ceased. The world around her glistened with moisture, and the air was fresh and sweet—a unique smell that only appeared after rain.

Heaving in a lungful of air, Colombia closed her eyes and gave a long, languid stretch, easing her joints.

What a relief it was to feel herself again. She'd been worried the fever would worsen and that Aedan would be stuck with a sick woman. This wasn't the place to get ill; they were far from a physician out here. And she didn't want him to have to carry her to Onnum.

Onnum. Nerves tightened her belly then, shattering the moment. Gods, her destination was drawing ever closer, and self-doubt was creeping back in. *What if Linus doesn't want me to join him?*

When she opened her eyes, she found that Aedan had cast aside his knife and stood up. He was standing just a couple of feet from her, his gaze upon her.

And the look on his face made Colombia's breathing catch.

It was a naked blend of hunger and longing, and her heart started pounding in response.

No one had ever looked at her like that—not even Linus on the day they'd said their farewells before he departed Italia for the northern frontier.

It was a look that made the world shrink to this spot, this moment. It made Colombia forget her worries about survival, and her gathering dread at how her betrothed, and her father, would respond when she arrived at the Wall.

All that mattered was the awareness that now crackled between them.

Wordlessly, Aedan moved closer. "I'm relieved you are better," he said softly, although the hoarseness to his voice made Colombia suppress a shiver. "You had me worried."

"Did I?" She tried to smile, to lighten the mood between them, yet her face muscles wouldn't cooperate. All she could do was hold Aedan's gaze as his hand rose to her cheek, and his fingertips traced a gentle path down to her jaw.

Colombia started to tremble, yet it wasn't a fever that had her in its grip now, but wanting.

And when the pad of his thumb skimmed across her lower lip, she swayed toward him.

XIII. I HAVEN'T FORGOTTEN

AEDAN BENT HIS head, his lips brushing Colombia's.

Curse him, he knew he shouldn't be doing this. There were a hundred reasons why he should keep his distance from this woman, but at this moment, all of them had scattered like leaves in the wind.

Colombia had slept deeply throughout the night, nestling into the cradle of his arms like a wolf cub seeking reassurance and comfort. The feel of her against him had aroused him initially, so much so that his bollocks had ached for a long while afterward, but once she'd fallen asleep, another—and even more discomforting—sensation had stolen over him.

Tenderness, and the fierce urge to protect the woman in his arms, swept over him in a tide. Of course, he shouldn't be letting himself feel anything for Colombia Juventus. She was a Roman noblewoman and promised to another. He'd only get himself in trouble if he continued down this road.

And yet, here he was walking it.

He'd slept poorly for the rest of the night, reeling from the sensations. They were both unwelcome and exhilarating, and when the dawn light filtered into their makeshift camp under the stone overhang, he faced it with gritty eyes and an ill temper.

Nonetheless, as he'd watched Colombia stretch, watched her turn her lovely face up to greet the morning sun, something had given way inside him. He'd risen to his feet to face her, and now he was doing what he'd told the darkness the night before he wouldn't.

He was kissing her.

His lips whispered over Colombia's once more, testing her reaction.

With a sigh, she leaned closer, her long, tawny, dark-tipped eyelashes fluttering closed again. And then, when a sigh escaped her, the last of his self-control unraveled.

A groan rumbled low in his throat as he increased the pressure of his lips on hers, both hands coming up to cup her face. He then traced the seam of her lips with the tip of his tongue and was rewarded when they parted for him.

He kissed her deeply then, yet reverently, his tongue and lips exploring her mouth as if she were an exotic fruit he would only be allowed to taste once.

And she was.

Even as his tongue entwined with hers, even as he reveled in the softness of that small, lush mouth, his chest began to ache. Colombia was forbidden, but there was no denying it any longer: he wanted her.

Ever since they'd set out on this journey together, he'd been fighting a growing awareness. He'd rebelled against it, yet this morning, his will was weak.

Colombia reached out, her small hands flattening against his chest. He was wearing a leather vest, yet he was sure she could feel the thunder of his heart against her palm.

His blood now roared in his ears.

With another sigh, she kissed him back, tentatively at first, with untutored enthusiasm. However, when her teeth grazed his lower lip, his rod jerked against the confines of his bracae.

His body's violent reaction made good sense filter in through the haze of desire that was close to consuming him.

Aedan slid his hands down to rest on her shoulders, his grip firming as he broke off the embrace and gently pushed himself away from her. Breathing hard, he met her gaze.

Colombia's eyes had a glazed look—but not one that had been caused by the fever she'd battled with the eve before. Her lips were swollen from their kisses, her cheeks slightly flushed.

Gods, she was beautiful—but she wasn't his.

"We should stop there," he said hoarsely.

Disappointment flared in her eyes, even as she nodded.

"I shouldn't have done that," he continued, biting the words out. "I'm sorry."

Her gaze remained on his face. "Don't apologize," she whispered. "I liked it."

Muttering a curse, Aedan released her and stepped back, putting much-needed distance between them. "You're promised to Linus Calix Aurelius, remember?" His tone was harsher than he'd intended, and her eyes widened.

She was probably surprised he'd recalled her betrothed's full name—but he had.

"I haven't forgotten."

Turning away from her, Aedan stooped under the overhang and retrieved his weapons. "The sun's up," he said tersely. "We need to be on our way." He then slung his quiver of arrows across his back, his bow over one shoulder, and began strapping his dagger to his thigh.

Colombia didn't reply. Instead, she ducked back under the lip of the rock and retrieved her woolen shawl, wrapping it around her shoulders. When she emerged to join him, her expression was taut, her gaze shadowed.

Aedan's chest constricted at the sight.

He'd been unnecessarily brusque with her. It was unfair to punish her. After all, he'd initiated the kiss, not her. "Sorry," he muttered again. "I'm not myself this morning."

Colombia's mouth tightened a fraction, the grey of her eyes deepening to the color of storm clouds. "Neither of us is," she replied.

It was a silent journey northwest.

Colombia didn't mind. She walked a few yards behind Aedan, content to retreat into her own thoughts. In truth, ever since that kiss, her senses had been reeling. She was trying to make sense of her own reaction to the Brigante warrior who was taking her to safety.

I shouldn't be surprised at my response, she told herself as she picked up her skirts to clamber over a large, lichen-covered rock that blocked their path. After all, she'd been acutely aware of her growing attraction to her protector.

But even as she tried to rationalize things, even as she tried to put that sensual embrace out of her mind, a treacherous voice whispered to her.

Linus doesn't kiss like that.

Linus doesn't look at you like that.

Swallowing hard, she balled her hands into fists at her sides and plowed doggedly on after Aedan. Enough. She wouldn't let her thoughts linger on a fantasy. Instead, she needed to focus on what was real.

On the man she'd promised herself to, and on the world she'd soon be part of once more.

This journey with Aedan was like stepping out of time. With him, she was someone else, and for a few moments, she'd let herself forget.

But it would be risky to do so again.

Jaw set, she marched after Aedan while the sun warmed her back and the breeze ruffled her hair. It was a relief to feel herself again. The fever had weakened her and clouded her mind—as had that heady kiss.

They soon left the rocky valley behind and walked over grassy, windswept hills.

But despite Colombia's resolution to put their embrace behind her, she soon weakened. Memories of the heat of Aedan's mouth, the feel of his body pressed against hers, kept returning to torment her. That kiss shouldn't have happened, but that fact only made excitement flutter low in Colombia's belly.

The Gods forgive her, she longed to taste him again.

The morning drew out, and at noon they rested on the banks of a glittering burn. Clear water ran through peaty soil, and they drank thirstily. Initially, Colombia had been nervous to drink from rivers, without boiling the water first; but since they were on the run, and couldn't ensure the water was clean before drinking, they had no choice.

Aedan seemed confident they wouldn't sicken, and she trusted him.

Colombia's pulse quickened then. Yes, she did trust him. Implicitly.

It hadn't started off that way. Initially, she'd been afraid he'd turn on her once he got her to safety. But it hadn't taken her long to realize he meant her no harm. Instead, he'd become her protector. And then, once she'd relaxed in his company, she'd become aware of the pull between them.

An awareness that was now intensifying.

Pushing aside the vivid memory of how she'd boldly grazed his lower lip with her teeth, Colombia cupped the cool water in her hands and took another gulp. She then glanced over her shoulder at where Aedan sat on the bank above her. "Will we be sleeping rough again tonight?" she asked, breaking the long silence between them. Curse it, her voice was far too breathy.

His mouth quirked. "No, we're making better progress than I thought ... and should reach Coria by nightfall." He paused then. "It's a fort just under three miles south of the Wall, set at the junction of two major roads."

Colombia's spine straightened, surprise creeping over her. "We'll reach the Wall tonight?"

He shook his head. "We'll walk the last stretch to Onnum tomorrow morning." Aedan pushed himself up then and climbed to his feet, dusting himself off. "I suggest that when we arrive at Coria, we pretend to both be Britons." His gaze traveled over her before resting on her face once more. "Your looks can pass as local."

Colombia nodded. Her mother's family had hailed from Rhaetia, a province north of the alps that bordered Italia. She was far paler than the dark-haired, tanned relatives on her father's side of the family.

"But since you don't speak Briton, it's best you keep silent when we get to Coria," Aedan continued.

"Wise idea," Colombia replied. Turning, she climbed the bank toward him. "I'd rather not draw attention to myself until I get to the Wall."

Aedan watched her approach, his gaze hooded. "A woman like you will never go unnoticed," he replied, voice lowering, "but if the soldiers at Coria think you're my Briton wife, they should let us pass unmolested."

Heat flushed over Colombia's chest. She hadn't realized they were going to pose as husband and wife at the fort. At Achwig, everyone had thought them lovers, but pretending to be married was something else. Her breathing grew shallow then as it dawned on her that she liked the idea. Even if it was a fantasy, she found herself imagining what it would be like to belong to this man.

The silence that followed Aedan's suggestion grew heavy, and Colombia's pulse quickened. They'd both done their best to pretend that kiss hadn't happened, but the wanting was still there.

And now it pulsed between them.

XIV. ONE LAST TIME

"IT'S BUSIER THAN I expected," Colombia whispered to Aedan as they crossed into Coria, over a stone bridge spanning the River Tin, amongst a throng of travelers. A golden gloaming settled around them.

"It will be ... this close to the Wall," her companion replied.

In truth, Colombia had forgotten how noisy civilization could be. Over the past few days, she'd been traveling across empty hills, remote valleys, and peaceful woodland, but now noise assaulted her from every direction: the rough shouts of men in both her own and the native tongues, the clang of iron in nearby forges, and the rattle of carts across the large flat river stones that paved Dere Street—the great road that cut a swathe north.

They now traveled upon the same road the supply convoy had been traveling on when the outlaws had attacked.

Colombia suppressed a shiver as haunting memories flooded back. It was a relief to know they'd almost reached Onnum—and that the outlaws hadn't caught up with them. Aedan had told her that, with any luck, their pursuers would head for the mouth of the River Tin once they spoke with Enid. It had been a clever ruse on his part.

The crowds grew thicker still as they walked into town. Of course, there were plenty of soldiers about—men clad in tunics, breastplates, pleated leather skirts, and heavy sandals—but Colombia also spied many civilians, both Roman and Briton, going about their end-of-day business. Roman ladies with pallas draped around their shoulders walked amongst native women in ochre or blue sleeveless tunics. Some of the native women wore bronze arm rings or torcs around their necks.

They passed by neat rows of long, rectangular dwellings with tiled roofs—a sight that made Colombia feel at home. However, unlike other forts she'd visited, there appeared to be little distinction between the vicus—the civilian town—and the military compound. The residential buildings merely became higher and better built the closer they drew to the center.

As they approached the heart of Coria, walking between military barracks to the right and a temple to Jupiter on the left, Colombia caught sight of the high, white-washed walls of a massive portico looming before her. The portico, with its burnt-orange roof tiles glinting in the setting sun, housed the two most important buildings of any fort: the praetorium, or commander's residence, and the principia, or military headquarters.

Of course, she could go there, could throw herself at the mercy of the fort's commander.

Colombia cast aside the thought. She was so close to her destination now; it was best she kept a low profile and pretend to be a Briton woman passing through.

Walking close to Aedan, she noted the interested looks one or two of the soldiers flashed her. Skin prickling, she stepped closer to her companion and linked her arm through his. Immediately, her tension eased a little. "Do you mind?" she whispered. "You were right about me attracting attention."

"It's hardly surprising," he murmured back. "Men well outnumber women in a frontier town like this."

"Do soldiers really take up with local women then?" she asked as they crossed the wide street before the massive portico. Through the colonnaded archways, she spied soldiers on parade. The rattle of armor and the shouts of their commanding officers drifted through the gathering dusk.

"Of course," he replied. "Many soldiers posted out here take Briton lovers ... and a few of them marry their women too." He cut her a veiled look. "It's frowned upon, but this far away from Rome, who really cares?"

Colombia fell silent. In their missives, both her father and betrothed had described their soldiers as too dedicated to furthering the glory of Rome to let themselves be distracted by local women.

Her cheeks warmed then. Of course, she should have known better than to believe them.

They left the center of the fort behind them, continuing along Dere Street to where a row of wine shops and shabby-looking tabernae sat.

Aedan appeared to be studying their façades with interest, as if deciding which tavern to stop at for the evening.

"We don't have any coin to pay for lodgings," Colombia pointed out. It was true: when she'd fled, there had been no time to grab her purse, filled with gold, silver, and brass coins.

Nonetheless, Aedan merely flashed her a grin and dug into the pouch at his belt, producing two brass sestertii. "These should be enough to buy us some bread and cheese, and a room for the night at the cheapest establishment we can find."

Colombia favored him with an arch look, and Aedan's smile faded. "I didn't take this off a Roman corpse if that's what you're thinking."

Her cheeks flushed. "I wasn't—"

"When I left his service, Aquila gave me some coins," he cut her off, "and these are the last of them."

Colombia nodded. "Well, I shall make sure my father pays you well when we reach Onnum tomorrow morning," she assured him.

A groove appeared between Aedan's brows, and Colombia immediately regretted bringing up the payment she'd promised him. She hadn't meant to, but she'd unwittingly reduced their relationship to a financial exchange—the last thing she wished to do.

Aedan meant much more to her than that.

"This tavern will do," he announced, angling them toward a narrow establishment squeezed between two rowdy wine shops. At this hour, it was busy. The gentle strum of a lyre filtered out, fighting to be heard over the rumble of voices.

The establishment's name, *Diana's Tavern,* was painted above the door, and Aedan and Colombia ducked under the lintel into a dimly lit space.

One glance inside and Colombia's gaze narrowed. This looked like a popina. Frequented by the lower-classes and slaves, such places often doubled as brothels. Indeed, half-clad local women perched on the laps of soldiers.

Curious gazes flicked in their direction as Aedan made his way to the squat, balding man behind the stone counter. He was pouring wine from one of the clay amphoras that lined the space. A brazier burned behind him, the aroma of roasting blood sausage mingling with the less pleasant smell of stale sweat.

Unlike the reclining couches that the better taverns boasted, this one only had a scattering of stools around circular stone tables, and most of them were occupied. The soldiers who weren't fondling the women on their laps were dicing. Raucous laughter rang through the popina. Ignoring the rowdy patrons, Aedan and Colombia perched on stools at the bar.

"What will it be?" the proprietor greeted them tersely. He had a pugnacious face and deep-set eyes that narrowed when they settled upon Aedan, taking in the tribal tattoos that marked his upper arms.

Colombia wagered they didn't see many Britons in here.

"Supper and a room for the night, for me and my wife," Aedan replied in fluent Latin, placing his two sestertii on the bar.

The man's piggy eyes widened. However, his expression didn't warm.

Taking the coins, he nodded before moving away to fetch their wine and food.

"Apologies for bringing you here," Aedan whispered to her when the proprietor was out of earshot. He then flashed her a sheepish smile. "As soon as we've eaten, we'll retire to our room."

Colombia nodded, swallowing her response. She had to remember they'd agreed she wouldn't speak.

The tavern owner returned then with two cups of wine, which he slammed down in front of them. Two dishes of bread, cheese, and dried plums arrived moments later.

Colombia fell upon her supper, as did Aedan. It was simple fare, and she'd likely tasted better—but the bread was fresh with a salty crust, the cheese tangy, and the dried fruit pleasantly tart.

The wine was rough, yet she enjoyed that too.

They cleared their plates quickly and then left the common room behind, ignoring the leering comments from two drunken legionaries sitting at the bar, down from them.

Colombia was relieved that Aedan wasn't the sort of man to raise his fists at the slightest provocation. The soldiers' comments were rude, yet they washed off her companion. Aedan's experiences over the years had given him a tough hide, indeed.

Diana's Tavern had an annex out back that housed a handful of tiny chambers.

As expected, their room wasn't luxurious. The chamber was cramped, with stained lime-washed walls. The linen on the narrow bed, which was fashioned out of wood and shaped like a reclining couch, was clean enough, yet worn. There was no window, or brazier to warm the air if the temperature dropped overnight. But at least they were able to bar the room from the inside, which made Colombia feel a little more secure.

Outdoors, the sun had now set, and the sounds of drunken revelry from the tavern itself and the wine bars that flanked it had grown louder.

Nonetheless, they were safely locked away until dawn.

Aedan divested himself of his weapons, placing his quiver, bow, and sword in a corner before settling himself down onto a low stool by the door with a sigh. Meanwhile, Colombia hovered, throwing him a questioning look.

Now that they were alone together again, she felt awkward. Before that kiss, she'd been at ease with him. Yet now they stood in a cubiculum together, it was difficult to meet his eye.

"Take the bed," he murmured. "I'll sleep on the floor."

Colombia's gaze shifted to the dusty strip of tiles between the bed and the door. They didn't look comfortable at all. She could give him her shawl as a blanket, yet he had nothing soft to lie on. "You'll never be able to sleep there," she replied.

He snorted a laugh. "I can sleep *anywhere*." His mouth quirked then. "I'm so tired right now, I could drop off even stretched out on a bed of nails."

"Are you sure? I can shift over to the edge of the bed … and make space for you."

Their gazes did meet then. "After what happened this morning, it's best I don't," he said quietly.

Colombia stared back at him, heat washing over her. Her mouth went dry. Did he regret that kiss? Minerva forgive her, she was drawn to this man. Every time his gaze fastened on her, her pulse went wild, need sharpening her senses. She knew it was wrong, yet her body didn't care. She hadn't seen Linus in five years— and she didn't recall him ever affecting her like the man seated a couple of feet away did.

Holding Aedan's gaze, she shrugged off her shawl and handed it to him. "Take this, at least."

He nodded, although their fingers brushed as he took the garment, and a shiver of pleasure went up her arm at the contact.

Colombia gasped, and Aedan froze.

The tension that filled the small chamber intensified. And as their stare drew out, something shifted within Colombia. A little wildness broke free.

"Colombia," Aedan said roughly. "This isn't—"

"About what happened this morning," she whispered. "I can't stop thinking about it." Aedan's lips parted in surprise, yet she pressed on, breathlessly reckless now. "Tomorrow, we must say goodbye, but before we do, can you kiss me ... one last time?"

XV. DON'T TEMPT ME

AEDAN SLOWLY LET out the breath he'd been holding.

"Colombia," he murmured. "Don't tempt me."

"It's just one kiss," she whispered back, her gaze never leaving his. "What harm can it do?"

Heart pounding, he rose to his feet. Did she truly have no idea? Even so, her request lured him like a fairy maid's song, and he found himself unable to resist. "Come here then," he murmured.

She did, and, reaching out, Aedan drew her into his arms. His mouth then slanted over hers in a hungry, possessive kiss.

With a groan, Colombia's lips parted under his, welcoming his questing tongue. Reaching out, she slid her hands up his chest before her arms linked around his neck, pulling him close.

And Aedan pulled her hard against him.

The Reaper strike him down, her body felt good pressed along his. Too good.

He grazed his teeth over her lower lip, nipping gently. Her soft, answering whimper made a groan rise in his throat. She nibbled at his mouth in return before sliding her tongue against his.

Her response was bold, and he loved it.

An instant later, Aedan tore his mouth from hers. "Gods, Colombia," he growled, "we have to stop."

Breathing hard, she drew back slightly. However, their bodies were still pressed flush.

"Why?" she whispered.

His breathing caught. "But what about your betrothed?"

"He belongs to another world," she replied, her gaze steady and bright. "Tomorrow I shall step back into my old life … but tonight, I'm free to be with you."

He dragged in a deep breath, trying to fight the hunger that thundered through his veins. "But there could be consequences. Tomorrow you might regret giving yourself to me."

She shook her head, stubbornness flickering across her face. "Never. I'd regret *not* doing this more." She sucked in a deep breath. "Do you want me, Aedan?"

A wave of dizziness swept over him. "Yes," he rasped.

"Then take me. I want this too."

A heartbeat passed, and then he hauled her against him. Their mouths collided once more, ravenous now. Aedan parted her lips with his tongue and explored the heat of her mouth, while his fingers delved into her hair, tangling in its silkiness.

Aedan's heart began to thud against his ribs.

He couldn't believe this was happening.

Colombia's tongue was tangling with his, her fingers sliding across his chest. She was making soft, mewling sounds in the back of her throat. Her small hands slid down to the waistband of his bracae and plucked at it impatiently.

Aedan smiled against her mouth.

It was clear what she wanted.

Colombia thrilled at her own courage.

Never would she have spoken thus to a man—never would she have made her desire so clear.

But this evening, in the back room of this squalid popina, she was fearless.

Some moments were meant to be seized or the opportunity would never come again.

And so, she stepped back from him and wriggled out of her tunic before shedding her wispy underwear.

Moments later, she stood before Aedan naked.

Goosebumps rose upon her skin, her nipples pebbling. It was cool inside the tiny room, but that hadn't caused her body's swift reaction. Instead, the heat of Aedan's gaze bathed her and brought all her senses alive.

Aedan stood there watching her, his blue eyes dark in the flickering light of the single lantern that burned by the bed. "The Maiden be blessed, you're lovely," he whispered, his voice catching slightly.

He shrugged off his tunic and started to unlace his bracae.

Colombia swallowed, her mouth going dry as a blend of nerves and excitement churned through her.

Minerva, she couldn't believe they were doing this—and that *she* had instigated it. Who was this lusty, bold woman?

Aedan's clothing fell to the floor, and he kicked it aside.

Breathing shallowly, Colombia raked her gaze down his body, as he had with her, drinking him in.

He was tall, lean, and long-limbed, yet well-muscled and strong. His skin was pale, with a light scattering of freckles across his smooth chest.

He was simply beautiful.

And when her gaze traveled lower, Colombia stopped breathing altogether.

Thick, long, and tapered, his shaft thrust toward her from a nest of light-auburn curls. It was even bigger than she'd expected, and a deep throbbing ache started to pulse between her thighs.

He was going to push *that* inside her?

Aedan moved close then, drawing her into his arms, and capturing her mouth with a wild kiss. His hands slid down her back, cupping her backside, before he hauled her hips hard against him.

And unlike when they'd kissed moments earlier, there were no layers of clothing separating them now.

The heat of his rod throbbed against her belly.

Colombia whimpered, desperate for more of him. Her hands smoothed over his skin, tracing the hard planes of muscle that sculpted his body.

Tearing his mouth from hers, Aedan left a trail of kisses down her jaw and neck before he cupped her breasts with his hands. He then lowered his head and started to suckle one. He worked the nipple gently at first before drawing it deeper into his mouth.

"Gods," Colombia gasped, her legs trembling under her. Each suckle sent pleasure arrowing through her core and turned her weak.

"You have delicious tits," he murmured as he tore his lips from one swollen nipple and focused on its twin.

He walked her backward then, moving her toward the bed.

Colombia lowered herself onto it, lying upon her back. Her breathing came in ragged gasps as he stretched out next to her, his hot gaze sweeping over the length of her trembling body.

And she *was* trembling—not from fear but want.

Propping himself up onto one elbow, Aedan gently stroked his fingertips down the valley between her breasts, tracing a path over her ribcage and her belly to the soft flaxen hair between her thighs. "Open for me, little dove," he murmured.

Little dove. The intimacy of the name made Colombia catch her breath.

Heart pounding in her ears, she spread her thighs. She couldn't stop shaking. This was the most exciting, forbidden thing she'd ever experienced.

"Have you ever touched yourself … here?" he asked, his fingers parting her gently.

Heat flushed over Colombia at the question. "No," she squeaked.

Aedan's liquid gaze held her fast. "And why not?"

"I d … don't … know," she stammered. "I just never … really …" Her voice trailed off as he parted her legs wider still, opening her to him. "I don't know what to do," she admitted.

His eyes, dark-blue with desire, glinted. "Well ... let me show you."

He began to stroke her before his thumb found a hard nub of flesh.

Colombia gasped, her hips lifting off the bed. "What was that?"

His mouth quirked. "Just the beginning."

The pad of his thumb concentrated on that spot, circling, stroking, and rubbing until Colombia was writhing against him. Pleasure was coiling, right there.

"Aedan," she gasped. "I don't know ... I can't ..." She choked out a soft cry then. "It's building ... but just out of reach."

"Follow it," he murmured. "Chase the feeling ... let go."

Eyes fluttering shut, Colombia obeyed, giving herself to the sensation and chasing the pleasure that swelled with each passing moment. He increased the pressure with his thumb, rubbing faster now, and a short while later, warm, shuddering, delicious pleasure exploded low in her belly, rippling between her spread thighs.

Colombia writhed on the mattress, and her raw cry filled the room.

She opened her eyes to see Aedan smiling down at her.

The man looked pleased with himself—and she understood why.

"I had no idea," she gasped.

His smile widened. "As I said before ... that's just the beginning."

Aedan shifted then, rolling onto his back, and drawing her up so that she sat astride him. "We'll take this slow," he promised her. "I don't want to hurt you."

"You won't," Colombia breathed, wriggling against the hot, hard shaft nestling between her thighs. Her body felt liquid, and pleasure still pulsed gently deep in her core.

She wanted him. There.

Aedan took hold of her hips, lifting her up and stroking her with the tip of his shaft.

Colombia gave a needy groan, circling against him.

However, he held her fast, continuing to stroke her. He then settled the swollen head of his rod into her entrance.

Colombia sighed before attempting to push down on him.

"Wait," he grunted. "We need to go slowly."

Inch by inch, he settled her upon him. He slid in easily at first, but then he stopped. An aching, stretching sensation rippled through Colombia's lower belly. He was big, and she was a maid.

She'd heard that a woman's first time could be sore. However, there was no pain, just a tight discomfort.

Aedan gripped her hips then, rotating her on his shaft—before he slowly pushed her down on him further.

Colombia sank against him, and the sensation of being stretched intensified. He filled her up, and when she eventually settled at the root of his member, so that their bodies were flush, a dull ache pulsed through the cradle of her hips.

Her pulse quickened then, sweat beading upon her skin. Perhaps he was too big for her.

"Just relax now, Colombia."

She looked down to find Aedan's gaze riveted upon her face. "Let your body go."

Reaching between her thighs, the pad of his thumb found that nub of flesh once more, and he gently started to stroke it.

Warm, pulsing pleasure rippled through her core, and the ache turned into something delicious. She gasped his name.

"That's right," he crooned, taking hold of her hips then and rolling them against his. "Just surrender."

Her body started to tremble as he lifted her, sliding her up the length of his shaft, nearly to the tip, before pushing her back down on it again.

"Oh," she whimpered. "That feels good."

He huffed a laugh. "Glad to hear it."

Aedan continued to move her up and down his rod, in slow, steady strokes—and after a short while, Colombia found herself arching hard against him every time he drove home.

Having him inside her felt incredible—yet she found herself chasing something again.

Curving her back, she changed the angle, and when he thrust up into her this time, he hit a place deep inside her that turned her liquid.

She cried out, writhing against him. "Aedan," she gasped. "I need more … please!"

Rasping a curse, he flipped her over on her back, raising her legs high and wrapping them around his shoulders—and then he thrust deep.

He'd gone gently in the beginning, showing great restraint. But the last of it had unraveled now. He took her hard, and with each thrust, Colombia lifted her hips to meet him.

This position was incredible. Every time he drove home, he touched that sensitive spot that made her writhe against him. Wild pleasure tumbled through her, and she surrendered utterly to it—and to him.

Arching back against the bed, she cried his name. Moments later, Aedan climaxed hard, his spine snapping back, his hoarse shout echoing through the room.

Breathing hard, he held himself up over her, his arms shaking, his lean body trembling in the aftermath. And when their gazes met, his eyes gleamed.

XVI. FORBIDDEN

AEDAN AWOKE SLOWLY. And as he drifted into consciousness, he became aware of a warm, naked body pressed against his. For a moment, he thought he was lost in a delicious dream, one he didn't want to wake from, but then a soft voice roused him. "Aedan? You're awake?"

Eyes flickering open, he looked into Colombia's smoky gaze. She was lying facing him, as if she'd been watching him sleep. An instant later, everything—every delicious, forbidden detail of the eve before—flooded back.

Aedan groaned, rolling over onto his back. He then muttered an oath in his own tongue. He should regret plowing Colombia Juventus, but he didn't.

He glanced over at her. The glint in her eye and the curve to her mouth told him that she didn't have any regrets either.

"You didn't move all night," Colombia noted. "You really *were* tired."

Aedan huffed a laugh. "I was *exhausted.*"

A flush rose to Colombia's cheeks then. Of course, they both knew it wasn't just the journey that had tired him out. After their coupling, he'd slept so deeply that his head now felt as if it were packed with wool. Light was filtering through the cracks in the shutters, letting them know dawn had indeed broken.

A smile lingered on his lips at Colombia's pretty blush. "Did you sleep well?"

"Better than I expected ... although I woke up early." She shrugged then, her expression shadowing. "Nerves."

Colombia's admission made the last vestiges of sleep clear. Aedan propped himself up onto an elbow before reaching out and combing his fingers through her dark-flaxen hair. Last night was behind them—a stolen moment in time—yet he found himself reluctant to let it go. "Everything will be fine," he murmured. "You'll see."

Colombia's gaze lowered then. "Maybe I should have sent word ahead." She broke off there, nibbling at her lower lip. "Some men don't like surprises."

"It's too late to worry about it now," he reminded her. "Just remember the reason you set out from Italia in the first place. You must want to marry this man ... you've crossed the empire to reach him."

Colombia nodded, her throat bobbing. "But five years *is* a long while ... what if we've both changed?" She winced then, her gaze flicking up once more. "What if he doesn't want me any longer?"

Aedan snorted. "Then he's a *stulte*."

A fool.

And he meant it too.

Linus Calix Aurelius was fortunate indeed.

There was a part of Aedan—a part he wasn't proud of—that secretly wished Colombia's betrothed would turn her away. Yet he took care not to let his mind travel in that direction. Even if Linus didn't wed Colombia, she would never choose to bind herself to an outlaw Brigante. Some things were impossible, he knew that. After all, hadn't he told her it was better to face the reality of life than live in a world of fantasy?

Their time together was drawing to a close, and he couldn't prevent that. Lazing abed with the lovely Colombia wouldn't make their farewell any easier.

Aedan rolled off the bed and stooped to pick up his clothing. "Right then," he said briskly, pulling on his bracae. "We'd better get going."

They stepped out of *Diana's Tavern* and onto the wide cobbled street beyond. The row of taverns and wine bars slumbered at this hour. However, the rest of the town was slowly waking up.

A cockerel crowed nearby, and the shouts of centurions taking their men through drills drifted out from the parade ground at the heart of the town.

A stone trough, used for watering horses and oxen passing through Coria, sat at the roadside, and Aedan used the wooden hand pump to bring up fresh water from the well behind it. They both drank deeply, slaking their thirst before setting off north toward Onnum.

Two and a half miles separated the two forts—but as Colombia walked at Aedan's shoulder along Dere Street, she found herself wishing the distance were longer.

Suddenly, she didn't want this journey to end.

The past days had been exhausting and yet exhilarating—and last night had forever altered her. The heat, the abandon, had been a revelation; Aedan had shown her another world.

As they traveled, striding out on the well-traveled road, she cast a look in his direction. The warrior walked tall, gaze fixed north, his expression shuttered.

Colombia's pulse quickened. She hoped he didn't regret last night; she certainly didn't.

As she'd lain awake watching him sleep, she wondered at the consequences of her impulsive act. Her womb could quicken. However, the thought hadn't filled her with terror. Instead, a strange calmness descended upon her.

Whatever happened now, she'd deal with it.

They didn't converse during the last stretch to Onnum, as the pair of them retreated into their own thoughts. And when the Wall finally hove into view, Colombia emerged from her reverie, her breath catching.

She'd been prepared for it, yet the sight of the great stone and timber fortification that snaked over the hills, east and west for as far as the eye could see, was even more impressive than she'd expected.

Colombia's breathing grew shallow.

At least eight feet tall, topped by the outlines of soldiers moving about upon it, the Wall was a monument to the might of the empire. It slashed across the land, forming a boundary between Britannia and Caledonia.

Her attention shifted then to the palisaded fort that interrupted the flow of the Wall. Onnum. A civilian township of tightly-packed, low-slung dwellings—the vicus—clustered inside its southern entrance.

Aedan and Colombia entered the south gate by crossing over the vallum—an earth and turf rampart with a wooden palisade on top and a deep outer ditch. The gates were open, although helmed figures watched them from the ramparts, spears bristling against the pale morning sky.

Surprisingly, there weren't any guards to stop them at the gates. They seemed content to let travelers flow in and out of the fort this morning.

However, Colombia felt gazes track their path, and the skin between her shoulder blades prickled in response.

Within the vicus, citizens thronged the narrow streets, and like Coria, there was a mix of Romans and Britons about. The clang of a smith's forge echoed off the surrounding walls, blending with the chatter of women's voices as they shopped at the market. Mounds of fresh produce sat on the backs of carts, and the aroma of baking bread wafted through the market, making Colombia's belly growl.

"I like this town." She glanced right to where a butcher was haggling with a man dressed in a slave tunic over a side of mutton. "It has a prosperous feel."

"The vicus at Vindolanda is similar," Aedan replied, moving closer to her side as locals favored them with curious looks. "Communities thrive wherever the Caesars build forts."

Colombia cast him a sidelong glance. "Admit it … as much as you resent us … you respect us too."

He snorted in response yet didn't contradict her.

They were approaching the southern entrance to the inner compound now. A great oaken and iron door loomed before them, blocking their way. There were a few yards distant when Aedan reached out and put a hand on Colombia's arm.

Slowing her stride, she glanced at him. "What is it?"

"This is as far as I go," he said softly.

Colombia halted and turned to him. "But you need to come inside with me." Her pulse quickened. She wasn't ready to say goodbye to him yet.

His mouth kicked up into a half-smile. "It's best I don't enter the compound. The commander won't welcome me. He'll jump to conclusions." His expression sobered then. "And they'd be the correct ones."

Colombia's cheeks warmed. Of course, she hadn't thought of that. Her father would see the pair of them together and assume Aedan had taken liberties. It seemed obvious now, and she felt a little foolish.

"What about your payment?" she asked, struggling to keep focused. "*Pater* will reward you for helping me."

He shook his head. "I don't want to be paid for helping you, Colombia," he murmured. "It was a pleasure."

She swallowed. "But coin will make things easier for you, surely?"

His lips lifted at the corners. "Don't worry about me."

She cleared her throat, wishing she were more composed. In truth, she wasn't prepared for this farewell. An ache rose under her breastbone as it hit her that she wouldn't see Aedan again. "What will you do now?"

"I don't know … to be honest, I haven't given it much thought."

"Will you return to your people?"

He shook his head.

"But the outlaws will be hunting you."

He flashed her an arrogant smile. "Yes, they'll always be on the lookout for me, but they won't catch me."

Colombia moved toward him so that little more than a foot now separated them. They stood in the midst of the busy market crowd. This close, she could feel the heat of his body. She dragged his spicy, intensely-male scent deep into her lungs and quashed the urge to reach up and touch his shaggy hair, to push it off his face.

"I will never forget you," she whispered, her voice catching. Suddenly, she wanted this moment in time to freeze. If only they were still out in the wilderness together. For a short while, the rest of the world had ceased to matter—who she was, who he was, hadn't been important. But now, reality shattered the bond that had formed between them. "May the Gods watch over you, Aedan."

He stared down at her, and in his eyes, she glimpsed a hunger. It wasn't just carnal, but something deeper, something she'd always longed to see upon a man's face when he looked at her. And when he spoke, his voice was husky. "And you, Colombia."

XVII. FORTUNA BE BLESSED

TWO LEGIONARIES ESCORTED Colombia up the
street inside the compound, past a bathhouse, stables,
and barracks on the left, and granaries and the
headquarters on the right. The commander's residence
sat next to the courtyard principia building.

She noted an odd atmosphere within these walls.
Unlike the vicus, which had been bustling and cheerful,
voices were subdued here. And a few of the soldiers she
passed—those that didn't gawk rudely at her—wore
disgruntled expressions.

Ignoring the stares she was attracting, Colombia tried
to do the same with the ache in her chest and the sting
behind her eyes. One night with Aedan wasn't enough,
and yet that was all the Gods would give her. She had to
look forward now, to her future with Linus.

Linus. She'd avoided thinking about him this
morning, for fear that guilt would barrel into her. He was
here, and soon she'd be reunited with him.

Her pulse accelerated, anxiety fluttering up.

I'm not ready.

Reaching her father's residence, she climbed the
stone steps of the praetorium and made for the
colonnaded entrance. A servant met her in the atrium.
Tall and thin, his fine green tunic contrasting with

burnished walnut-colored skin and peat-dark eyes, the man regarded her with thinly veiled distaste. "I'm Marcus Amulius, the commander's house steward," he introduced himself. "Who are you and what business do you have setting foot in here?" He cast a sharp, accusing look at the two soldiers who'd accompanied the newcomer into the praetorium—as if he couldn't believe they'd let a scruffily dressed Briton woman inside the compound.

"I'm Colombia Juventus," Colombia replied once the steward's gaze had returned to her. "And I'm here to see my father."

The man's narrow shoulders stiffened, and horror rippled across his features.

A moment later, he remembered his manners and bowed. "M... my lady," he stuttered. "We weren't expecting you."

"I didn't send word ahead," Colombia replied coolly. "Fetch my father ... I wish to greet him."

Marcus bowed once more. "Of course, my lady." He then took a step backward and motioned for her to follow. "The commander is next door meeting with his officers ... if you wish to wait in the tablinum, I shall let him know you're here."

Colombia followed him out of the entrance hall and onto a covered portico. They circuited a paved courtyard, a rectangular space dotted with urns filled with flowers and herbs, and low stone benches.

However, Colombia didn't pay her surroundings much attention. She was too busy trying to keep her breathing even. From the moment they'd entered this residence, her pulse had started to pound like a drum.

Her father would be angry with her—she knew that— she just hoped his joy at seeing her alive and well would soften his response.

Marcus led her into the tablinum. The windowless, white-washed living space was simply, yet tastefully, decorated, with a mural of rolling hills, blue sky, and rows of olive groves painted on one wall and a woven rug upon the tiled floor. Reclining couches covered by colorful cushions dominated the space, and a desk and chair sat against the rear wall. A long table, where a row of drinking vessels and a tall ewer of wine perched, lined the wall opposite the mural.

Colombia was tempted to go straight to it and pour herself a huge calix of wine to settle her nerves.

Instead, she turned and nodded to the steward briskly, letting him know he was dismissed.

Head bowed, Marcus hurried from the tablinum.

Colombia watched him go. The pale morning light flooded into the room through the open doors leading out into the courtyard, pooling on the gleaming tiles.

"Minerva grant me the courage to face him," she murmured, beginning a slow circuit of the tablinum. She then reminded herself. "He's a man … not a god."

The truth was that her father *was* intimidating—and in the years since her mother's death, she'd spent little time with him. She continued walking, for movement helped ease her nerves, doing several circuits of the room before the scuff of approaching footfalls made her skid to a halt.

He's coming.

And no sooner had she turned to face the open doors when a tall, broad-shouldered figure, deep-red cloak fluttering behind him, strode into the tablinum. Her father then halted, his smoke-grey gaze raking over her from head to foot. Severus Valerian Juventus was as imposing as she recalled, although his dark hair, cropped close to his scalp, was shot through with more grey than the last time she'd seen him.

"Colombia." The commander's voice was deep and powerful—and there was no mistaking the censure in his tone. "What is the meaning of this?"

"Good morning, *pater*," Colombia greeted him softly, bowing her head. His presence filled the room, cowed her. "I apologize for my disheveled appearance … and the manner of my arrival. I was traveling with a supply convoy on Dere Street … but we were attacked a few days ago."

Silence rippled through the tablinum, and when Severus replied, it was with a muttered obscenity. "*Futuo!* You were traveling in *that* convoy, daughter?"

Colombia nodded. "My guard and my maid were both killed."

His gaze raked over her. "How in Hades did you survive then?"

"A traveler came to my rescue," she replied. Aedan was right. It was best her father knew as little about him as possible. "He saved my life ... and escorted me here."

The commander's eyes snapped wide, his lips parting. "Have you taken leave of your senses?" he growled. "Why, in Jupiter's name, would you embark on such a journey?"

Colombia swallowed to ease the sudden tightness in her throat. "It has been a long while since Linus and I were betrothed. I wished to see him ... and you ... again."

Heat flamed across her cheeks as she spoke, especially when her father's gaze narrowed. Until a few days ago, her reason for departing Asculum had seemed a noble one, a romantic one. Yet now she knew what a risk she'd taken.

Indeed, she was lucky to be alive.

Suddenly, she was ten years old again and staring down at her scuffed slippers as her father scolded her.

"And why didn't you send ahead word of your arrival?"

"I wanted it to be a surprise."

Severus growled another curse. "Well, it certainly is that."

Heart beating hard in her throat, Colombia forced herself not to drop her gaze. "This land is different to how you described it, *pater*."

His scowl deepened. "What?"

"You told me Britannia was a peaceful territory ... where Roman and Briton live in harmony." She halted then, swallowing. "But they hate us."

Her father stared back at her, a nerve flickering in his cheek. "Not all of them do," he muttered. "They just need a firm hand."

Colombia continued to hold his eye, heat igniting under her ribcage. "Why did you lie to me?"

His mouth tightened. "Women need to be protected from the harsh realities of life on the frontier," he replied. "I didn't want you to worry."

Silence fell then, and Colombia was tempted to push him further. However, she sensed his rising anger. It was best she changed the subject. "Is Linus still at Onnum?" she asked huskily.

Severus grunted. "Yes ... and you'll see him soon enough."

Crossing to the table, the commander poured two cups of wine before passing his daughter one. However, his expression was severe. *Severus*—he'd been aptly named. Her father's handsome face looked carven from marble when he was angry.

Raising the calix to her lips, Colombia took a fortifying gulp. The wine was sweet and delicious, reminding her of home. Yet she nearly choked on it when her father spoke once more. "Were you raped during the attack, daughter?"

Colombia coughed before wiping her mouth with the back of her hand. Eyes smarting, she met her father's gaze. His eyes were no longer the color of smoke, but that of pewter.

"No," she gasped.

His stare didn't waver. "You weren't harmed in any way?"

She shook her head, deciding it was best not to tell Severus how close she'd come to being raped.

It occurred to her then that this journey had indeed changed her. Her father looked upon her as if she were made of fragile pottery, like he always had her mother. But she wasn't a delicate flower, she never had been. Ever since the attack on the convoy, Colombia had discovered that beneath her admittedly pampered exterior, she was resilient and strong.

Oblivious to her realization, Severus's expression softened then, some of the tension in his broad shoulders releasing. "Fortuna be blessed."

Aedan walked the dusty streets of the vicus, heading for the southern gates.

It was done. He'd delivered Colombia to safety, as he'd promised, yet his feet dragged.

He'd never enjoyed farewells, but that one had been tough.

Colombia had parted with dignity and grace. Nonetheless, he'd seen the emotion glistening in her eyes. It had been difficult for her too. She was strong though and determined. He respected her for that.

Last night hadn't been wise—for it had awakened something best left alone—but they hadn't spoken of it since.

There was no need. Words wouldn't change who she was, who he was. They'd walked the same path for a few days, but their road ended here.

Of course, like the proud fool he was, he'd refused payment for escorting her to Onnum. He was now entirely without funds. His decision had been for the best though. Severus Juventus wouldn't welcome him into his home, and Aedan didn't want to see Colombia shamed.

He passed a tavern then. It was still early, yet he wished he had coin to buy himself a cup of wine. He could have done with a drink right now.

Up ahead, the gates out of the fort loomed, and Aedan's stride faltered.

Coming to a halt, he murmured an oath under his breath.

He needed a plan. He couldn't return to the life of an outlaw—and had no interest in doing so anyway. Nor could he keep roaming from place to place, as if he was trying to outrun his bitterness and disappointment. And he had to stop believing fate was out to get him.

That wasn't what Colombia would do.

His mouth lifted at the corners.

No, that indomitable woman faced life head-on with no regrets. Maybe he should be a little more like her, instead of nursing his disappointments like bruises.

Glancing around, Aedan watched a wagon weighed down with sacks of grain, towed by a large ox, make its way toward market square. The farmer, perched up front, whistled merrily to himself as he flicked the reins.

Aedan's smile widened. Colombia was right—Onnum was a vibrant town. It was a place where a man could make a fresh start.

Of course, if he was staying on here, he'd need to learn a trade. He'd never needed one in the past, for he'd been born a chieftain's son. However, he was strong and fit, and his years as a slave had taught him several useful skills. He could wield a hammer, use a saw, and had always worked well with wood.

Surely, there were carpenters and builders here in Onnum. Perhaps one of them needed an assistant.

His smile turned rueful then. At six and twenty winters, he was a little old to start out as an apprentice. But he needed to do so if he wanted to step away from his outlaw's life.

Decision made, Aedan swiveled on his heel and headed back toward the center of the vicus—in search of work.

XVIII. LET HIM GO

MACCUS VIEWED THE sweaty group of warriors gathered before him.

One of them, a huge man with a scowling face, had just finished talking.

Maccus sighed. "So, what you're saying, Lucon, is that Aedan and the woman led you on a merry dance?"

Lucon's face flushed. "The crone at Achwig told us they were headed for the mouth of the Tin ... but we found no trace of them there."

"Perhaps she lied to you."

Lucon pulled a face. "She's a wise woman ... she spoke the truth."

There was a belligerent edge to the warrior's voice that irritated Maccus. Lucon had been in a vile temper ever since they'd found him, blood running down his leg, by the transport wagon a few days earlier.

Maccus hadn't been impressed that his men had wasted precious time trying to rape a Roman noblewoman. They should have just taken her prisoner—should have handed her over to him so he could decide her fate.

Instead, they'd been blinded by lust.

Smoothing his mustache, Maccus rose to his feet. He'd been enjoying a horn of ale by the fire in his makeshift village deep in the woods when the band he'd sent to track down Aedan and the Roman woman had returned.

They'd been camped here, surrounded by the riches they'd taken from the Caesars, while the dust settled.

Word would have reached the Wall by now that the convoy had been attacked, and their supplies—and pay wagons—seized. The lands south of Onnum would be crawling with patrols. The Romans would be out for blood this time.

But Maccus would wait them out—as he always did—while he planned his next attack.

For there would always be another attack while Maccus drew breath. He wasn't done punishing those who'd taken his beloved Bree from him. And if he died fighting the Romans, so be it. He'd be reunited with his love in the afterlife, for The Warrior would reward him for his valor.

"I'm disappointed in you, Lucon," he rumbled.

His words made the warrior's broad shoulders tense, while the men surrounding them went quiet, all gazes riveted upon the man who was the focus of their leader's displeasure.

None of them wanted that.

"I will continue the search," Lucon muttered, his meaty hands clenching into fists at his sides. "I will find the shit-weasel ... and when I do, I will gut him ... slowly."

Lucon's bloodthirsty threat made a few of the men around him murmur in agreement. Indeed, Aedan's betrayal had outraged them all.

However, Maccus wasn't focused on the former slave he'd never entirely trusted.

"Aedan's not important," Maccus announced, his voice carrying through the trees. "Not when we have struck the Caesars such a heavy blow."

Surprise rippled over the faces that stared back at him. As much as they respected their leader, they were shocked he wasn't going to pursue the man who'd betrayed them, who'd killed their own and robbed them of their prize.

Maccus stifled another sigh. Sometimes his warriors lacked vision. He gestured then to the glade they sat in. It was a beautiful spot—hidden far from the Roman roads, and far from their forts—nestled in the mountains that formed a spine between the east and west of Britannia. It rained often up here, and mist wreathed through the trees every morning, yet it was their haven.

"The time for blending into the shadows is coming to an end," the outlaw leader continued. "For years, we have raided our enemy … and we have earned ourselves a fearsome reputation." He paused, motioning to the line of carts parked under the trees behind him. "This is our richest plunder yet … for we now have sacks of Roman coin at our disposal." His mouth curved into a slow smile. "Summer is ending … but before Mid-Winter Fire arrives, we will strike the Wall. We shall burn one of their great forts to embers. The Hag will dance upon Roman corpses."

A shocked silence fell. A heartbeat followed, and then Maccus's men responded.

A great roar rippled over the glade and across the narrow burn that cut its way through the peaty ground to the north of their camp.

"This is a fine spot to grow roots," Maccus continued, his skin prickling as the shadowy plans that had been gathering in his mind for a while now started to take real shape. "No longer shall we rove from place to place … instead, we shall call warriors to us." Maccus's attention rested upon Lucon then. "Instead of hunting Aedan … you'll be traveling the north, telling our people that Maccus, son of Ferix, and leader of the 'Scourge of the North', calls them to his side."

Lucon's eyes burned bright in reply. He then silently nodded.

Still smiling, Maccus swept his gaze around the gathered warriors. He saw the savage pride upon their faces. This was what they'd been waiting for, what he'd been building toward, over the past years.

And this successful raid had provided an opportunity he wouldn't squander.

"Which fort on the Wall shall we attack first, Maccus?" One of the warriors asked, a squat, bald man who was grinning widely.

Maccus met his eye and pretended to consider the question.

There was no doubt in his mind which of the forts he'd strike. The Roman soldiers who'd attacked his wife, who'd raped her and left her to die, were from the Second Legion. They'd been under the command of Severus Valerian Juventus.

"Onnum."

Colombia settled herself down on the bench inside the bathhouse and poured oil on her palm. The scent of rose filled her nostrils. With a sigh, she rubbed the oil over her naked skin before scraping off the grime of the past few days with a strigil, a curved metal implement.

Alone in the bathhouse, she relaxed into the ritual. Meanwhile, steam rose from the waiting bath just a few feet away.

A fort commander was fortunate indeed, for he had a private bathhouse attached to his praetorium. The others in this fort had to share the public bathhouses—of which there were two, one inside the compound for the soldiers, and one in the vicus beyond.

Yet Colombia got to bathe alone.

Moira, her father's house slave—a red-headed Brigante woman—had offered to aid her, yet Colombia declined. As such, Moira had placed a soft, folded drying cloth next to the tiled pool and left Colombia to it.

The scrape of the strigil caused the tension to slowly ebb from her, and when Colombia finally cast the implement aside and rose to her feet, her belly no longer felt tied in knots.

Later, she'd be reunited with Linus again—but first, she had to make herself presentable. Before returning to his meeting she'd interrupted in the principia, her father had raked a critical gaze over his daughter. "Get yourself cleaned up, daughter," he'd muttered. "You can't greet Linus dressed like a Briton."

The comment had been offhand, yet the superiority of it vexed her. No wonder Aedan resented men like Severus Juventus.

Lowering herself into the pool, Colombia sighed. The water was warm and silky, and she sank up to her chin in it.

Gods, how she'd missed her baths over the past days.

Leaning up against the tiled edge of the pool, she let her eyes flutter closed. Her thoughts should have shifted to her impending meeting with her betrothed, but it wasn't his face that drifted into her mind.

It was Aedan's.

Colombia's eyes opened. The heat of the water, which soaked into her muscles like a balm, reminded her of the languor that had enveloped her after they'd lain together. She'd never felt so at peace.

Inhaling slowly, she allowed herself to think of Aedan for a few moments. That was a mistake, for longing, and worry, wreathed up.

Where will he go now?

It was best she didn't know, and yet the ache that had pulsed in her chest when she'd said goodbye to him rose once more. Reaching up, Colombia rubbed her breastbone with her knuckles.

Jupiter, she missed him already.

"Foolish woman," she muttered. "Let him go."

With a sigh, she closed her eyes once more and slid under the water.

"That's it, *domina* ... I've finished."

"Thank you, Moira." Colombia picked up her small hand mirror of polished silver and inspected her appearance. The slave had braided her long hair and wrapped it around the crown of her head. She'd left a few strands free though, oiling them into pretty curls upon Colombia's cheeks. "You've done a lovely job."

Glancing at Moira, she noted the woman observed her with a veiled expression. Since they'd met earlier in the day, Moira hadn't smiled once. She was polite, and although her knowledge of Latin was halting, she managed to communicate well enough.

Moira was older than her, by five years, at least. She was tall and strong, with an even-featured face, bright blue eyes, and hair the color of flame. She wore a neat, knee-length slave tunic, belted at the waist, and sandals. Her bright mane was tamed in a tight braid down her back.

Motioning to the dark-green garment spread out on the recliner behind her, Moira nodded. "Do you wish to wear the *stola* over your tunic, *domina*?"

Colombia nodded. She didn't tend to wear the dress over her tunic when she was at home, but today was an exception. She'd also wear her palla—her shawl.

Linus was due to arrive shortly. She had to look her best.

Moira helped her dress, although the Brigante had trouble adjusting the folds of the palla. After the death of his wife, Colombia's mother, over a decade earlier, Severus hadn't remarried. Moira no doubt wasn't used to helping ladies with their clothing—as such, Colombia was happy to show her how a palla needed to drape over one shoulder.

It was strange, for as much as it felt good to wear clean clothes again, she now found the heavy folds of fabric covering her a little smothering compared to the simple tunic she'd worn over the past few days.

However, Moira had taken away the garment Enid had given her. No doubt it would be thrown on the fire.

The women stood in a small cubiculum—the sleeping space that would be Colombia's now. The windowless chamber lined the courtyard and had large doors opening onto the portico. The doors were open at present, letting in the pale noon light. The day was overcast, the air humid, as if a storm was brewing.

Out in the courtyard, Claudia the cook was watering the rows of herbs and flowers growing in pots and urns. The scent of rosemary and thyme drifted into the cubiculum, easing the nerves that fluttered under Colombia's ribcage.

Not long now, and she'd be reunited with the man she'd traveled half the world to see.

Flashing Moira a brittle smile—one that wasn't returned—Colombia moved toward the doors. "I should go to the tablinum ... father will be expecting me."

XIX. REUNITED

INDEED, SEVERUS WAS already seated on one of the couches in the living space, calix of wine in hand, awaiting his daughter.

He was alone; Linus hadn't yet arrived.

Even so, anxiety tightened Colombia's breathing as she stepped inside the tablinum. "*Salvē, pater.*"

The commander glanced her way, and his gaze swept over her. After a pause, he favored her with a nod of approval. "That's better, daughter," he murmured. "I finally recognize you again."

Colombia entered the room, moving to the couch opposite her father. "It was always me," she replied, unable to prevent herself from responding. "Surely, you could see beneath a bit of grime?"

Severus's eyes narrowed. His daughter's tone was gentle, yet he hadn't appreciated her pert response.

Colombia's pulse quickened at his silent disapproval.

Her father had lived away from Italia for many years now. Not long after losing his beloved wife, he'd accepted a posting to Britannia. Although he'd been back to Asculum a few times over the past years—certainly more than Linus had—he was becoming a stranger to her.

A stern-faced man sat before her now. Severus had always been strict with his only child, yet when Colombia's mother had been alive, he'd been softer, warmer. Perhaps this cold northern land, and the things he'd witnessed here, had hardened him.

Silence fell between them, and Colombia was searching for something to say that wouldn't rouse his disapproval further when the heavy tread of approaching footsteps made her look toward the portico.

A tall, dark-haired man appeared, drawing to a halt in the doorway.

Colombia's breathing caught.

Linus Calix Aurelius was even more handsome than she recalled. His lantern jaw, dark gaze, and widow's peak of night-black hair had always made him stand out in a crowd. Yet dressed as he was today, as if he'd just come from the parade ground, the sight of him made her pulse flutter in her throat.

He wore a blood-red tunic, and a cloak of the same color hung from his broad shoulders. The tunic reached to just above his knees, revealing strong, muscular legs. Metal greaves covered his shins, and heavy mailed sandals shod his feet. Over his tunic, he wore a pleated leather skirt and a leather harness, while his gleaming lorica, plate armor, covered his broad chest. A helmet, crested by a crimson fan that ran from left to right, completed his outfit.

Of course, as primus pilus—the commanding centurion of the first cohort of the Second Legion—he would be dressed accordingly.

Colombia couldn't help it; she stared.

Linus's gaze met hers, the moment stretching out before his mouth curved into a smile. "Greetings, Colombia."

The man squinted up at Aedan. "You're a bit old to be looking for an apprenticeship, aren't you?"

Swallowing a sigh of irritation, Aedan kept a smile plastered upon his face.

His decision to remain in Onnum had been the easy part.

Finding work here was proving to be a challenge.

There were a handful of builders, coopers, and carpenters in the vicus, but all of those he'd visited so far had turned him away. The last one, a carpenter, had snorted a laugh when Aedan had asked him if he needed an apprentice. "Why would I need one of those?" the man had jeered, jerking his thumb at the three strapping youths toiling in the workshop behind him. "I've three strong sons."

Aye, his search for work was turning out to be a humbling enterprise, yet Aedan persisted.

Nothing could be as humiliating as living as a Roman slave, having his identity torn from him. He'd spent years residing within forts, being insulted and sneered at by soldiers whenever he ventured out of the commander's residence.

Being turned away when he asked for work was nothing in comparison.

However, the carpenter who looked up from the window frame he was sanding wasn't sneering. Nor had he insulted him.

The man had merely stated the obvious. A man of Aedan's age didn't usually ask for an apprenticeship. Such positions were badly paid; often, in return for learning his trade, the apprentice would receive no wage at all, just a roof over his head and meals.

"I admit, I'm a bit old to be starting at the bottom," Aedan replied, bracing himself to be sent away. "But I've skill with wood … and I work hard." His gaze traveled over the workshop the man toiled in. A thin layer of sawdust coated everything, and the work benches were cluttered. It didn't appear as if this carpenter had an assistant. "And you look as if you could do with some help."

The man sighed before standing up and stretching his back.

It was hard to guess his age, for his leathery face was lined with care, and his blue eyes had the faded look of someone who'd weathered much in his life. "My son once worked at my side, and my wife used to keep this place tidy," he admitted, his voice lowering as he glanced around the workshop. "But both died two winters ago when a fever rampaged through this fort."

The grief in the man's voice was still raw, and Aedan's smile faded. "I'm sorry," he murmured. He too knew grief, and how it cast a long shadow.

"So am I," the carpenter said gruffly, clearing his throat. His watery blue gaze focused on Aedan once more, and this time, when he appraised him, his expression turned thoughtful.

"But I *am* in need of assistance," he admitted, his mouth curving into a rueful smile. "My joints are paining me these days ... and it's taking me too long to complete projects." He paused then, his expression sobering. "However, I can't pay you much ... to begin with at least ... a sestertius a week, plus food and lodgings, of course."

Relief barreled into Aedan, and he nodded. "Agreed."

The carpenter smiled once more, moving away from the window frame he'd been working on, and walked over to the doorway, extending a hand. "The name's Keir, by the way."

The two of them clasped arms, and Aedan found himself grinning. He'd only spoken briefly with this man, and he wasn't someone who trusted easily, yet there was something about Keir, the carpenter, that told him they'd be friends.

"And I'm Aedan."

"Some wine?"

Linus's voice was just as she recalled—deep and as warm as honey.

"Yes, thank you," Colombia replied, wishing her own voice didn't sound quite so strained. She'd waited for so long to see her betrothed again, yet now he was finally standing in the same room as her, she couldn't relax.

After witnessing their reunion, her father had left them alone in the tablinum. She'd both been pleased and unnerved by his departure, for while the commander had been present, the exchange between Colombia and Linus had been polite, yet formal.

Now they were alone, they could speak frankly.

She watched her betrothed's broad shoulders as he poured the wine and turned from the table, handing her a calix.

Colombia took it, her fingers brushing his as she did so.

Linus's hands were strong and warm, but her heart didn't start kicking against her ribs at the contact. It had been so long—too long. They both needed time to get used to each other again.

Linus's eyes, which were the color of the finest mahogany, roamed over Colombia's face. He stepped closer to her then and raised his calix in a toast. "Here's to my betrothed's arrival in Onnum." His tone was soft, yet she caught the wry edge to it. He'd been all smiles while her father was present, yet his expression sobered now they were alone.

Colombia's pulse did quicken then as anxiety tightened her throat. "Are you angry with me, Linus?"

His eyes widened. "Hades, I don't remember you having such a blunt tongue," he murmured.

Colombia swallowed, her cheeks warming. Of course, she'd been on her best behavior during their meetings prior to his departure from Asculum. She'd taken great care to speak demurely.

However, that had never been the real her. And after the events of the past few days, she found she no longer had any patience for male pomposity. She wished to speak to Linus on an equal footing.

"Apologies, if I come across as overly direct," she replied, her tone cooling. "But it's been a tiring, and fraught, journey north."

Linus sighed, a crease forming between his dark brows. "I'm not angry with you," he rumbled. "However, I do wonder why you're here."

A lump formed in her throat, the heat in her cheeks intensifying. "Is it not obvious?"

He inclined his head before taking a sip of wine. "No, enlighten me, Colombia."

Dragging in a deep breath, her grip increasing around the stem of her calix, Colombia considered her next words. Linus had asked her to explain herself, and she would. She wouldn't temper her speech.

Strangely, when she'd been traveling with Aedan, she hadn't once felt as if she had to rein herself in or fret about coming across as too opinionated. She didn't need to worry about social rules and propriety. She'd felt she could just be herself.

Colombia focused then on the dashing man standing a few feet back from her, awaiting her response.

"It has been a long while since you proposed to me, Linus," she said eventually. "You promised to return to Asculum regularly during your posting … but you never did."

The crease returned between his brows, deeper this time. "I've written to you regularly, haven't I?"

She nodded, her throat tightening. "Indeed, and I have enjoyed your letters, Linus … they have sustained me when I had nothing else to cling to … but the fact remains the years pass, and we are still betrothed. Do you not wish to make me your wife?"

That question was a mistake; she realized it the moment it slipped from her lips. Yet it was too late to call it back—and Linus's full mouth flattened.

"If you had read my missives, you'd know how busy I've been," he replied, irritation creeping into that smooth baritone.

"I know you've been busy," she said softly, "but—"

"Of course, you have little idea of what a man in my position has to deal with," he cut her off. "The building of Hadrian's great wall has been a monumental project ... and now that those outlaws have stolen our pay wagons, the soldiers grow restless." His handsome mouth twisted then. "Do you think I've had the time to think about marriage?"

Colombia swallowed once more. "You could have called for me," she pointed out. "Surely, having a wife with you would make life here easier?"

Linus gave her a withering look. It was hard not to lower her gaze. Nonetheless, under the embarrassment, the hurt, an ember ignited in her belly. After all she'd endured to reach this man's side, she didn't appreciate being spoken to as if she were a halfwit.

"The frontier is no place for a woman," he growled after a lengthy pause.

Colombia's mouth pursed. "Is that so? You never mentioned that in any of your letters."

Silence fell in the tablinum. Linus stared down at her, a nerve flickering under one eye. The hand gripping his calix had tightened, and unease curled through her.

It occurred to her then that even before his departure from Asculum, she'd known very little about this man. All she'd seen was his dashing good looks, his charm, and his smooth words. But standing before him now, a little of that veneer was tarnished.

As Aedan had once asked her—who was the man beneath it all? Was he quick to temper or the sort to raise a hand to his woman? She had no idea.

"I didn't want to worry you," Linus replied after a weighty pause. "But after your ordeal, surely you understand what a wild land this is."

Colombia held his gaze. "I'm not as easy to break as you believe," she replied, her voice barely above a whisper, even as the ember started to pulse hot now. "I may have encountered outlaws on my way north, but I survived, didn't I?"

His dark brows crashed together. "You did ... but only by the grace of the Gods."

XX. THIS BELONGS TO YOU

COLOMBIA'S HEART WAS pounding when she retired to her cubiculum. Sinking down upon her bed, she whispered a soft curse.

That hadn't gone as she'd hoped.

She let her temper get the best of her, and Linus hadn't responded well.

In the end, he'd stalked from the tablinum without even bidding her good day.

"Damn it," she muttered. "What have I done?"

She wasn't referring to her argument with her betrothed—but to the fact she'd traveled all this way for a man she didn't even like.

The realization made her jolt.

She'd thought herself in love with him, but she'd been deluded.

Linus was as charismatic as she remembered, yet he was also supercilious and dismissive. And cold. He hadn't shown any real joy at seeing her, hadn't lifted a hand to stroke her cheek or tried to kiss her.

There was no warmth in his eyes as he stared down at her.

Colombia's throat constricted, a sickly sensation washing over her.

He doesn't want me here.

She'd hoped to fix a wedding date with Linus during this meeting, yet the conversation had deteriorated before she could get that far.

And it was just as well. Weakness flooded over her, pressing her down, and her already racing pulse quickened further.

Colombia had made a terrible mistake coming here, and she'd anger her father further if she rejected Linus. But there was no point in fooling herself. She'd already wasted too many years doing that. It was an irony that she'd worried of late he might not want her—but it went both ways.

Her time with Aedan had taught her the importance of not pulling the wool over her eyes, of not wrapping herself in pretty lies. The truth could be ugly, yet it was real.

She had to face it.

Rising to her feet, she wiped damp palms on her stola and squared her shoulders.

Another unpleasant encounter awaited her—but it was best to get it over with.

Colombia found Linus upon the western walls.

The shadows were growing long as the day waned. The sky had cleared, and the afternoon sun gilded the Wall that hugged undulating hills as it stretched to the horizon. The sun was warm on Colombia's shoulders, yet she pulled her palla close as she surveyed her surroundings.

Her gaze came to rest on the tall, proud figure standing upon a watch tower looking south.

Linus's silhouette was distinctive, even from a distance. He was watching a patrol return to the fort— presumably, they'd been out hunting for the outlaws.

The soldiers below—a surly pair who'd been leaning indolently against a wall instead of standing to attention at their posts—had told her she'd find the primus pilus here. But now that she saw him, her earlier determination faltered.

Maybe this could wait until tomorrow.

She stood there a moment, recalling their argument earlier. The scorn in Linus's eyes had cut her deep. Some men might be flattered that a woman would travel so far to see her lover, yet he'd bristled at the intrusion.

No, she needed to do this—now.

Linus turned, his brow furrowing when he spied her. "Colombia?" He stepped down from the tower and approached in long strides. "What are you doing up here?"

"I came looking for you," she replied. "We need to talk."

His jaw tightened. "Yes, we should discuss what to do with you," he replied. "However, this isn't the place."

What to do with me? Alarm tightened Colombia's ribcage. It sounded as if he intended to send her back to Italia, pack her off like something he was ashamed of.

"Here will do just fine," she replied, stopping before him. "No one can overhear us."

A deep groove appeared between Linus's dark brows as his gaze roved over her face. "What's come over you, Colombia? You weren't this outspoken back in Asculum. I must say I'm not fond of your scold's tongue. I don't—"

"I can't marry you," she cut him off, her pulse accelerating.

His dark eyes snapped wide, and for a moment, she could have sworn she saw relief flare in them before he scowled. "What?"

"We're not suited. I realize that now."

"You were happy enough to accept my proposal five years ago," he growled. "What has changed?"

"Me. I was infatuated with you once, but not any longer."

Linus's lips parted, shock rippling across his face.

Her bluntness no doubt stunned him—indeed, *she* was surprised by it. Nonetheless, there was a freedom in speaking her mind without worrying about what others thought of her.

Tension coiled under Colombia's ribcage as she waited for him to respond. And when he didn't, she exhaled sharply. "Do you love me, Linus?"

Their gazes met and held, the moment stretching out. A heartbeat passed, and then another, and then he slowly shook his head.

"So, why did you propose?"

He snorted. "Our union was never about love, Colombia," he drawled. "I'd been passed over for a number of promotions … and believed I'd spend the rest of my days training troops outside Asculum. But then I discovered that Commander Juventus was back from the frontier for a few weeks. I also heard he was intent on finding a husband for his daughter." Linus paused then, his gaze glinting. "As soon as you accepted my proposal, I received the promotion I wanted."

Colombia tensed. His admission stung, for, in her innocence, she'd believed he was as taken with her as she'd been by him. She'd had no idea she'd been a poor second choice to a glittering career. No wonder he'd never returned to Italia to visit her.

"Would you have ever called for me … if I hadn't taken matters into my own hands?"

His mouth pursed before he shook his head once more.

Colombia reached down and pulled off the golden band upon her left hand. "Here," she said softly, holding it out to him. "This belongs to you."

Linus hesitated. He didn't want her, yet he didn't like being bested by a woman either.

Moments passed, and then he reached out, and with ill grace, snatched the ring from her.

The commander stiffened, and his face hardened.

Watching her father's reaction, Colombia swallowed hard. She hadn't looked forward to telling him she wouldn't be marrying Linus. But like her confrontation with her betrothed, this couldn't be put off either.

They were seated in the triclinium, platters of salted bread, cheese, and dried fruit between them. Moira had just brought in their supper, although Colombia had delivered her news before she or her father touched it.

Severus's brow furrowed. "But you only just arrived here?"

Colombia drew in a deep, steadying breath. "I know, but all it took was one conversation with Linus to realize I'd made a mistake."

Her father muttered a curse. "One of many, daughter."

Colombia's cheeks flushed hot, and she dropped her gaze to the calix of wine she gripped. "I know I've disappointed you," she murmured. "But Linus didn't want to marry me either."

The commander snorted. "Nonsense. He had every intention of honoring your betrothal."

Her chin kicked up, her gaze ensnaring his. "He only proposed to me to gain favor with you ... to further his career. He admitted it."

Her father's expression veiled, and when he replied, his voice was dangerously quiet. "Did he?"

Colombia swallowed. "When I marry, I want it to be for love, *pater*."

He stared back at her, a shadow rippling over his face before he shook his head. "Your head is full of foolish notions," he muttered. "Marriage has nothing to do with love ... it's an arrangement."

"But you loved *mater*," she shot back.

Severus jolted, and she knew she'd hit a nerve. Her parents had been devoted to each other—so much so that her father hadn't remarried in the twelve years since his wife's death. "I did," he admitted roughly, "but not right away. We were strangers to each other in the beginning." His frown deepened then. "Real love doesn't happen overnight. It has to grow, like the roots of a tall oak."

"I understand," Colombia replied. And she did now. Her time with Aedan had lifted the rose-tinted veil from her eyes. Was it any surprise she'd broken things off with Linus after being reunited with him? The reality of the man could never live up to the image she'd painted in her mind. "But I could never love Linus. As soon as you left us alone … and we spoke privately … I realized we'd be miserable together."

Of course, her decision was far more complex than the explanation she'd given her father—the problem was that Linus couldn't hold a candle to Aedan.

The realization made her throat start to ache.

Gods, she couldn't believe she'd never see him again.

Her father surveyed her a moment before slowly lowering his calix to the table between them. "So, what now, daughter? You picked a poor time to arrive at the Wall. The attack on our supply convoy … and the robbery of our pay wagons … has left us vulnerable. I can't spare the men at present to escort you home."

Colombia's pulse quickened. His admission was a relief. After such a long journey north, she wasn't ready to set out for Italia so soon. She'd spent so little time with her father over the years, she didn't want to say goodbye to him yet. Leaning forward, she continued to hold his eye. "Then let me stay awhile please, *pater*." A muscle flexed in his jaw, yet she pressed on. "I shall help manage your household … I will make myself useful and won't get underfoot. I promise."

Father and daughter stared at each other a long moment before Severus Juventus murmured another oath, raking a hand through his short hair. "Damn it, Colombia. You look so much like your mother … but you're as stubborn as a boar."

A smile lifted the corners of her mouth. "*Mater* always said I took after you."

The commander snorted. However, he didn't deny her words. Leaning back in his recliner, he huffed a deep sigh. "Very well … you can stay on until the spring."

XXI. LETTING THE PAST LIE

"WE'RE LOWER ON olive oil than I thought," Colombia noted, peering into the last clay urn sitting on the larder floor. "This is barely half-full."

"Really? I thought there would be enough to last us until Saturnalia," Claudia replied, her voice tight.

Colombia glanced over her shoulder at where the cook hovered in the doorway leading out into the kitchen. Over the past month she'd been in Onnum, she regularly met with Claudia to plan meals and check the stores. After the attack on the supply convoy, the cook had done her best to conserve food, yet she couldn't work miracles.

Claudia's thin face was strained this morning, her gaze flicking around the empty shelves within the larder.

Unfortunately, olive oil wasn't the only thing they were running out of. Everything that couldn't be easily sourced locally—dried fruits, wine, and spices—was dwindling. They were also down to their last two sacks of spelt—concerning indeed, for Claudia ground the grain for bread and pastries.

Colombia sighed. "It looks like the next couple of months are going to be very lean."

Claudia's brow furrowed. "Saturnalia ... and the next supply delivery ... can't come soon enough," she grumbled.

The two women returned to the kitchen, where the toothsome aroma of simmering boar stew greeted them. Usually, Claudia would have added a little clove and dried fruit to the dish, yet she wouldn't today. Nonetheless, it still smelled delicious. Claudia could do much with very little.

Picking up her wax tablet and sharp stylus, Colombia started scratching out notes to herself, a reminder of what they needed to conserve. "Father warned me yesterday that the principia's strongroom is nearly empty," she told the cook. "We need to cut back on our food shopping and economize ... will that stew do for two days?"

Turning from where she'd been adding some chopped rosemary to the cauldron, Claudia's brow furrowed. "I suppose so ... if I bulk it out with carrots and onions." She paused then, biting her lower lip. "But I don't usually serve the commander the same meal twice in a row. What if it displeases him?"

Colombia gave a soft snort. "The commander knows we have to tighten our belts. Don't worry, he'll understand."

Claudia's thin shoulders visibly relaxed at this assurance. She then flashed Colombia a grateful smile. "He seems more at ease since your arrival, my lady ... even if he's been a bit stressed of late, what with his men demanding their pay."

Surprised by the cook's candor, for Claudia was usually painfully formal with her, Colombia smiled back. "It's good to be able to spend time with *pater* again," she admitted. "He took this posting less than six months after my mother died, and I've barely seen him since."

"He's dedicated to his service to the empire," Claudia murmured. "But I've always wondered why he hasn't remarried."

Colombia caught the curiosity in Claudia's voice and sensed that the cook had many unanswered questions about the man she served. Severus must have appeared an enigma to many in this fort. He was self-contained, and when he wasn't working, he did little socializing.

"I too have wondered that," Colombia replied with a half-smile. "I'll have to ask him why one of these days."

In truth, she hadn't brought up anything personal with her father when they relaxed together in the evenings. After supper, they'd retire to the tablinum, where they often played a game of Latrunculi as they sipped a little wine.

Being able to spend time with her father again, after so many years apart, was a gift indeed, and she was loath to spoil it with questions that would discomfort him. Initially, she'd worried he'd be irritated by her presence in the fort, but Severus had surprised her.

He not only tolerated her living here but seemed to appreciate it.

"I imagine he must have loved your mother very much," Claudia said, still trawling for details.

"Yes, *pater* adored her," Colombia replied. Her mood shadowed a little then. "He despaired when she died."

She tried not to think about her mother's illness and death. Her father had tried to keep reality at bay while she was sick, calling physicians from far afield to treat her, and arguing with any who gave a grim diagnosis. After her death, he'd raged for a few days, unable to accept that his beloved wife was gone, before falling into a black mood that ensured everyone in his household—servants, slaves, and his daughter—kept their distance.

Claudia's face creased into a sympathetic expression. Her lips parted then, as she readied herself to ask something else. Colombia's answers had encouraged her; there was clearly much she wished to know about Commander Juventus.

Colombia's stomach tightened. She wasn't sure she wanted to tell her anything else—not at present, anyway.

However, the cook was forestalled from asking further questions when Moira strode into the kitchen. The slave carried a large shopping basket under one arm. Halting, she glanced from Claudia to Colombia, realizing that she'd interrupted something. "Are you ready for market, *domina*?"

"Yes," Colombia replied, relieved. "Just let me fetch my *palla*."

Outdoors, the air was fresh and the scent of woodsmoke hung in the air. Autumn was creeping over the north, and the warmth of summer was abating. Soon they'd have to light the furnace that warmed the hypocaust system, for the evenings grew cool.

Leading the way out of the compound into the vicus, Colombia stifled a sigh.

She enjoyed her life at Onnum, yet something was missing.

Or more correctly, *someone*.

Aedan.

A lingering ache had taken up residence in her chest of late, one that sharpened whenever she thought of the Brigante warrior who'd escorted her to safety. Her menses had come five days after her arrival at the fort, a relief indeed. She truly hadn't wanted to explain to her father why she was with child.

Nonetheless, she cherished that night she'd spent in Aedan's arms. Often, she'd lie abed reliving it—yet the memories held sharp edges.

They made her miss him.

I wonder where he is now, she thought wistfully as she entered the busy market. *Or if he misses me too.*

Raising her hand, she rubbed at her breastbone, as she often did when she thought of Aedan, willing the ache to subside. There was no use in pining over what could never be.

Colombia turned to Moira then. "We need eggs," she told the slave. "Claudia has promised to bake one of her custards for *cena*."

Moira nodded, her gaze scanning the surrounding stalls. On the far side of the colorful sea of awnings stood a woman selling eggs. Usually, she had a number of wicker baskets spread out before her, yet this morning, there remained just one. "They're selling out fast, *domina*," Moira noted, her tone brisk. "We should buy some first."

The two women made their way across the crowded marketplace, weaving in amongst other shoppers, women mostly, who carried baskets under their arms and chattered together as they went about their morning ritual.

A smile tugged at Colombia's mouth. Roman noblewomen didn't usually shop at market, sending their servants or slaves out to do the task instead. However, she relished any opportunity to leave the compound. Apart from Moira, and Claudia, the cook, the interior of the compound was an almost exclusively male domain, but beyond she enjoyed hearing the lilt of female voices and mixing with other women.

An angry shout carried across the market square then.

Colombia halted, swiveling to see a legionary sprawled on the ground, clutching his groin. A heavyset woman with bright-red cheeks stood over him, quivering with outrage. Claudia recognized her. She was the magistrate's wife.

Forgetting the eggs for the moment, Colombia approached the matron.

However, the woman hadn't yet seen her. Instead, she glared imperiously down at the groaning man. His face was flushed, his eyes glazed. The tunic he wore under his leather harness was stained and crumpled. It was only mid-morning, but the legionary was well into his cups.

"*Caenum!*" the magistrate's wife choked out, her bosom expanding like forge bellows. "How dare you touch me."

Colombia halted before them. "What happened, Portia?"

The matron's chin kicked up. "Lady Colombia," she gasped. "This ... *filth* ... just groped me."

Colombia stiffened at this news. Since her arrival at Onnum, she'd marked an increasing sense of disorder within the fort. Usually, her father's men were respectful, yet one or two leered at her these days when she was out and about. She hadn't said anything to Severus, for she knew he'd punish them for it. Nonetheless, it made her a little wary about stepping out alone for a stroll.

It didn't surprise her that this legionary was drunk when he should have been at his post—for her father had been forced to deal with a growing amount of disorderly conduct of late—yet the fact he'd dared lay a hand on the magistrate's wife did.

Meeting the legionary's glazed stare, Colombia frowned. "What's your name, soldier?"

"*Futue te ipsum!*" he growled.

Both the matron and Moira, who'd stopped behind Colombia, stifled gasps. Around them, the market went quiet.

The legionary had just cast a gutter insult her way.

Stepping closer to the soldier, Colombia held his eye. "*Malum*," she growled, her answering insult causing a titter in the crowd behind her. "You're speaking to Commander Juventus's daughter. Now give me your name."

Across the square, Aedan watched Colombia stare down the drunken soldier.

He didn't normally venture out to the market at this time of day—for mornings were the busiest time in the workshop—yet Keir had a bad cold at present, and had asked Aedan to pick up some fresh milk and vegetables.

He'd been casting an eye over the stacks of cabbages, carrots, and onions at a stall, and wondering how many Keir actually wanted, when a commotion on the other side of the wide space drew his eye.

And there she was.

Over the past month, Aedan had tried not to think much about Colombia Juventus. He knew she resided within the fort, yet he deliberately kept away from places where he might see her.

However, as the altercation between the two women and the legionary drew out, Aedan tensed.

He couldn't hear what had passed between them, for he was too far away, yet he could tell from the belligerence of the soldier's stare and the high spots of color that appeared upon Colombia's cheeks that he'd insulted her.

Aedan's mouth thinned, and he took a step away from the vegetable stall. That bastard looked like he needed his nose flattened.

An instant later, he checked himself. *What are you doing?*

Ever since settling in Onnum, he'd known his and Colombia's paths might cross again. Yet, it wouldn't be today.

Not enough time had passed since they'd parted ways. Aedan was settling in well here. He enjoyed working with Keir. The man was a patient and able teacher, and Aedan was able to explore his gift for woodworking. It was a good life, and he didn't take it for granted.

Yet the sight of Colombia made him feel restless—made him feel as if, despite his newfound contentment, something was missing.

She was missing.

His gaze devoured her, noting the way her slender frame tensed, and her grey eyes narrowed imperiously as she said something else to the soldier.

The drunk's face stiffened, and he lowered his gaze, mumbling a few words.

Colombia looked down her nose at him as she continued speaking. Moments later, the soldier climbed gingerly to his feet, nursing his crotch as he did so.

Aedan's gaze widened. Had she kneed the man in the cods?

Face screwed up, the soldier limped off toward the compound, while Colombia turned to the portly Roman matron standing a few feet away. They exchanged a few words before Colombia moved off. A statuesque, flame-haired Brigante woman fell in behind her. Dressed in a plain tunic and sandals, the redhead was clearly a house-slave.

Aedan's gaze tracked them across the square. They were heading with purposeful strides toward an egg vendor on the far side.

Pulse quickening, Aedan turned back to the vegetable stall and hurriedly made his purchase.

Catching sight of Colombia had unbalanced him. She didn't know he had settled at Onnum, and despite that he longed to approach her, to hear her soft voice and have that smoky gaze settle upon him, he knew it wasn't wise.

No doubt, she was wedded to her Roman by now. She was moving on with her life, and he had to do the same.

It was best to let the past lie.

XXII. FATHER AND DAUGHTER

"YOU DID WELL telling me about that legionary's coarse behavior and drunkenness, daughter," Severus said as he ripped off a piece of crusty bread and dipped it in his stew. "Rest assured, Darius Gavia has been punished."

Colombia met her father's eye across the table. "How?"

When the soldier had insulted her earlier, she'd wanted to kick him in the face—yet now her father's grim expression made queasiness churn in her gut. There was a reason she'd deliberately not told her father about the leers and lewd comments some of the men had whispered as she'd walked by over the past weeks.

Severus Juventus ran this fort with an iron fist—and he wasn't a man known for his mercy.

Her father's dark brows drew together. "Drinking on duty and then insulting two high-ranking ladies is punishable by death," he replied coolly. "However, we're short on men these days, so I took the *flagrum* to him instead."

Colombia stifled a wince. Back in Asculum, she'd seen a soldier beaten with a flagrum once. The whipping had been brutal, for the three long leather straps tipped with metal hooks had torn chunks of flesh off the soldier's back.

Swallowing bile, she reached for her calix of wine and took a large gulp.

Noting her reaction, her father's expression softened. "I'm sorry you have to hear such things, Colombia," he murmured, his voice roughening. "A noblewoman should not have contact with the brutality of military life."

Colombia sighed, her fingers tightening around the stem of the calix. "It's all right, *pater* ... I'm not going to faint."

Severus's mouth thinned, his brow furrowing. "If your mother were alive, she'd be aghast that you were living here with me," he muttered. "You should be in Asculum, in comfort and safety."

Colombia set her wine down with a resigned sigh and took a mouthful of stew. She knew her father was only trying to protect her, yet she did find his views tiresome at times.

As she'd expected, the stew was delicious. Claudia had been tending it all morning, seasoning it to taste.

"Do you like the stew, *pater*?" she asked then. "We've run out of spice, but Claudia has made a few tweaks to the recipe."

"It's good," he replied.

Her mouth curved. "That's a relief ... since you'll be having it tomorrow too. We're trying to make our stores go a bit further."

Colombia's father gave a rare smile then, his expression softening. "Like your mother, you know how to manage a household ... although you're much more strong-willed and opinionated than Antonia ever was."

Colombia cocked an eyebrow. "And that's a bad thing?"

Severus snorted. "Such traits are expected in men ... but they are unfeminine in women."

"Why?" Her gaze held his.

Surprise flickered across Severus's face at the directness of her question. There was a time, not too long ago, when she would have quailed at speaking so boldly to her father, but these days, she had the courage to let her true character show.

She wouldn't leash her tongue just so that the men around her didn't feel challenged.

"No man likes a stroppy woman," Severus grumbled, taking a bite of bread. He chewed and swallowed before continuing. "We value gentleness … obedience. Not your opinions. You'd do well to remember that, Colombia."

Colombia fought a scowl, her playful mood dissipating. *Aedan liked to hear my opinions.*

Pushing aside thoughts of the man she couldn't forget, she sighed. "*Mater* was both gentle and obedient, wasn't she?"

His expression shuttered. "She was."

Silence fell between them, drawing out while they continued to eat their stew. Eventually, wiping her bowl with a scrap of bread, Colombia met her father's eye once more. "I don't think my aunt and uncle liked me living with them," she admitted softly. "Neither looked sad to see me leave … or tried to dissuade me from traveling here."

Severus's features tightened. "I shouldn't have left you with them for so long," he muttered, "but there was no one else." He paused then, a groove etching between his brows. "They didn't mistreat you, did they?"

She shook her head. "No … but Aunt Livia has a wicked temper if crossed."

Her father sighed before shaking his head. "Livia is nothing like your mother … it always amazed me they were from the same family."

"You miss *mater* still … don't you?" It was a direct question, yet since they were having a frank conversation, Colombia felt emboldened to ask it.

Their gazes held for a few moments before Severus huffed a sigh of his own. "I do … it was hard losing her … no one could replace Antonia." He looked down then, a finger tracing the decorated edge of the dining table. "I blamed myself, you know?"

Colombia stiffened. She hadn't realized that. "Why?"

"When she started having stomach pains, I should have called for a physician sooner." He was avoiding her eye now. "I thought she was just having digestion problems."

"We *all* thought that," Colombia reminded him. "Including *mater* … it wasn't your fault."

He shook his head, his jaw tightening. "I was dismissive, taken up with work as usual. I regret that now." His throat bobbed then. "That was why I took that posting shortly after her death. I couldn't bear to stay in Asculum, surrounded by memories."

Or to be near me. Colombia swallowed too, as she realized how much it would have pained him initially, every time he looked at her. Everyone said she was the image of her mother—no wonder he'd departed so swiftly.

Silence fell between them once more before Colombia eventually broke it. "You could marry again, *pater* … you could have more children."

Severus snorted, his chin kicking up. "The frontier isn't right for a gently bred woman … or for a family … or for you, Colombia. Come spring, I shall send you back to Italia."

Colombia's shoulders slumped, although she nodded. She hadn't expected to stay here forever, yet the reminder disappointed her, nonetheless. "I know I can't remain with you," she admitted. "But I'm grateful for the time we've had together."

His mouth lifted at the corners. "So am I."

Moira entered the triclinium then, wine ewer in hand. Approaching the table, she dipped her head to Severus. "More wine, *dominus?*"

Severus nodded, holding out his calix.

Moira refilled it and Colombia's cup. "Claudia has prepared baked custards," she told them. "Shall I bring them in now?"

"Yes, thank you, Moira," Severus replied.

Moira departed the triclinium to fetch the custards, and Colombia flashed her father a wry smile. "I don't think I've ever heard you thank a slave before," she observed.

Severus's mouth pursed at her teasing. "Moira serves me better when I show a little gratitude," he rumbled, flashing Colombia a rueful look. "You might have noted that the Brigantes aren't particularly deferential."

"Do you often have problems with them?" she asked, curious now.

Severus took a gulp of wine. "At times, yes. That recent attack on our supply convoy wasn't the first one we've weathered … although it hit us the hardest. It was ill fortune that they struck our pay wagons." He pulled a face then. "We haven't been able to recover anything they took … or catch the filth responsible."

Colombia's pulse quickened at this news, for his words reminded her of Aedan, and the fact he'd run with the 'filth' he spoke of.

She hoped Aedan had chosen another path—one that wouldn't put his life in danger.

Over the past weeks, she'd also marked the hardness that had crept into her father's voice when he'd spoken of the outlaws who'd escaped justice.

"Do you hate them, *pater?*"

It was another blunt question, yet since her father was in a chatty mood today, she seized her chance.

Severus glanced up. "Who?"

"The Britons … those you rule."

Their gazes held for a few moments, and surprise rippled over her father's face. Once again, her directness had caught him off-guard.

Colombia wondered if he'd answer, or merely brush her question aside as he often did if she overstepped.

But, to her surprise, he replied. "*Hate* is a strong word, daughter. Nonetheless, ever since we set foot in Britannia, the people of this land have fought us … every damn step of the way. It gets tiring … not being able to take them at their word." His expression darkened then. "You can't trust any of the bastards. They'll shake your hand one moment and stab you in the back the next."

Colombia swallowed to ease the sudden tightness in her throat. She thought once more of Aedan, of how he'd rescued her, how he'd escorted her to safety and refused to take payment for it. He was an honest man, a good one. "Surely *some* of the Britons are trustworthy," she murmured, chagrin creeping into her voice.

Severus pulled a face. "Perhaps ... but I've yet to meet one I'd rely on."

XXIII. HONORING MARS

DRAWING HER PALLA close, Colombia stepped under the shelter of the grand portico that ringed the headquarters building and the parade ground. Moira ducked in next to her—and both women watched as the neat rows of soldiers came to a rattling halt on the parade ground.

A trumpet echoed through the fort, the mournful sound causing the fine hair on the back of Colombia's forearms to rise.

Linus was there, of course, striding down the ranks, his gaze sweeping over his men. They straightened as he moved by, before they saluted him by slamming their fisted right hands over their hearts.

The primus pilus hadn't noticed the two women observing the parade from the shadow of the colonnade. As always, when Linus was at work, he was focused on that and nothing else.

Two months had passed now since Colombia had arrived at Onnum, and she hadn't spoken to him since the day she'd given back his ring—and he hadn't sought her out either. Their lack of contact had been a relief.

"I've never seen a soldier wearing flowers around his neck before," Moira observed.

Cutting her companion a sidelong look, Colombia noted the slight curve of the woman's mouth. Indeed, it was an incongruous sight to see Roman soldiers wearing garlands of flowers.

Moira had wondered what the baskets of wildflowers she'd helped Colombia and the other women pick the afternoon before, from the hills that stretched around Onnum, had been for—and now she knew.

"It does look a little strange," Colombia admitted. "Especially since so many of them are scowling."

It was true. Despite their gleaming armor, which they'd have spent all morning polishing for the purification rites for Armilustrium, a great number of the men wore sour expressions.

Colombia tensed as her gaze traveled along the line. Today marked the end of the campaigning season. Indeed, the garrisons stretched out along the Wall were all getting ready for the long, cold winter. Armilustrium honored Mars, God of War. Just the day before, they'd sacrificed a horse to celebrate Equus October. Usually, the men would be in high spirits. Once night fell, there would be a procession with torches around the fort, which would conclude at the shrine to Mars in the praetorium. After that, there would be feasting and drinking.

"I hope the festivities sweeten their tempers," she murmured, voicing her worries aloud. "Of course, the men are angry about missing their last wages. Their hunt for the stolen pay wagons has been unsuccessful ... and there isn't enough coin in the strongroom to pay them until the next convoy arrives at Saturnalia."

"Most of them would only gamble it away, anyway," Moira pointed out. "Although I hear the taverns in the vicus aren't doing well these days. They rely on the patronage of hard-drinking legionaries."

Colombia glanced back at the slave, noting her wry smile. It had taken a while for Moira to warm to her, yet these days, the two women were much more at ease in each other's company. The Brigante woman had a dry sense of humor that Colombia appreciated.

"You're right ... most of them waste their salaries," she replied. "However, their loyalty to my father comes at a price. None of them work for free."

Moira nodded, her attention shifting back to the rows of legionaries, and to the man wearing a blood-red cloak, who'd just stridden out onto the parade ground. Commander Juventus's deep voice echoed across the space. Despite that he was nearing the end of his fourth decade, Colombia's father carried himself like a man half his age.

She wasn't surprised that he'd caught Moira's eye now. Although the boldness of her stare did surprise Colombia a little. Whenever the woman served them at mealtimes in the triclinium, the slave rarely looked the commander's way.

A gust of biting wind barreled across the compound then, whipping strands free from Colombia's tightly braided hairstyle. As always, Moira had done a fine job with her hair that morning, yet it wouldn't survive the blustery weather.

Glancing up at the slate-colored sky, Colombia frowned. She wanted to visit the cloth merchant in the vicus, although she didn't wish to get rained upon.

"Come on," she murmured to Moira. "Let's get our errand done before the rain arrives."

Leaving the portico, the two women took the street to the gate leading into the civilian settlement. The guards patrolling there weren't paying much attention to the comings and goings. Instead, they were casting a pair of dice in the dirt and exchanging insults.

Colombia frowned at their lack of attention.

The two women emerged into the bustling market square. The vicus was even busier than usual today. The locals were also celebrating Armilustrium in their own way. Streamers of flowers hung from doorways and windows, although the gusty wind had dislodged some of them.

Walking through the square, Colombia inhaled the aroma of spit-roasting boar. The Romans who lived within the vicus had set up spits around the perimeters of the square and were slowly cooking them in preparation for nightfall. Dusk was still some way off, yet a row of torches had already been driven into the ground to be lit after dark.

A drop of rain caught Colombia on the cheek, and she glanced once more up at the sky. Hopefully, the weather wouldn't douse the revelry.

"I hope the cloth merchant hasn't closed his doors early," she muttered, quickening her stride. "Since there's a festival."

"We can always go back tomorrow, *domina*," Moira reminded her gently. "The fabric will still be there."

"I know," Colombia replied. "But we both need new tunics ... and I'd like to get started on making them in the morning."

The two women navigated the streets toward the cloth merchant's shop, hurrying their step as more raindrops wet their cheeks. Along the way, they passed a rowdy tavern. Drunken laughter filtered out onto the street.

Colombia and Moira walked on, passing the carpenter's workshop a little farther along. The scent of freshly cut wood wafted out from the open doors, and Colombia inhaled deeply. Glancing into the interior of the workshop, she spied an older man hunched over a high-backed chair he was decorating, hammer and chisel in hand. His brow was furrowed in concentration as he worked.

Shifting her gaze away, Colombia hurried onward.

Farther down the street, she was relieved to find the cloth merchant still open.

The small, pot-bellied man, who hailed from Italia, welcomed them inside with a broad smile. "I have just the thing, my lady," he assured Colombia before bustling to the back of his shop to retrieve a bolt of fabric.

While she waited, Colombia glanced around her at the stacks of colorful cloth that lined the walls of his shop. Moira reached out and stroked one of the silks, her blue eyes widening at its feel. However, when the shopkeeper returned, she snatched her hand back.

Ignoring the slave, the merchant flashed Colombia another smile and placed a bolt of pale-yellow linen on the table in the center of the shop. "What do you think?"

Colombia moved forward and touched the fabric, noting its softness and fine weave. "Yes, this will do nicely," she said after a moment.

A short while later, Colombia and Moira emerged from the shop, the coin purse at Colombia's waist considerably lighter, while her companion carried a bulky, yet carefully wrapped, parcel.

Moira glanced up at the grey sky as they walked back down the street. "It looks like the rain might hold off a little longer."

Relieved, Colombia nodded. She didn't want to get the costly fabric soaked on the way home.

The poignant call of a trumpet echoed once more through the fort then as the light started to dim. Not long now before the torches were lit. Even a few streets back from the market square, the rich aroma of roasting boar filled the air. Colombia smiled. She was looking forward to the celebrations. Things had been lean of late in the fort, but her father had agreed to put on a good show this evening, in an effort to boost morale.

They passed by the carpenter's workshop again, and Colombia found herself glancing through the doorway once more.

She expected to see the older Briton, still hard at work—but instead, another, younger, man had replaced him.

Colombia gasped, her heart slamming against her breastbone, and she skidded to a halt.

XXIV. HIS PLACE

AEDAN STOOD AT the workbench, sanding a stool, his brow furrowed in concentration.

He hadn't yet seen her.

Colombia's heart started to pound like a drum. *What in Hades is he doing here?*

And despite that Moira was now asking her what the matter was, her gaze devoured him.

He looked well. His bare arms, decorated in blue tribal swirls, gleamed with sweat as he worked, the muscles flexing with each movement. His hair, curling from the day's dampness and sweat, had been trimmed since she'd seen him last. It was still shaggy, yet a little less unruly.

"Aedan."

He stopped his sanding and glanced up, his gaze swiveling to the doorway—and the moment those sea-blue eyes fastened upon her, Colombia stopped breathing.

Minerva protect her, his gaze still had the power to scatter her wits.

Aedan's lips parted then. "Colombia."

Pulse racing, she took a step forward. Moira was still standing in the street, yet her companion had stopped asking her if anything was wrong, since Colombia hadn't responded.

Her attention remained fixed upon Aedan now. "I didn't realize you'd stayed on in Onnum?" Her voice was unnaturally high and breathy, yet she couldn't help it. She was still reeling from seeing him.

He smiled, a dimple forming on his cheek. "After we bid each other farewell, I decided I might as well try my luck here."

"Are you a carpenter now?"

"More like a carpenter's apprentice. I'm learning fast though."

"I visit the vicus often … I'm surprised I haven't seen you?"

Aedan stepped away from the workbench and approached her. "That's not so surprising … I spend most of my time in here, learning my trade." He halted a few feet back from her, his gaze roaming across her face, and when he spoke once more, his voice had lowered. "It's good to see you, Colombia."

"And you," she whispered back. She wet her lips then. Her mouth had gone dry, and she felt oddly lightheaded. "And do you like this new life you've made for yourself?"

"I do." Reaching up, Aedan massaged a muscle in his shoulder, although his gaze never left hers. "Keir is a good teacher and a fair master. I hope to one day run my own workshop, although I've still got a lot to learn."

A soft cough sounded behind Colombia then, reminding her that they weren't alone.

Cheeks warming, she turned, beckoning her companion forward. "Moira … this is Aedan. He's the man who rescued me a couple of months ago."

The slave stepped into the workshop, her blue eyes bright with curiosity. She then greeted Aedan in his own tongue, and he did the same.

Colombia's chest constricted, an irrational arrow of jealousy stabbing her between the ribs. The two fellow Britons exchanged words with such ease that she felt like an outsider. Of course, she *was* an outsider, one of the invaders who'd taken control of these lands by force. However, she'd never felt quite so excluded until this moment.

She wished she'd learned more than just a few words of Aedan's tongue when they'd been traveling together.

Aedan's attention drifted to the package Moira was holding. He then shifted back to Latin. "Have you been shopping?"

"Yes," Colombia replied. "We've just visited the cloth merchant."

Aedan nodded. He then met her gaze once more. "And how are things with your centurion?" he asked, his voice carefully bland. "I suppose you're a wedded woman now?"

"Linus and I aren't married," she replied softly. "I broke off our betrothal shortly after arriving here."

Aedan's eyes snapped wide. "Why?"

"We weren't suited."

He arched an eyebrow, inviting her to continue. However, Colombia flashed him an embarrassed look. She didn't want to go into things—not with Moira listening in on their conversation. Moira didn't know about the true nature of their relationship, and it was best she didn't, just in case word got back to her father.

Colombia's relationship with Severus had improved greatly of late, yet if he learned she'd taken a Brigante warrior to her bed, he wouldn't look so kindly on his daughter.

"I have to get back to the compound." Colombia then gestured to the stool he'd abandoned. "And you look busy." She paused, her mouth curving into a slow smile. "But I'd like to drop by again ... may I?"

Aedan's gaze held hers. "Of course."

Watching Colombia and her companion exit the workshop and turn right onto the street, Aedan stood there, stunned.

He couldn't believe Colombia had ended things with Linus. When she'd told him of her husband-to-be, Aedan wondered if the man was a blockhead—but now he was sure of it. The man should have been humbled by the fact she'd traveled across the empire to reach him.

Instead, the fool had let her go.

Dragging a hand through his hair, Aedan murmured an oath. Gods, he was tempted to run after the lovely Colombia and kiss her on the street, under the eyes of all.

Nonetheless, he checked the reckless impulse.

Commander Juventus would have him horsewhipped for taking such liberties.

Aedan's mouth thinned at the sobering reminder.

Over the past month, he'd told himself that Colombia wouldn't remain in Onnum forever, and that he'd be wise to forget her.

Yet the Gods seemed to be playing with him—for they'd brought her to his door.

Returning to the stool he'd promised Keir he'd finish this evening, Aedan picked up his sander and resumed work. Although he used blocks of sandstone for rougher jobs, the gentle curves of the stool needed something finer—as such, he used a sheet of sharkskin wrapped around a stone. The stool was close to being done, although Aedan found it difficult to concentrate on his work now.

Thoughts of Colombia made it hard to focus.

Once again, seeing her had unsettled him. He wondered then if he'd been wise to settle down in Onnum. If he'd chosen another of the many forts that dotted the Wall, he'd have found it easier to move on. To let his longing for the smoke-eyed Roman beauty go.

Colombia's free to wed whomever she chooses now ... she might choose me.

The thought brought him up short.

Cursing under his breath, Aedan tossed his sander to one side.

The Reaper take him, what was he thinking? He was a Brigante living in a Roman fort, entertaining the thought of asking for the hand of Commander Juventus's daughter.

His mood soured then. Out in the wilderness, there had been no barriers between him and Colombia—but inside the walls of Onnum, she was as untouchable as the stars.

Once again, the Caesars were showing him his place.

"Colombia, we're having guests for supper this eve ... can you ensure Claudia prepares something special?"

Glancing up from where she was dipping a piece of salty bread in a drizzle of olive oil—for they were rationing it these days—Colombia met her father's eye. They sat in the triclinium, eating ientaculum—the first meal of the day.

Outside, a misty grey dawn was breaking. The mornings had gotten chilly of late, yet the hypocaust system ensured these rooms remained warm.

"Of course," she murmured. If they were having guests for vesperna, they would have to put on something a little more elaborate than the usual soup. "I'll see to it. Will they be staying overnight?"

Severus nodded before he smiled. "You've done a fine job of managing my household since your arrival, Colombia," he admitted after a brief pause. "I think Marcus is starting to feel redundant."

Colombia huffed a laugh. "Hardly." The house steward was always bustling around the praetorium, organizing everyone. However, he liked it when Colombia planned meals with the cook. She inclined her head then. "Whom are we hosting?"

"The fort commander of Vindolanda ... Justinian Aquila ... and his wife."

Colombia straightened up on the recliner she'd been lying on. "The Eagle is coming here?"

Her father's smile turned rueful. "Ah, so you've heard about him then?"

"There are few who haven't, I'd wager."

"You would have heard too that he married one of the *Picti*."

Colombia nodded. "Have you met her?"

"No ... but today should remedy that." Severus's mouth pursed then, making it clear he wasn't looking forward to being introduced to the woman.

Colombia watched him steadily. "Has his choice of wife made him unpopular?"

Her father pulled a face. "In some quarters ... although since Hadrian gave his blessing for this union, they can't grumble too loudly."

Colombia inclined her head. "Why is Aquila paying us a visit?"

Severus reached for a cup of milk and drained the dregs. "They've been having trouble amongst the garrison at Vindolanda too. Aquila and I need to find a way to raise morale before the next pay wagons arrive."

"The men do seem ... restless," Colombia admitted, her brow furrowing. "Perhaps they believe you're deliberately withholding their wages."

"Well, I'm not." Her father's expression tightened. "I thought yesterday's festivities might have picked up their spirits ... especially since we made a special effort with the feast ... but there was a brawl last night. Two men are dead, and five are in the *valetudinarium* ... the medics are doing their best to tend them, but one's not likely to make it." He muttered a curse under his breath then. "The last thing I need is my men turning on each other."

Emerging from the triclinium, Colombia watched her father's broad-shouldered figure disappear through the door to the atrium. He would be heading for the principia building next door, where he met every morning with his officers. No doubt, they'd be discussing the continued unrest within the fort. As always, his stride was long and purposeful, although he'd departed with a scowl upon his face.

Colombia understood his dark mood.

Although she usually enjoyed her strolls around the compound and the vicus beyond, she'd become uneasy of late. A shadow had fallen over Onnum, and it showed no sign of lifting.

Colombia drew her palla close and stepped out into the courtyard, raising her chin to view the foggy morning. Mist had risen from the nearby burn for the past few dawns, yet it usually burned away by noon.

She set off toward the kitchen then. The sound of voices drifted from the open doorway, where the rest of the household would be finishing up their own ientaculum. She needed to let Claudia know they'd have company for supper. After that, Colombia would help Moira ready a cubiculum for Aquila and his wife.

Aquila.

Aedan's former master.

Her thoughts turned to the Brigante then. She was tempted to pay him a visit to tell him his former master would be her father's guest this evening. However, she quickly dismissed the thought with a rueful shake of her head.

It was just an excuse to see him.

Not even a day had passed since she'd discovered he was living in Onnum, and already she longed to visit him again. But Aedan wasn't going anywhere, and she had much to do today.

Her visit would have to wait.

XXV. GOOD ADVICE

"THIS IS A fine meal ... compliments to your cook." Commander Aquila's deep voice rumbled across the triclinium.

Inclining her head, Colombia smiled. Indeed, Claudia had done well at such short notice. A spread of sausages, roast grouse, eggs poached in honeyed wine, cheeses, and fresh bread lay upon the table in the center of the space. Wooden recliners, where the diners lounged as they consumed their supper, lined the rectangular table, while Marcus and Moira waited to one side, ewers of wine in hand. "I shall be sure to tell Claudia," Colombia promised Aquila.

In truth, she'd hardly noticed the food this evening—she was too fascinated by their guests to focus on much else.

Justinian Aquila was one of the most striking, attractive men she'd ever seen. Tall and dark-haired, with penetrating golden eyes, he held himself with supreme confidence. His wife, Fenella, was equally remarkable. Small and lithe, with silky brown hair pinned high, the *Picti* woman wore a fine stola, while precious stones sparkled upon her throat and earlobes. She was a beauty indeed, and her midnight-blue eyes were full of sharp intelligence.

And when Fenella had entered the praetorium, Colombia had marked the swell under the folds of her tunic and stola. The woman was with child.

Severus had noted it too—for his mouth had thinned.

"Our larder is getting a bit sparse ... but Claudia knows how to make do," Colombia's father said then, holding his empty calix for Moira to fill. "We're all looking forward to the arrival of the next supply convoy at Saturnalia."

Aquila's penetrating gaze shifted to Severus, his head inclining. Colombia could see why people called him 'The Eagle'. It wasn't just his name 'Aquila'—but those eyes gave him a predatory look. "Our patrols haven't been able to recover any of the stolen goods or coin," he admitted. "Have you had any luck?"

"No ... I expected to find some of it scattered across Brigante settlements. But it seems that the 'Scourge of the North' aren't sharing their bounty." Severus paused then. "At a guess, they're using it to build their strength."

Aquila held his gaze. "That's also my concern," he replied. "I've put more men on the wall at Vindolanda ... it pays to be vigilant."

Colombia glanced across at where Fenella was helping herself to a poached egg. Her expression was composed, yet her gaze was keen. She was listening intently to the conversation.

Shifting her attention to her father, Colombia noted that he'd not once looked Fenella's way since the meal had begun. Since her and Aquila's arrival, he hadn't been rude to the woman. However, he hadn't been welcoming either.

Colombia's cheeks warmed, embarrassment flooding over her. Her father didn't host often, but he seemed to have forgotten his manners.

Severus huffed a sigh then, his focus still upon Aquila. "And that brings us to the reason you're here, Justin. Our garrisons grow increasingly unruly. What are we going to do about it?"

Aquila winced. "I've enforced stricter discipline, but I'm not sure I'll be able to keep the men in check until

Saturnalia. They work hard and expect to be compensated.”

“We *all* do,” Severus grumbled. “They seem to forget that none of us are taking a wage at present.”

“Have you told them that, *pater?*”

Severus’s gaze cut to his daughter. “Excuse me?”

Colombia tensed. Over the years, she’d been discouraged from intruding on male conversation, from offering opinions on matters outside a woman’s realm. However, this evening, she couldn’t help herself. “Perhaps the answer at times like this is to talk to your men,” she said softly, aware that Fenella was now watching her, a curve to her lips. “They need to know you’re on their side ... and that you understand them. After all, everyone likes to be heard.” Her attention then flicked to Aquila. “If you become too strict, they’ll only grow to resent you.”

“That was good advice you gave during supper.”

Colombia shifted her gaze from where she was watching her father and Aquila play Latrunculi to see that Fenella was smiling at her.

After finishing their meal, they’d moved next door to the tablinum. The men were now halfway through their first game, moving counters across the wooden board, while the women sat on a couch a few feet away, sipping cups of wine.

Colombia pulled a face. “Do you think so? Neither of them looked impressed.”

Fenella huffed a soft laugh. “Men ... they like to think they have all the good ideas.” She leaned closer then, her gaze glinting. “But we know different.”

Colombia smiled back, warmth spreading across her chest. “We do. Men might rule the world ... but we women know how to negotiate, how to build trust. They'd do well to listen to us better."

Fenella's dark-blue gaze glinted at this admission. "I don't meet a lot of high-born Roman women," she admitted then. "Although those I have been introduced to aren't like you."

"I've always been somewhat of a black sheep," Colombia replied, her smile turning rueful as she looked to where the two men were engrossed in their game. "Much to my father's frustration."

Glancing back, she found Fenella still watching her steadily. The woman had an unnerving look, direct and penetrating, not unlike her husband's.

"What's it like living amongst us?" Colombia asked, deciding it was time to take the focus off herself.

Fenella smiled. "Strange at first ... but I've gotten used to it." She paused then. "It's certainly easier being Aquila's wife than his slave."

Colombia huffed a laugh. "I imagine it is ... but are we really so different though, my people and yours?"

"I suppose not." Fenella's expression turned thoughtful. "When you strip away our different ways of living, our different tongues and gods, we have more in common than most people think." She jerked her chin toward Severus, making it clear she'd marked his poor welcome earlier. He was focused on his game with Aquila, yet he'd not said a word to Fenella all evening.

Heat crept up Colombia's neck. She was just about to mutter an apology for her father when Fenella spoke once more. "What brings you to Onnum, Colombia? Surely, a woman of your age has better things to do with her time than accompany her father at the frontier?"

Colombia sighed before taking a sip from her calix. The woman had artfully turned the conversation back to her again.

The urge rose within her then to tell Fenella about Aedan.

Surely, Aquila would be curious to know where his former slave had ended up. However, she checked herself. Perhaps Aedan wished to remain hidden. This wasn't her news to tell.

"It's a long story," she replied. "Are you sure you have the patience for it?"

Fenella flashed her another smile. "Lucky for you, I have a fondness for lengthy tales … go on, I'm listening."

"Look at the pretty *lupa* … I wouldn't mind climbing on top of her."

"I wouldn't, Cartesius … that's Juventus's daughter you've just taken for a whore."

"*Futuo!* Really?"

"Yeah … watch yourself. The last man who messed with her had the skin flayed off his back."

Casting the two men a scowl, Colombia drew her palla closer around her and hurried past the noisy tavern. The two off-duty legionaries, who lounged against the wall of the building, cups of wine in hand, discussed her as if she were deaf. She felt their gazes track her path as she walked away.

Suddenly, Colombia wished she'd brought Moira along; she wasn't used to venturing into the vicus without her. A heavy atmosphere, one that had nothing to do with the overcast skies, hung over Onnum this afternoon. Indeed, it wasn't wise to go anywhere unescorted while discontent persisted within the fort—and yet Colombia had slipped out alone.

Colombia hoped her father and Aquila had come up with a plan to deal with the poor morale—and that they might consider her advice. Severus's guests had left that morning, after Aquila and her father had stayed up late discussing what to do about their common problem.

Approaching the carpenter's workshop, Colombia's gait slowed. Worries about the unrest melted away, and her belly fluttered, in anticipation of seeing Aedan again.

Halting at the door, her gaze settled upon the tableau within.

Two men labored side by side this afternoon—Aedan and the older Brigante she'd seen when she'd passed by on the way to the cloth merchant. They were working on a beautiful oaken table. Both men were carving intricate designs around the edge of it using small chisels, talking together as they worked.

Aedan's face was relaxed, and he laughed now at something his companion had just said.

Suddenly, Colombia was loath to interrupt them. Two days had passed since she'd seen him last, and she'd told herself she should wait before visiting the workshop again. Yet here she was. Maybe she should slip away, unnoticed.

However, an instant later, Aedan glanced her way. Straightening up, his mouth quirked into another smile. "Colombia?" he greeted her. "What are you doing here?"

"I was taking a stroll," she lied, plastering an answering smile upon her lips to mask her discomfort. "And thought I'd stop by."

Aedan's smile widened, his eyes crinkling at the corners before he motioned to the older man. "Colombia ... this is Keir." He glanced over at the carpenter then, switching to his own tongue. Over the past couple of days, Moira had been teaching Colombia a little of the Briton language, at her request. And although she had only learned a handful of words and sentences so far, Colombia gleaned that he'd introduced her—telling Keir that Colombia was the fort commander's daughter.

Keir nodded to her, smiling. "Good day, my lady," he greeted her in halting Latin.

Colombia smiled back. Her gaze then shifted to the table between the two men. "That's an exquisite piece of furniture," she observed. "Who's it for?"

"A farmer outside Coria." Aedan pulled a face. "A pompous retired centurion ... the man's a donkey's ass."

Keir flashed his apprentice a quelling look. "A job's a job, lad," he muttered. "Vidius is paying us well ... that's all that matters."

Aedan snorted at this yet didn't comment further.

Keir shifted back from the table and put his chisel and hammer to one side. "The day is nearly done now," he announced. "Shall I fetch us all something to drink?"

Aedan nodded, flashing the carpenter a grateful smile. "Thanks."

With a nod to Colombia, and a grin, Keir disappeared out back.

When he was gone, Colombia stepped inside the workshop, while Aedan picked up a broom and swept wood shavings out into the street. Outdoors, the gloaming was settling. It was later than she'd realized, and they were clearly shutting up shop for the day.

I should really get back. Once it got dark, her father would mark her absence and send Moira out looking for her. Nonetheless, Colombia didn't move. She wanted to remain here just a while longer.

"They're making a lot of noise at that tavern," Aedan observed as he pulled the heavy doors closed. "There's a group of them drinking on the street."

Colombia pulled a face. "Although coin is scarce these days, it seems a few legionaries can still afford a cup of wine."

She didn't mention the things she'd overheard those two legionaries saying about her. Maybe she should ask Aedan to escort her back to the compound once her visit here concluded.

Aedan turned from closing the doors, his pursed lips making his opinion of Roman soldiers clear. The past two months hadn't softened his attitude, it seemed.

Awkwardness stole over Colombia. Suddenly, she felt as if she were intruding. "We had guests last night," she admitted then, flashing him a shy smile. "Commander Aquila and his wife."

Aedan's gaze widened. "You met them?"

She nodded. "I don't think I've ever met two such charismatic people."

He snorted, although his gaze was warm. "Justin and Fenella make quite a couple, don't they?"

"They do ... you can see they're devoted to each other. Fenella's pregnant."

Another smile lifted the corners of his mouth. "I'm glad to hear they're both well." He moved across to the workbench behind the table and leaned against it, folding his arms across his chest.

Curse her, she noticed how the muscles of his upper arms flexed under his smooth skin, the way the blue woad tattoos danced. Aedan was tall and lean, yet his body was hard and sculpted. She remembered what it had felt like pressed up against her, how his skin had tasted.

Her pulse started to race.

"They are," she replied, clearing her throat once more as she tried to focus. "I wanted to tell them you were living here ... but I decided not to. I hope that was what you wished?"

His smile faded, and he nodded. "Thank you," he murmured. "I don't bear either of them ill, yet it's best our paths don't cross."

She inclined her head. "Why are you so reluctant to see Aquila again?"

He huffed a sigh. "Awkwardness, I suppose. I was once his slave, yet I'm not any longer. I wouldn't know how to act around the man, or what to say."

Colombia studied his face, wondering at his answer. Aedan was confident, arrogant, and didn't seem to care what people thought of him; yet something about Aquila made him a little insecure. She wouldn't be surprised if Aedan still harbored some resentment toward his former master.

Keir appeared then, bearing a tray with three wooden cups balanced upon it. His gaze flicked between the two of them, curiosity lighting in his eyes. "Ale?"

XXVI. TAKING THE RISK

THE THREE OF them drank together while Aedan and Keir talked of daily life in the fort. They made the effort to converse in Latin, even though Keir wasn't nearly as fluent as Aedan. Colombia appreciated them including her.

It was cozy inside the workshop; a lantern hung overhead illuminating the shelves of tools and the table they'd almost finished. The fruity scent of olive oil, which they used to preserve wood, hung heavily in the air, and Colombia inhaled it deeply. The smell reminded her of Asculum.

Eventually, Keir heaved himself up off the stool he'd been perching on and drained the dregs of ale from his cup. "I'd better clean up in here ... before I finish preparing supper," he announced, flashing Colombia an apologetic look.

"You go through," Aedan answered. "I'll put the tools away."

Keir nodded, yet there was a knowing glint in his blue eyes as his gaze shifted from Aedan to Colombia once more. Although his apprentice's expression was veiled, it was clear Aedan wanted some privacy with his guest.

If she'd been in a Roman household, Colombia wouldn't have been allowed to spend time alone with an unmarried man—especially since Aedan wasn't her betrothed—but the Brigante people did things differently.

As such, Keir left them to it. "I put a mutton and turnip stew on earlier," he informed Aedan as he headed toward the door. "I just need to make some dumplings to go with it."

"I'll be through shortly," Aedan assured him.

Keir left, shutting the wattle door behind him.

When they were alone in the workshop, an awkward silence fell.

Aedan finished his ale and set the cup aside before he started to pick up the various tools scattered over work surfaces and replace them on the shelves and hooks upon the walls.

Colombia watched him work, nervousness stealing over her. She suddenly was at a loss for words.

"It's a pleasure to see you again, Colombia," he said eventually, glancing over his shoulder at her after hanging a saw up on the wall. "But is it wise for you to keep visiting me?"

"Probably not," she murmured.

He turned to face her fully. "What if your father hears of it?"

She grimaced. "No doubt, he'd be angry."

"And yet you'd defy him anyway?"

Colombia sighed. "Now that I know you live here, I don't think I can keep away."

Aedan's gaze widened. Her candidness had clearly surprised him.

It surprised Colombia too, yet at the same time, it thrilled her. Aedan always made her feel brave.

He moved away from the far wall then, skirting the table and coming to a halt just a couple of feet from her. "Maybe I should have moved elsewhere."

"I'm glad you didn't."

Aedan's mouth thinned. "We're playing with fire, Colombia." He paused then, looking around, and she noted the tension in his jaw, neck, and shoulders. "And if we're not careful, we'll get badly burned."

Colombia's throat tightened. "You're right," she whispered. "I'm being reckless visiting you at this hour … on my own … it's just that" —she broke off there, her breathing suddenly shallow— "I miss you."

He stared back at her. "You think I don't miss you too?" he replied huskily. "Every moment of the day since I left you at the gates to the compound, I've felt your lack." He fisted his hand and slammed it against his breastbone. "Here." He swallowed hard then. "But it's pointless. You're the fort commander's daughter … and I'm a Brigante turd he'd happily flatten under his boot."

Colombia's pulse fluttered at the base of her throat. "That's not true … he wouldn't treat you like that."

Aedan's gaze narrowed. "Wouldn't he?"

She recalled then how Severus had ignored Fenella the previous evening, and unease prickled her skin. "My father's as arrogant as you are, and just as proud," she replied, pushing the thought aside. "Yet he's not unreasonable."

Aedan folded his arms over his chest. "Well, if that's the case, why don't you take me to him now … and tell him you want to marry me. See how he reacts."

Colombia stared back at him, her lips parting.

Aedan's frown deepened into a scowl. "I thought not."

"That's not fair."

"Maybe not, but it's the truth."

Silence swelled between them before Colombia whispered, "Do you *want* to marry me?"

Aedan muttered a curse in his own tongue and raked a hand through his hair. "Damn it, Colombia, we can't travel this road."

"Why not?" She took a step toward him, holding his gaze.

A muscle ticked in his cheek, yet he didn't reply.

Her heart was pounding now, yet she held her ground. She certainly hadn't visited Aedan expecting this, but now they stood toe to toe, she wasn't going to let him retreat from her.

She was suddenly aware of his closeness, the scent of leather and wood on his skin, and the vibrant sea-blue of his eyes. She ached to reach out and touch him, but she forced herself not to.

"I was scared to break things off with Linus," she said then, her voice lowering, "I thought *pater* would send me away, but he didn't."

"Severing your betrothal is one thing," he growled, "but taking me as your husband is another. He'd disown you."

"And I'd take that risk … for you."

And she meant it too. She could talk her father around.

Aedan drew in a sharp breath. A faint blush had risen to his cheeks, and his eyes glittered.

Colombia didn't move. Instead, she let silence fill the space between them.

Aedan stepped forward, and his hands closed around her shoulders. An instant later, he hauled her against him, his mouth claiming hers.

It was a wild, hot kiss—one that held nothing back.

Their lips, tongues, and teeth clashed. Groaning, Colombia leaned into him, wrapping her arms about his neck.

Gods, she'd missed this too.

She'd thought about Aedan far too often over the past two months, even knowing she'd never see him again. And although she was happy at Onnum, a hollow sensation vibrated through her chest when she relived the days they'd spent together. It was a sweet kind of torture—and so was this.

Aedan tore his mouth from hers then, trailing kisses down her jaw and neck. "Colombia," he groaned. "Do you have any idea what you do to me?"

She whimpered an incoherent reply.

"I can't be near you without wanting you," he went on hoarsely, his tongue flicking the hollow between her collarbones. "I ache for you."

"I'm yours," she gasped in return. "And if we can't stay at Onnum, we'll go somewhere else … we'll find a place where no one cares that I'm Roman and you're Briton. All that matters is that we're together."

Another groan rumbled up from his chest, and Aedan pulled her closer still, the hard length of his body molding against hers. He then swung her around and walked her backward. The small of Colombia's back hit the edge of the table, yet before she could shift away from it, Aedan's hands had cupped her backside, and he lifted her up onto its surface.

Heedless of where they were, or the fact that Keir was preparing supper next door, Aedan nudged her legs apart with his knee, stepping between them.

The dominant move made hunger twist once more within Colombia, and she wriggled closer.

A soft groan escaped her when he pushed up the heavy folds of her stola and tunic, freeing her legs. Wrapping them around his hips, she drew him nearer still. He pressed himself hard against her, his hands stroking the outside of her naked thighs—and the feel of the hard rod pressing into her, even through the thick material of his bracae, made her writhe against him.

Although Briton women went naked under their skirts, Colombia wore a subligaculum, a skimpy undergarment. And the friction of the silky material against her, as Aedan rolled his hips, made her bite her lip.

Her head fell back as his lips grazed up the column of her throat to her jaw. And then, an instant later, he was kissing her again, his tongue tangling with hers.

Colombia's hands roamed across his chest. Her shawl slid down, yet she was still wearing far too many clothes. Curse all the layers of fabric that separated them. She wanted to be naked right now—she wanted those strong yet gentle hands to touch her everywhere.

Fumbling in her eagerness, she unlaced his bracae, freeing his shaft. It pulsed, hot and eager, in her hands, soft skin stretched over iron; and she whimpered, need thrumming through her.

Muttering a curse, Aedan spread her thighs wider still and pushed aside the silky material of her subligaculum.

And then, with one driving thrust, he seated himself inside her.

Colombia arched into him, biting down hard on her bottom lip to stop herself from crying out.

Gods, she thought she remembered how good this felt, but she hadn't. It was even better than she recalled. He stretched her, filled her, the tip of his shaft touching a place that made aching pleasure throb through her womb.

Sliding his hands under her backside, and gripping tight, Aedan took her there, on the edge of the table, in deep, hard thrusts. And within just a few strokes, she was quivering.

She couldn't control herself. She writhed and pushed against him, biting down on her lip until she tasted blood—for otherwise, she'd have screamed.

Likewise, Aedan's face was contorted with hunger.

Colombia shattered then, clutching at his vest as waves of blinding pleasure pulsed out from her core, turning her inside out. She collapsed against the hard wall of his chest as he too climaxed. The heat of his release filled her, and Colombia bit back a sob, burying her face in his neck. Aedan's arms clamped around her, and he hauled her against him.

They clung together there, panting in the aftermath—unable to speak, unable to move—for a while.

"Aedan ... the dumplings are nearly ready!" a man's voice intruded then, filtering through the wattle door. Faint, off-tune whistling followed, accompanied by the clatter of iron pans. Colombia dazedly realized that Keir was still next door, preparing supper.

Still breathing hard, she drew back, lifting her gaze to meet Aedan's.

His eyes were dark in the glow of the lantern hanging from the beams behind him. And what she saw in his gaze made her still-pounding heart leap.

Raw, fierce tenderness glittered there. "Very well, little dove," he rasped. "I shall take the risk."

XXVII. WHAT NEEDS TO BE DONE

THEY LEFT THE workshop and made their way down the street. Small clay lamps hung from the eaves of buildings, bathing the vicus in soft gold.

Colombia and Aedan walked hand in hand. Keir had promised to keep Aedan's supper warm, but they'd left the carpenter with little explanation.

They didn't talk now, as they both prepared themselves for the coming meeting with Severus Juventus.

Colombia glanced at Aedan's profile, noting how his gaze focused forward. Shadows played across his proud features.

They passed the tavern farther down the street. Earlier it had been rowdy, with a milling crowd of soldiers gathered before it. But now it was silent. Lamplight flowed out onto the cobbled street.

The sight surprised Colombia. Perhaps those men had run out of coin after all and returned to the barracks.

It wasn't late, although most of the residents of Onnum were indoors at present, having supper. As such, the streets Colombia and Aedan walked through were largely empty.

However, as they crossed the market square, Colombia was surprised to see the gate to the compound was open—and that no sentries were watching their approach.

She squeezed Aedan's hand. "Something's wrong," she whispered.

"You're right," he murmured. "Where are the guards?"

They slipped into the compound.

Aedan released her hand and moved a couple of steps ahead, his gaze flicking left and right as they walked toward the heart of the fort. The principia building glowed pale up ahead.

The eerie quiet splintered then, angry voices filtering toward them. And as they drew nearer still, Colombia spied a mob gathered inside the principia's wide courtyard, before the entrance to the headquarters building itself.

Colombia's pulse trebled. *Jupiter, what are they doing?*

She caught sight of a familiar figure then. Her father stood on the steps to the principia, his cloak wine-red in the lamplight. He didn't wear his helmet or lorica this eve—and his expression was thunderous.

A handful of high-ranking officers, Linus among them, spanned out behind him.

With a jolt, Colombia realized they were blocking the way into the building.

Naked blades glinted in the crowd below, and Colombia's chest constricted. Many of the soldiers had drawn their pugiones, their fighting daggers—yet her father had yet to draw his own.

"Hades take them," she whispered. "They're mutinying."

Aedan grunted his agreement, and as they stepped under the portico, which ran around the edge of the principia, they both slowed their pace.

"Sheath your blades, and go back to your beds." Her father's voice, hard and angry, rang across the courtyard. "You're wasting your time here."

"Give us our wages!" came a rough, answering shout. "You're holding onto them for yourselves, you greedy bastards."

"There's nothing to give," the commander countered. "Our strongroom has nothing … only enough coin to buy essential supplies for your rations left."

"We don't believe you," another soldier called out.

Shouts of "liar" echoed against stone.

"Show us then!"

Severus drew his pugio, his brows knitting together. "You demand nothing from me," he rasped. "None of you are setting foot inside this building."

"Just try to stop us," someone else shouted.

"We'll get coin out of you, one way or another," a legionary added, taking a threatening step forward and brandishing his pugio.

"Stand down, *caenum!*" Severus roared at him.

Colombia's blood started to thunder in her ears. The Gods save them, things were about to get ugly. Her father and his officers weren't giving an inch. The aggression that shivered through the air scared her, yet she couldn't just stand here and watch.

She had to do something.

Leaving Aedan's side, she crept around the edge of the portico, moving toward the narrow gap between the mob and her father.

"Return to the barracks," Linus shouted, his voice cracking with outrage. "And we'll deal with you in the morning."

That was the wrong thing to say, for a collective growl went up amongst the crowd. They all knew what 'deal with you' meant.

Colombia's father had told her what happened to soldiers who rebelled. They'd be turned over to those who hadn't taken part in this mutiny—to be beaten to death with clubs and stones.

"Colombia!" Aedan caught hold of her arm as she crept forward farther still. "What are you doing?"

She glanced over her shoulder, her gaze meeting his for an instant. "What needs to be done … stay here!" And with that, she twisted free of his grip and darted forward into the gap.

She heard Aedan curse behind her and hoped he would indeed heed her. Having a Briton in their midst wouldn't calm the men's tempers—but maybe *she* could.

Skidding to a halt between the bottom step and the crowd of angry men, her heart quailed.

Up close, they looked incensed, maddened—faces taut, eyes glinting. They appeared capable of murder.

"Colombia!" Her father boomed. "Get back!"

Ignoring him, Colombia drew herself up, letting the gazes of the soldiers settle upon her.

"Haughty bitch!" someone yelled from the back. "Stand aside, or we'll trample you too!"

Fear beat in Colombia's chest like a panicked bird, but she held her ground. She needed to provide a distraction, for these men were just instants away from surging forward and coming at her father with their daggers. The commander was a formidable fighter, but even he couldn't withstand such an assault.

Inhaling sharply, she let the moment draw out. She had to speak carefully now. The wrong word would get her killed. She couldn't talk down to them or manipulate them—instead, she had to remind them of why they were here on the frontier, of the common purpose they shared.

"Wait!" she called out, her voice echoing across the courtyard. "Think about what you're doing." Dozens of hard stares bored into her, yet she plowed on. "I understand why you're angry. You should have received your wages two months ago. Life is hard up here … and without coin to spend, you wonder what the point of it all is."

Angry rumbling rippled across the crowd, but Colombia pressed on. "Yet there *is* a point … there is a reason you're all here." She broke off then. Her heart was beating so fast it was difficult to think. But she had to. Everything depended on what she said next. "None of you signed up to further the glory of Rome." Her gaze slid across the faces amassed before her. Indeed, few of them were swarthy Romans like her father and his officers. Most of them didn't hail from Italia, but from its colonies. There were copper-skinned soldiers from Numidia, with dark hair that curled tightly against their scalps, and big fair-haired men with ruddy complexions from Germania and Gallia. "You did so for a chance at a better future."

A few of the men at the front of the crowd nodded, and one or two of them lowered their daggers slightly.

"You agreed to give the empire five and twenty years of your lives … and in return, we promised to clothe you, feed you, and pay you." She paused then. "I know it's not easy on the frontier. You're all far from your homelands, and Britannia can be bleak and unwelcoming … but look at all you've achieved." She gestured around her then. "This magnificent wall, worthy of the Gods themselves. It will stand long after the last of us is gone."

"What do we care about that, woman?" An aggressive voice carried across the crowd. A tall legionary with dark-tanned skin and hawkish features had stepped forward. "The Wall is meaningless to us."

"No, it's not," she replied, meeting the soldier's eye. "It's a symbol of your bravery … your resilience." She dragged in a deep breath then before plowing on. "You will be paid as soon as the pay wagon arrives—you can be sure of that. And if you remain loyal, and once your service ends, you will receive a parcel of land or its equivalent in coin. You will be a prominent member of society … and you can settle anywhere you choose within the empire. Isn't that worth your loyalty?" She drew in another deep breath. "Step away now, return to the barracks, and I give you my word no punishment will fall upon you."

Silence fell then, swelling as the moments passed.

Colombia didn't glance over her shoulder at where her father's gaze bored into her back, or right at where Aedan no doubt watched from the shadow of the portico.

Instead, her attention remained on the men before her.

"My daughter speaks boldly." Severus Juventus spoke then, his voice hard-edged. "But I *will* honor her promise. Stand down and the most you'll get is a grade decrease and extra duties." He bit out these words as if they cost him dearly—and they likely did.

Those were soft punishments, indeed.

Another hush settled over the principia, and then— one by one—the legionaries sheathed their pugiones. Some of them still wore disgruntled expressions, but the danger that had crackled in the air when Colombia stepped before them had lifted.

They were no longer out for blood.

Colombia watched, hardly daring to breathe, as the crowd filtered out of the courtyard.

And only when the last legionary departed did she turn to face her father.

Severus was staring at her, his smoky eyes wide, his lips parted. Colombia had a moment's satisfaction of knowing that she'd rendered her father speechless.

Likewise, the officers that flanked the commander all looked poleaxed. Linus was staring at her as if Medusa stood before them.

Colombia didn't care. Her knees were starting to wobble now, as the fire that ignited in her veins, that had propelled her between her father and the mob, subsided.

"Colombia," Severus finally rasped. "I can't believe you did that."

Neither could she.

"It looks like you have a glittering career ahead of you in the senate, Lady Juventus," one of the officers, Optio Carbo, murmured, a wry edge to his voice. "With oratory skills like that, you'd go far."

Colombia gave a soft snort. Women didn't speak in the senate; they all knew that. Nonetheless, she appreciated the sentiment.

"You took a great risk, daughter," Severus said gruffly then. "One that could have ended badly."

"I know, *pater*," she whispered. "But I had to do something. They were a heartbeat away from savaging you. I couldn't stand by and let that happen."

Her father's gaze shifted right then, and Colombia tensed.

He'd seen Aedan.

Indeed, her lover now moved to her side. Aedan's expression was shuttered, his tall, lean body tense.

"Who's this?" her father growled.

Colombia drew in a slow, steadying breath as her pulse, which had just started to steady, accelerated once more. "May I present Aedan," she said, meeting her father's eye once more. "He rescued me when the supply convoy was attacked two months ago ... and he's the man I wish to marry."

XXVIII. THE CHOICE IS YOURS

THE COMMANDER'S GAZE snapped wide. "What?" he rasped.

"I love him, *pater*."

Another silence, this one brittle, fell before the headquarters building. Colombia was aware they had an audience, for her father's officers hadn't left with the other men. All of them, including Linus, looked on as she declared her feelings for the man standing at her side.

But she didn't care.

Let them bear witness to this.

"Colombia," her father finally ground out her name. "Please tell me you haven't lain with this man."

"Commander," Aedan spoke up now. "I love your daughter and wish to make her my wife."

Soft snorts followed this admission, and heat spiked under Colombia's ribcage. How dare they mock Aedan.

However, her lover ignored them. His gaze never left the commander's.

After a long pause, Juventus replied, "I think not."

Aedan's features tightened. "Do you believe I'm unworthy of her?"

The curl of the commander's lip gave them his answer. He then cut his attention to Colombia. "Return to the praetorium, daughter."

"No." Colombia stood her ground, hands balling into fists at her sides. "I'm not going anywhere. Not until you—"

"Centurion Aurelius, Optio Carbo … escort this man back to the vicus," her father barked. "Now."

Linus and the optio who'd complimented Colombia on her oratory skills stepped forward swiftly, each grabbing hold of Aedan by the arms.

Snarling a curse, Aedan tried to shake them off. However, they held him fast.

"Release him!" Colombia lunged forward, reaching for Aedan—but her father caught her by the shoulders and hauled her back. He then wrapped an arm around her waist, holding her fast.

"Arrogant Roman dogs!" Aedan shouted, struggling violently now. "You all think you're better than me … but you aren't fit to kiss my arse! You won't—"

His tirade cut off as Linus jabbed him sharply in the ribs.

Moments later, Aedan recovered. "You won't keep us apart, Juventus," he wheezed, his gaze burning into the commander. "Colombia and I *will* be together."

Severus was unmoved. "If you truly love my daughter, you'll want what's best for her," he replied coldly. "Keep away from her." With that, he towed his daughter out of the principia courtyard.

Colombia fought her father all the way home.

It was pointless though. He was far stronger than her. His grip around her waist was immovable.

He propelled her up the steps to the praetorium and through the atrium, where Marcus watched them, wide-eyed.

The commander didn't greet his house steward. Instead, he pushed his struggling daughter along the portico and into the tablinum. Releasing her, he then hauled the doors closed.

Panting from outrage, Colombia turned on him. "Stop this, *pater!* You can't—"

"Have you lost your wits, girl?" Severus cut her off. His angry gaze pinned her to the spot. "You can't marry a Briton!"

"Why not? Aedan's a good man, brave and honorable."

"But you're a Roman noblewoman. You must marry a man worthy of you ... not that foul-mouthed lout."

"He is worthy! Aedan's a chieftain's son, and he's—"

"Enough!" Under his deep tan, her father's cheeks glowed red.

Fear curled in the pit of Colombia's stomach. She'd never seen him this angry. Even so, desperation clawed up her throat. She couldn't let him shout her down or bully her.

"I don't need your blessing," she said, even as her voice wobbled. "I don't wish it to be this way, but if you won't accept my decision, I shall walk from your home, never to return."

His face went slack, as if he couldn't believe his ears.

Colombia's heart started to pound. She'd thought facing down an angry mob was difficult, yet this confrontation with her father was so much worse. It was personal. She'd enjoyed living with her father over the past months and getting to know him again. But she'd not give up Aedan to remain in his favor.

She wasn't lying. If he resisted her over this, she'd cut ties with him.

Moments passed, and when her father replied, his voice was iron-edged. "You speak as if you have some control over your life, Colombia. But you forget—as my daughter, you are my property. *I* say whether you stay or go. *I* decide what your future holds." He broke off then, breathing hard as his anger sought to boil over. "And as soon as I can arrange it, I'm sending you back to Italia."

"Keep your filthy hands off the commander's daughter."

Linus Aurelius's fist slammed into Aedan's mouth, knocking him off his feet.

Aedan picked himself up off the cobbles, ignoring the burning pain in his lower lip, and glared up at the man who'd once been betrothed to Colombia. Of course, he'd recognized the name when Juventus had barked his orders inside the principia courtyard.

"*Futue te ipsum!*" Aedan growled, hoping the insult would make the centurion come at him. He badly wanted to fight someone right now. However, Linus merely sneered at him and stepped back, motioning to the guards to close the gate.

Aedan spat on the ground. "This isn't over," he rasped, wiping the blood that trickled down his chin with the back of his hand. "You'll not get rid of me that easily."

The gate closed with a dull boom, sealing him out.

Glaring at it, Aedan sought to rein in his fury. They'd bested him tonight, but this was a temporary defeat.

They wouldn't keep him from Colombia.

Limping home, his hands clenched at his sides, Aedan silently cursed the Caesars. Their arrogance. Their disdain. He'd made a mistake living amongst them, for the bastards would forever look down their aquiline noses at him.

Keir was waiting for him by the fireside.

The carpenter's gaze narrowed as Aedan lowered himself gingerly onto a stool opposite. "What happened to you, lad?"

"I've just come from asking Juventus for Colombia's hand," Aedan growled back.

"It didn't go well, I take it?"

Aedan pulled a face before wincing as his cut lip stung. "You don't sound surprised."

Keir sighed. "I'm not."

Aedan glowered at him.

Their gazes held then before Keir slowly shook his head. "You're like a bull let loose in a market, lad. There are other ways to get what you want. You don't have to rush in, head lowered and ready to charge."

Aedan snorted. "It's the only way to deal with the Romans. They'd walk right over us otherwise."

Keir huffed a deep sigh before gesturing to the pot still simmering over the coals between them. "Do you want any stew?"

Aedan shook his head. His gut had closed. He was too angry to eat anything right now. All he wanted to do was ram his fist into Severus Juventus's face. Right after he broke Linus Aurelius's nose.

Raking both hands through his hair, he muttered a salty curse. "You'll never guess what *else* happened inside the compound," he said then, meeting the carpenter's eye once more. "Colombia and I were on our way to see her father when we found a mob of angry legionaries trying to force entry into the principia building. They seemed to think Juventus was hoarding their money in the strongroom. They looked ready to lynch him."

Keir's gaze widened. "How did—"

"Wait, there's more," Aedan went on. "Before I could stop her, Colombia strode into the midst of it all and faced them down. She convinced the soldiers to walk away without drawing blood." He gave a bemused shake of his head then. "I've never seen the like of it."

It was the carpenter's turn to utter an oath. He then raised a greying eyebrow. "But things still ended badly for you both?"

Aedan nodded, his stomach clenching as the commander's parting words rang in his head.

If you truly love my daughter, you'll want what's best for her. Keep away from her.

The pig-headed bastard. Colombia had just prevented a mutiny, possibly even saved his life, and all he cared about was her choice of husband.

Moments passed, and slowly the fight ebbed out of Aedan. Crushing fatigue followed, pressing down onto his shoulders. "This is my fault," he ground out, shifting his gaze to the glowing embers in the hearth before him.

"You're right. I should have thought things through before I went before Colombia's father. Our timing was terrible."

"It was," Keir replied. The carpenter then heaved himself up off his stool and walked stiffly over to where a clay amphora sat against the wall. "I think we could both do with a cup of wine, lad."

Aedan nodded numbly. He needed a bucket of it.

He fell into mutinous silence then, brooding as Keir poured them generous cups. His companion returned to the fireside and handed Aedan his wine.

Raising the cup to his lips, Aedan took a large gulp. The wine was rough, made of sour plums, yet he welcomed its heat pooling in his stomach, tempering the fury that still boiled there.

"I hate them," he muttered then, his fingers clenching around the cup. "For years now, the Caesars have been my curse. Every time I find anything worth living for, they destroy it." Keir didn't reply, and eventually Aedan looked up, spearing him with his gaze across the fire. "Why don't you despise them too?"

The older man heaved a deep sigh before smiling. "I've lived among the Romans for years now. I learned my trade at Eboracum, but when I heard about the prosperous forts upon the Wall, I moved my family here." His smile turned sad then. "Maybe if I hadn't, my wife and son would still be alive ... but I don't blame the Caesars. They weren't responsible for the sickness that raged through Onnum that winter."

Keir broke off then, lifting his cup to his lips and taking a deep draft. "I had a hard upbringing, lad," he said finally. "I lost both parents and all my siblings early to illness and war. When I turned up at Eboracum, I had nothing but the ragged clothes I stood up in, yet I was allowed to make a life for myself there. I've always found safety and peace amongst these people." His gaze flicked up, meeting Aedan's once more. "And you can too if you let go of your pride ... your resentment."

Aedan snorted.

"Hate is a canker, lad," Keir said softly. "And it'll rot your life. Whether you like it or not, the Romans are here to stay. You can either work with them or against them ... the choice is yours."

XXIX. IT CAN'T END LIKE THIS

COLOMBIA LAY AWAKE in her cubiculum, staring up at the darkness.

It can't end like this.

And it wouldn't.

She'd fight her father with every bit of guile she possessed before she'd let him take Aedan from her.

Her breathing caught then, and her throat started to ache. This was her doing. She'd let her impulses rule, had pushed Aedan into an impossible situation. Her father's blood had been up after the attempted mutiny, his pride bruised. He was standing before his officers too.

It was the worst possible moment for her to tell him she was in love with a Brigante warrior and planned to marry him.

Yet she had.

The back of Colombia's eyelids stung, and she blinked rapidly.

This evening had been a wild one. Her visit to the workshop had set off a chain of events that quickly spiraled out of control.

She needed to put things right, needed to speak to her father once he'd calmed down. She told Aedan he wasn't an unreasonable man, and she believed that. If she could approach him with the same gentle hand she'd used with the mutinous soldiers, he'd listen to her.

He'd relent.

He wouldn't send her back to Asculum.

Swallowing to ease the lump that had risen in her throat, she tried not to think of that. Her father hadn't told her when he was sending her away. A couple of months earlier, he'd told her he couldn't spare the men, yet she imagined he'd manage to organize an escort for her now.

However, it would take a day or two.

She had time to change his mind.

The night stretched out, and Colombia continued to lie there, her mind churning.

Eventually, muttering a curse under her breath, she got up and reached for a heavy robe. There was no point in lying there, willing sleep to come. Not while she was in this state.

Perhaps some warm milk from the kitchens would help—it always had in the past when she'd had trouble sleeping. Morning was still a way off; she desperately needed to rest.

There was no one about now. Nonetheless, Colombia knew her way around the kitchen. The fire would be low, yet the embers would have enough heat in them to warm a small pot of milk.

Opening the door to her cubiculum, she slipped out onto the covered walkway. Moonlight bathed the courtyard beyond, and a chill breeze feathered across the portico. They were well into autumn, and Colombia reckoned a frost would settle tonight.

Shivering, she drew the folds of her robe tightly around her. Hades, the wind could be cold this far north. She wouldn't linger over her warm milk.

She padded on slippered feet down the portico, heading toward the kitchen.

Along the way, her gaze flicked toward the atrium—and she caught sight of two shadowed figures standing erect, pilums at their sides.

Colombia's step faltered, her mouth thinning.

She couldn't believe it. Her father had posted guards at the entranceway to his residence. The rest of his household might think he was merely being security conscious after the near mutiny—but Colombia believed otherwise. It was to prevent his misbehaving daughter from running off to her lover.

Her skin prickled then. Jupiter, if he was putting her under guard, he was going to be harder to convince than she'd thought.

She needed to get some sleep, for she'd require all her wits about her in the morning.

Colombia quickened her stride as she skirted the moonlit courtyard. However, halfway along it, she spied movement on the other side of the paved space.

The door to her father's quarters was opening.

Moira slipped outside.

Colombia's breathing caught, and she froze.

Even from across the courtyard, she could see the woman was scantily clad and barefoot.

Incredulity wreathed up within Colombia.

Moira is pater's bed-slave?

It didn't matter to her whom her father bedded, it really didn't. Even so, this discovery knocked her off balance. Severus Juventus had insisted no woman could replace his wife's memory, but that hadn't stopped him from tumbling his slave.

Colombia remembered then the look she'd seen the slave give Severus when she'd watched him stride out onto the parade ground at Armilustrium. There had also been a moment a few days ago, when he'd thanked Moira for something before looking up and meeting her eye. Their gazes had lingered for a fraction too long.

Of course, it had been right under her nose.

Colombia should have shifted out of sight behind one of the portico columns, to spare either of them embarrassment, yet her feet wouldn't move.

As if feeling the weight of her stare, Moira turned and looked across the atrium. An instant later, the two women's gazes met.

Colombia walked across the courtyard and lowered herself onto one of the stone seats that dotted the rectangular space. It was a cold day, and unpleasant to linger outside for long, yet she didn't move.

Instead, her gaze swept the portico, marking the guards that now flanked the atrium.

They still barred the only way in or out of the praetorium.

It seemed unusually quiet inside the fort this morning—a subdued hush had settled over the nearby barracks in the aftermath.

Clenching her jaw, Colombia glanced around, hoping to catch a glimpse of her father. It was early; he didn't usually depart the praetorium yet. However, the commander was nowhere to be seen. She'd eaten *ientaculum* alone this morning.

Colombia knotted her fingers together upon her lap, clenching hard.

I have to speak to him.

Her pulse started to race then.

What if he keeps avoiding me? He could organize her escort and send her packing, and she wouldn't have the opportunity to change his mind.

Stubbornness formed a hard kernel within her, calming the erratic beat of her heart. "You won't win this battle, *pater*," she vowed aloud. "The more you tighten your grip, the harder I'll fight."

"*Domina.*"

Glancing up, she spied Moira walking toward her across the paved space. She hadn't yet crossed paths with the slave this morning, as Claudia had served her in the triclinium.

The slave wore a woolen mantle around her shoulders and thick leggings under her tunic to ward off the cold. As always, Moira's bright hair was tied back in a braid, although strands had come free, curling around her pale face. Steam rose from the surface of the cup she carried.

"Claudia has prepared you some hot, spiced wine."

Moira halted before her and held out the cup, her expression veiled. Her reserved manner reminded Colombia of her first days here, when Moira had been wary of her. They'd developed a friendship of sorts over the past two moons, but after last night, would Moira be wary around her again?

Colombia reached out and took the cup. "Thank you."

Moira nodded before backing away. Clearly, she was eager to retreat to the kitchens.

"You needn't worry," Colombia murmured. "I'm hardly in a position to judge you ... am I?"

Moira halted, her face tensing.

"My father is strong-willed," Colombia continued. "I just hope you go to his bed willingly. I'd hate to think you'd been forced into becoming his bed-slave."

Moira swallowed. "I go willingly," she admitted softly, pausing for a few moments before continuing, "When your father first bought me from a slave market at Eboracum, I resented him. Yet with the passing of the months, I discovered who he is beneath the hard façade ... a good man, but a lonely one." She paused then, glancing away. "And I was lonely too. He does still miss your mother, *domina*. He sometimes speaks to me about her."

Colombia studied her face for a few moments before replying, "You care for him, don't you?"

"I do."

Silence fell between the two women, stretching out until Colombia cleared her throat. "You'll have heard what happened yesterday evening?"

Moira nodded. "I heard you stood up to a mob of angry men ... and prevented them from laying siege to the principia." There was awe in Moira's voice, and despite everything, Colombia's spine straightened at the memory. Yes, she'd done that.

"I did," she admitted. "Although *pater* wasn't impressed enough to give Aedan and me his blessing … you learned of what happened afterward?"

"I did," Moira paused. "It didn't come as a great surprise. I suspected there was something between you and Aedan. When I saw you together that day at the workshop … you couldn't take your eyes off each other."

Colombia winced. "Yes, well, I've never been good at hiding my feelings, or checking them … a trait that's now landed me in trouble."

Moira's gaze shadowed. "Your father is a proud man, *domina*," she said with a shake of her head. "His opinions are not easily swayed."

Colombia's mouth curved into a tight smile. "We'll see about that."

XXX. A HEAVY WEIGHT TO BEAR

TOWING A HANDCART behind him, Lucon limped through the gates of Onnum and into the vicus beyond. And as he did so, he resisted the urge to flash the guards, who stood above the trickle of farmers and merchants arriving at the fort in the grey dawn, a toothy smile.

They'd just let a wolf into the fowl coop.

He glanced then, over his shoulder at where Tuathal followed. Unlike him, the warrior kept his gaze lowered. Nonetheless, his thin face was composed into a deliberately dull-witted expression.

The pair of them hauled rickety wooden carts, piled high with cabbages and turnips. Dressed in faded, work-worn clothing and threadbare woolen cloaks, the two outlaws blended in with the other Britons trailing into the vicus.

Leaving the southern gates behind them, the men made their way down a wide, cobbled street.

And as he walked, Lucon scanned his surroundings. He'd never been inside a Roman town before and was surprised by how prosperous it was. The houses, many of them rectangular in shape and white-washed, had bright fire-red tiles. The streets were clean, and the people he passed had a well-fed look.

A smile did curve Lucon's lips then. There would be rich pickings here.

Slowing his gait, he allowed Tuathal to draw level with him—and the warriors shared a look.

"We're in," his companion grunted. "What now?"

Lucon frowned. Although he wasn't showing any signs of nerves outwardly, anxiety was clearly getting to Tuathal. They'd already discussed their plan the eve before.

"We pretend we're two simple farmers selling our wares," Lucon replied. The rumble of the cartwheels on the cobbles masked their conversation, yet he was still careful. "And make our move at nightfall."

"The market ends at noon," Tuathal reminded him. "We're going to have to find something to occupy us afterward … or we'll draw too much attention to ourselves."

"We'll spend a coin or two at a tavern." Lucon frowned then. "Just don't get too drunk … we'll need our wits about us."

Tuathal nodded, his peat-brown eyes gleaming.

Both their carts appeared laden with produce, yet it was an illusion. They had false bottoms—and within carried clay pots of pitch.

During daylight, they'd play the role of farmers selling their vegetables before lingering for a few ales. But once night fell, the two outlaws had an important job to do.

"If he sends Colombia away, I'm going after her."

Silence fell around the hearth. Aedan and Keir sat on stools, fingers wrapped around warm cups of broth. It was nearly time to start work for the day, yet neither man was in the mood this morning.

Aedan had slept fitfully, and Keir also looked tired this morning—as if he too had spent a troubled night.

Their gazes held. The carpenter then huffed a deep sigh. "Curse it, I was afraid you'd say that." He shrugged then. "I understand though. You love the lass."

Silence fell in the dwelling, while both men sipped at their broth. Eventually, Keir spoke once more. "As selfish as it sounds, I don't want you to leave. I've gotten used to having you around."

Aedan swallowed the dregs from his cup, smiling. "And I've learned much from you," he replied, his voice lowering.

Indeed, although living amongst Romans chafed him, he'd still felt at home in Onnum and enjoyed working alongside Keir. He was like a kind uncle.

"Don't get too cocky, lad," Keir grumbled. "You're still an apprentice."

Aedan grinned in response.

The carpenter surveyed him over the rim of his cup. "If Juventus intends to send her away, it'll be soon."

Aedan nodded, his expression sobering. "I know … and I'm ready."

Keir's brow furrowed then, worry clouding his eyes. Aedan could tell the man had much on his mind— although he'd already aired his thoughts the eve before.

Aedan wasn't sure he wanted to hear it all again.

"Just promise me one thing," Keir said finally, breaking the heavy silence between them.

"What?" Aedan asked warily.

"That when you catch up with Colombia … and the two of you make a new life together … let the past go. Right now, you carry it upon your back like a tortoise. It's a heavy weight to bear, lad."

Aedan stilled. Keir was right. It was. However, releasing his bitterness toward the Caesars would be easier said than done.

Exhaling sharply, Aedan nodded. "I'll do my best."

Moira groaned, arching her back with the feline grace that had attracted Severus to her from the first. She tilted her face to the ceiling then, revealing the long, milky line of her neck.

Severus watched her, in rapt fascination, as she gave herself in to the pleasure. He loved to see her topple over the edge, and to know he'd brought her there.

Moira's statuesque body gleamed with sweat from their coupling, her magnificent breasts swaying as shudders of pleasure went through her. Her bright hair, which she usually wore tied back, cascaded over her pale shoulders.

Minerva, she was a sight.

Lying on his back, breathing hard from his own climax, Severus enjoyed the torpor that always followed a good tumble. He'd let her ride him tonight, one of his favorite positions, and their coupling had been wild and passionate, even more than usual.

"Come here," he said hoarsely, reaching for his lover and gently pulling her down so she lay cradled in his arms.

Wordlessly, Moira complied. She was still breathing hard, and she splayed a hand over his chest, her fingers threading through the crisp, sweat-damp hair there.

They lay together for a while, as their pulses and breathing steadied, and Severus clung to the sense of well-being that cocooned them. For a short while, he could forget the attempted mutiny and his daughter's flagrant behavior.

Nonetheless, Colombia had shown great courage and skill in standing up to those men. He'd looked on in amazement as she soothed their tempers. In the end, they'd walked meekly out of the principia courtyard.

Severus had remained true to his word. He'd only dealt out mild punishments for the legionaries responsible for the uprising. Nonetheless, he was keeping a close eye on those men now; he wouldn't be trusting any of them again.

Severus tensed then as the reality of life beyond the walls of his cubiculum crept back in. Even Moira, with her soft, supple body, and hair that smelled of rosemary, couldn't keep his troubles at bay for long.

Stirring against him, Moira propped herself up onto an elbow, while one hand continued to trace intricate designs across his chest.

Severus watched her for a moment, huffing a soft laugh. "What are you doing, woman ... giving me tribal markings?"

She glanced up, her mouth curving. "They'd suit you ... a warrior should bear tattoos."

"I have one, remember?" Severus shifted slightly, raising his right arm to show where the letters SPQR had been etched into his skin: Senatus Populusque Romanus. Underneath the letters was a design of Capricornus—the horned goat was one of the emblems of the Second Legion.

Reaching out, Moira traced her fingertips over the marking on his upper arm. His skin prickled at her touch. Her lips quirked once more. "And I've always liked it ... however, I would also give you another." Her hand moved to the right side of his chest. "Here."

"And what marking would you choose?" he asked. Severus was enjoying this game; it drew him out of his brooding and made him forget his cares for a short while.

"A Doire Knot," she murmured without hesitation, tracing a circle upon his chest. "Interlinking oak branches ... symbolizing strength, wisdom ... and immortality."

Severus snorted. "Immortality?"

Her smile faded. "My people believe our Gods were created from the saplings grown from fallen acorns. Oak trees are sacred to us ... which makes the Doire Knot a powerful marking indeed."

Severus's own expression faded as their gazes met and held. His slave had bestowed an unexpected compliment upon him tonight, and her words caused a kernel of warmth to germinate under his ribcage.

The Britons were strange folk. Fierce and yet highly emotional, they lacked the order and discipline of his own people. His red-haired slave had always been somewhat of an enigma to him—and he realized now that he was no closer to understanding her.

"Your daughter knows about us," Moira said then, catching him by surprise.

Severus tensed, the well-being and warmth enveloping him sloughing away. He then frowned. "You told her?"

Moira shook her head, her expression shuttering. "She saw me leaving your room last night."

Their gazes held, and the anger that had spiked within Severus drew back.

Jupiter, his temper was on a short leash these days. He'd been ready to scold his slave for her flapping tongue, yet this wasn't her fault.

In truth, he'd been increasingly careless of late when it came to Moira. Marcus and Claudia would likely know he'd taken his slave to his bed—but when Colombia moved into the praetorium, he hadn't wanted her to discover the arrangement.

Colombia, who looked so much like her mother, was a painful reminder of what he'd lost. He also hadn't wanted to see the judgment in her eyes at learning he bedded his Brigante slave. Would she think he was betraying her mother's memory, or would she judge him a hypocrite after the disparaging comments he'd made about Britons? However, she'd know too that there were different rules for men and women. He was a high-ranking Roman officer, and Moira was his slave. If he wished to bed the woman, he could. He wasn't breaking any conventions by doing so.

But Colombia's desire to throw aside propriety and wed a Brigante was disgraceful.

All the same, Severus's relationship with Moira had changed of late. At first, he'd tumbled her no more than once a week—but over time, his hunger for her grew. Eventually, he'd relaxed his guard.

And now Colombia knew about it.

His chest constricted then.

He'd dealt with his daughter harshly, yet she'd brought it on herself. Colombia's behavior had been outrageous.

Had she been meeting the man in secret? Had she lain with him?

Foolish girl. How would she ever find a decent husband now?

A heavy knock on the door intruded then, and Severus tore his gaze from Moira's. "What is it?" he barked.

"Sorry to wake you, Sir," a gravelly voice, muffled by the door, filtered into the cubiculum. "But there's trouble … the vicus is on fire."

XXXI. INFERNO

AEDAN DRIFTED INTO wakefulness to the sound of shouting.

Groggily, he pushed himself up on his sleeping pallet, blinking owllike as his eyes adjusted to the darkness.

No, he hadn't dreamed it—there were raised voices coming from the street.

Rolling out of bed, Aedan pulled on his clothing and yanked on his boots before leaving the lean-to—the small sleeping area Keir had given him—and emerging into the backyard behind the workshop.

Immediately, the acrid odor of smoke caught in the back of his throat.

Pulse quickening, Aedan strode to the front of the workshop, to find the carpenter awake and standing before the doors. Keir's gaze was fixed north, upon the rooftops just outside the compound—where a red glow lit up the night sky.

An instant later, a roar rumbled across the vicus and hungry red-gold flames exploded into the heavens. A misty rain fell tonight, although it was so soft and fine it made no difference to the fire.

Aedan cursed before meeting Keir's alarmed gaze. "Come on ... let's see if we can help."

The two men took off at a run, navigating the grid of streets toward the center. However, when they reached it, Aedan realized the fire was already more extensive than he'd thought.

Several of the dwellings packed in around the market square were alight, the magistrate's residence among them, as were the houses behind the square.

The fire was spreading fast, throwing out a wall of blistering heat. But despite that an inferno roared around them, the locals had formed rows from the stone well at the heart of the square. They feverishly passed buckets along a chain, before throwing water on the hungry flames.

Aedan and Keir joined them, but even as he grabbed a wooden pail and threw its contents upon the inferno, Aedan's stomach clenched.

This wasn't enough.

The fire was spreading fast, and there was nothing anyone could do to stop it.

"How did it start?" Aedan asked a man who handed him another bucket of water. He had to shout to be heard above the roar and crackle of the flames.

"Arson!" the man yelled back. "Some shit-eating bastard threw pots of burning pitch onto the roofs."

The loud boom of a roof giving way swiftly followed. Citizens of the vicus, and the soldiers who'd joined them to help fight the fire, reeled back as a shower of golden sparks rained down on the square, setting the night ablaze.

Fatalism pressed heavy hands down on Aedan's shoulders, even as he strode back to get another bucket of water. At this rate, the blaze would consume the whole vicus, including Keir's workshop.

Finding the carpenter, he grabbed him by the shoulder, squeezing hard.

"There's no point in staying here," he shouted over the din. "These houses can't be saved … but maybe your workshop can be. Get home and douse the roof and exterior with water."

Their gazes fused for an instant before Keir's jaw tightened. With a nod, he stepped back, turned, and ran from the square.

Turning, Aedan rejoined the line to refill his bucket from the well. However, as he waited, his gaze alighted upon the walls of the compound, where a row of soldiers had gathered.

His first thought, upon hearing it was arson, was that malcontent still festered within the fort—and that one of the disgruntled legionaries had started the fire.

However, the soldiers' gazes weren't trained on the burning vicus as he'd expected, but on the high palisade beyond.

Aedan's skin prickled as his warrior instincts stirred. The arson wasn't just some vengeful act, but a diversion.

Something else was afoot.

Aedan shoved the bucket into the hands of a woman waiting next to him and raced from the square, following the squads of legionaries that marched toward the palisade.

Even amongst the chaos, Roman soldiers didn't break rank, didn't panic. Despite the recent unrest within the fort, these men were well trained. When threatened, instinct kicked in, and they knew what to do.

Dark, acrid smoke drifted through the vicus now, like black fog, with the glow of the inferno lighting up the sky behind them.

Reaching the palisade, Aedan waited while the soldiers thundered up the steps to the guard tower and the walkway that circuited the fort. The barked orders of the centurions above reached him, and his chest constricted.

Aye, it was as he'd feared.

Onnum was under attack.

A ball of flame flew over the walls then and collided with a squad of soldiers who'd been approaching behind Aedan.

Howls of agony echoed through the vicus. A legionary, flaming like a candle, staggered across the street before colliding with a nearby wall. Another fireball flew over the walls, and the neat ranks of soldiers scattered.

Backing up toward the great oak and iron gates, where men were shoving metal braces into place, Aedan glanced around him.

He had to know what they were dealing with.

Scaling the steps and dodging the elbows of soldiers who tried to shove him out of the way, Aedan made it up onto the wall.

And when he gazed down at the vallum, the high turf ramparts and the deep ditch that protected the fort, his belly swooped.

A sea of figures, their naked torsos gleaming in the torchlight, swelled in a great tide to the south. And at a glance, Aedan knew they were Brigante. The tribes north of the Wall painted themselves in blue woad to go into battle, yet these warriors, some of them heavily tattooed, were clad only in bracae, their auburn and brown hair pulled back from savage faces.

They'd placed long ladders across the vallum and were scrambling across it. And some had already reached the southern gates.

Arrows flew from longbows, and Aedan ducked as a volley clattered against the palisade.

"What are *you* doing up here, Brigante?"

Aedan swiveled to see Severus Juventus bearing down on him. The commander wore a magnificent fanned helmet and gripped a gladius in his right hand.

"Friends of yours, are they?"

"No," Aedan replied, surprised at the swiftness of his response. The warriors attacking Onnum weren't his brothers. Like Juventus, he too was trapped within these walls. "Give me a sword, and I'll help you defend this fort."

Juventus's lip curled. "Leave the wall," he snarled. "You'll only get yourself trampled on up here."

"Commander!" A soldier shouted. "To your left."

Juventus whirled, just in time, as a lithe figure vaulted over the edge of the wall and came for him.

The attackers had managed to erect one of their ladders against the palisade and were scaling it.

Alarm jolted through Aedan. They couldn't get inside the vicus—if they did, it would be carnage. He might have resented the Caesars, yet he didn't want to see Onnum destroyed.

The commander dealt with the warrior swiftly, driving his gladius through his throat as he lunged for him. However, he had no time to recover, for two more men leaped from the wall, the whites of their eyes gleaming in the firelight.

The blaze in the vicus was so bright now that it illuminated the wall in sharp relief.

Aedan glanced around him in search of a weapon. Before coming to live at Onnum, he never went anywhere without a dagger strapped to his thigh and a sword at his hip. But a carpenter's apprentice didn't need to go about armed.

A violent scuffle was going on just a few feet away, and he had nothing to defend himself with.

Severus Juventus was in the midst of it, sweat gleaming off his bare upper arms as he stabbed viciously with his gladius.

The man might be a supercilious bastard, but he could fight; Aedan would give him that.

Juventus dealt with the attacking warriors before bellowing orders to his men. The legionaries formed a line, shields interlocking, just as another hail of arrows hit the wall.

Cursing, Aedan ducked low, flattening himself against the palisade.

He needed to find himself a blade.

A few feet away, a legionary took an arrow to the throat. The soldier crumpled, choking. Aedan crawled over to him and relieved the dying man of his gladius and shield. He then unbuckled the soldier's pugio and fastened it around his own waist.

Launching himself to his feet, Aedan turned to see a tide of Brigante warriors spill over the edge of the wall.

XXXII. CLOSE THE RANKS

"THE FORT IS under attack." Marcus's announcement made Colombia's breathing catch in her throat.

The sounds of commotion on the street outside the praetorium had woken her. Dressing, she'd wrapped a palla about her before venturing out into the courtyard.

There, she'd found her father's household—Marcus, Claudia, and Moira—gathered in a huddle, their faces ghostly in the light of the braziers that lined the portico. They all wore strained expressions, their gazes shadowed.

And now Colombia knew why.

"Where's *pater?*" she asked.

"He's joined his men," Marcus replied. "The vicus is on fire, and there's a horde attacking the outer palisade."

Colombia breathed a curse at this news, her gaze cutting to the two soldiers who still guarded the entrance hall. Spines ramrod straight, plate-armor gleaming, they held pilums at the ready.

Curse it, she needed to get out of here—needed to find Aedan.

If the vicus was ablaze, he and Keir would be at risk.

But she couldn't go anywhere, not with the exit blocked by her father's men. Shouting rang across the fort then, followed by the clang of clashing blades. And then howls and screams of agony rent the air.

Colombia froze.

The sound was feral. A few feet away, Claudia let out a whimper, wrapping her arms about her thin frame to still her shaking. Moira moved close to the cook and placed a reassuring arm about her shoulders.

Colombia's heart started to pound. What was she thinking? Did she really want to go out in that?

Aedan was a warrior; he knew how to handle himself. She couldn't help him now. And if she went into the vicus, she'd get herself into trouble. Instead of thinking about escape, she needed to focus on managing her father's household and keeping everyone calm.

Marshaling her thoughts, she turned to Marcus. "They're not in the compound, are they?"

The steward's throat bobbed before he shook his head.

Spots of water wet Colombia's cheeks then. She'd noted a misty rain was falling like a gentle veil when she'd emerged into the courtyard—but as she raised her face to the sky now, fat drops started to fall.

Perhaps if Aedan had been given time to think about it, he would have refused to raise a sword against his own people.

But in the heat of the moment, as Onnum blazed and Brigante warriors crawled over the walls of the fort, intent on slaughtering every soul inside it, he made a different choice.

Onnum had been his home.

Colombia was still here too, safe for the moment behind the high walls of the compound. He wasn't going to let these warriors reach her.

The irony that he was now fighting alongside those he resented wasn't lost on him though. But it didn't bother him as much as he'd thought it would.

Wedging himself into the line of soldiers, and holding his shield aloft, Aedan braced himself against another volley of arrows. A moment later, he rushed forward, joining the legionaries as they met yet more warriors.

There were so many of them.

Aedan didn't know who'd rallied this army, but he recognized the tattoos of many of the warriors. Indeed, they were all Brigante, hailing from south of the Wall.

And as he fought, stabbing with his short, vicious sword, Aedan became aware that the misty drizzle had changed to a downpour.

Cold needles of rain pelted the wall, driving against the bodies that writhed upon it.

What with the smoke, slashing blades, and the slippery wooden planks underfoot, it was perilous up here. Unlike the Romans, who wore heavy mailed sandals that gripped well, Aedan's soft-soled boots slid as he fought.

"*Futuo!*" Someone growled behind him.

Aedan had just driven his sword through the eye of a warrior who'd tried to sink a knife into his guts, when he swiveled to find Severus Juventus glaring at him. He'd lost his fancy helmet, and rain slicked his face, plastering his short greying dark hair against his skull.

"What are *you* still doing up here?"

"Fighting," Aedan grunted, blinking water out of his eyes. "What does it look like?"

Whirling around, the commander bellowed an order up the wall. "*Ad latus stringe!*"

Close the ranks.

Within moments, they'd formed another line—and Aedan joined them—just as yet more Brigante warriors scrambled over the edge of the wall, landing like agile cats on the wet planks.

"*Parati!*" Juventus shouted. *Get ready.* "*Percute!*" *Charge.*

The ringing sound of blades clashing echoed through the night, accompanying the rumble of thunder overhead.

The rain cascaded down now, slashing across the fort like a waterfall.

Aedan fought on, focusing entirely on holding the wall. Fighting shoulder-to-shoulder with the Romans was a new experience indeed; they approached battle differently to his own people. Despite that they were the defenders, that they'd been caught off-guard tonight by this attack, they rallied swiftly. And through it all, their lines never broke.

Was it any wonder their armies had conquered the world?

At first, the tide of Brigante warriors had seemed unstoppable, yet as they fought them off, the flow of attackers ebbed.

But when a tall and lanky warrior, with a thick brown mustache and long hair scraped back and fastened at the nape of his neck, lunged onto the wall, Aedan recognized him instantly.

Maccus.

Despite that battle fever held him in its thrall, Aedan's heart started to kick against his ribs.

He'd fought alongside the outlaw leader many times during his time with the band.

Maccus was the best fighter he'd ever seen.

Despite his height, he moved with almost boneless fluidity, at one with the long iron blade he wielded. Fighting two-handed, Maccus clove a path through the soldiers who barred his path.

Blood sprayed in his wake.

And as Aedan tracked his path, he saw that Maccus's gaze was riveted upon the tall figure who strode to meet him.

Severus Juventus was going to take the outlaw leader on.

From the moment their blades locked, it was clear that the commander had met his match.

Every strike Juventus made, the outlaw countered.

The commander's lean face was twisted as he fought, his gaze narrowed and glittering.

Aedan was forced to look away then, defending himself from a swinging iron blade. Ducking under his attacker's guard, he stabbed the man in the guts, shoved him back, and pushed him over the wall.

Swiveling around once more, he noted Juventus and Maccus were still locked in combat—neither giving any ground.

Maccus feinted then before kicking out viciously, catching his opponent in the shin. And despite that greaves clad the commander's lower legs, Juventus stumbled, slipping on the slick boards beneath his feet.

Pressing his advantage, Maccus lunged.

Juventus sprawled back, hitting the walkway. He rolled aside, just in time, avoiding the outlaw's slashing sword. However, Maccus had the advantage now, and he went in for the kill.

Juventus held him off with his own blade, yet the outlaw was quickly wearing him down with vicious strikes. All it would take was a few more blows, and Maccus's sword would bite his neck.

Without stopping to think, or second-guess his decision, Aedan lunged forward, drawing the pugio from his waist.

Catching Maccus by the hair with one hand, he drove his dagger through his leather vest, between his ribs, and twisted.

Maccus grunted, whirling away from Juventus, his fist catching Aedan in the jaw.

Aedan reeled back, yanking the pugio with him.

Recognition lit in Maccus's eyes, and he bared his teeth. He lunged then, coming after him.

Aedan shifted out of range. However, his boots slid in the rain, flying out from under him. His breath gusted out of him as he sprawled on his back.

Maccus grinned, knowing he'd won, and raised his sword to finish Aedan off. But he never brought his sword down.

His expression froze before agony flickered across his lean features.

The attack had given Juventus the reprieve he needed. The commander rolled to his feet and struck hard, driving his blade under Maccus's armpit as he lifted his sword arm.

His teeth set in a rictus, Juventus pushed the blade deeper still.

Maccus's eyes glazed, and his knees sagged. He went down like a sack of barley.

Breathing hard, Aedan got to his feet. His gaze met the commander's then—and to his surprise, Juventus flashed him a grin.

An instant later, they both swiveled away to face the last of the Brigante warriors that had climbed onto the wall.

XXXIII. GO TO HIM

"YOU HANDLE A blade well, Brigante."

The gruff voice made Aedan turn. They'd just killed the last of those warriors brave enough to breach the wall. Aedan had been craning his neck, watching below. Soldiers surged through the open gates, across the drawbridge they'd lowered over the vallum, and into the smoky, rainy night—to see off the remaining Brigante.

It had been a violent battle, and a number of soldiers had fallen on the wall, but they'd successfully defended it.

Not one attacker had managed to get through into the vicus.

However, Severus Juventus wasn't focused on the surrounding devastation. His blood-spattered face was set in a grimace, as if the admission pained him.

"My name's Aedan," Aedan reminded him. "Onnum has been good to me. I wasn't going to hide with the women and children while the fort was under attack, was I?"

He was aware then that they had an audience.

Now that the wall had been cleared, and the bodies of their attackers lay strewn over the walkway, the surviving soldiers turned to watch their commander face the Briton who'd fought at their side.

Juventus stopped before him, a nerve ticking in his rain-slicked cheek. "You don't fight like a common man," he noted, his gaze roaming over Aedan's face.

"I'm a warrior," Aedan admitted. "The first-born son of Colmus, son of Bel."

The commander inclined his head. "He rules Moedin fort, does he not?"

"He did … although my brother sits in the chieftain's chair now."

Juventus's grey eyes sharpened. "And why not you?"

Aedan swallowed a sigh. Of course, conversations about his origin always led to this point. "I led my men into battle against General Aquila a few years ago," he said gruffly. "We were defeated, and Aquila took me as his slave. When he freed Fenella, he did the same for me."

The commander raised an eyebrow. "Aquila's slave, eh? After such a history … I'm surprised you'd fight at my side … or come to my aid."

Aedan's mouth quirked. "I surprised myself."

They stared at each other a moment longer before Juventus cleared his throat. "It seems I may have misjudged you. It's time I humbled myself." He then thrust out a hand. "Thank you, Aedan, son of Colmus."

Clasping arms with the commander, under the watching and no doubt incredulous gazes of his men, Aedan's smile widened. "You're welcome."

Aedan descended the walls as the rain continued to patter down. He noted the ruddy glow from the blaze in town had dimmed. The deluge had extinguished the fire, although thick black smoke now drifted over the ramparts.

Severus Juventus had already departed, his crimson cloak, tattered and dark with blood, billowing behind him. He'd left his men to clean up the mess.

Aedan would do the same.

An eerie hush settled over the palisade, broken only by the patter of the rain, and the faint cries of dying Brigante to the south.

Reaching the vicus below, Aedan walked through smoky streets. He was relieved to see the outer streets weren't charred.

The heavy rain had arrived just in time.

He passed by the workshop, hoping to see Keir there, but the carpenter was nowhere to be found, and so Aedan made his way to the market square.

Through the haze of smoke, he could see the faint glow of dawn to the east. Soon the sun would rise, and the full effect of the devastation would become clear.

The buildings that had once encircled the cobbled space were nothing more than smoking, blackened skeletons, as were the houses two streets behind it. He expected to see the folk of Onnum clustered around the ruins of their homes, yet, instead, they were all gathered before the southern gate to the compound.

The gate was open, revealing two figures swinging by their necks from the watch tower.

Keir was among the jostling sea of men and women who craned their necks to get a better look.

"What's happened here?" Aedan asked, drawing to a halt beside the carpenter.

Keir cast him a quick look, relief suffusing his face. "The Mother be praised, you're alive." He glanced back to the two men hanging a few yards distant. "We found the fire starters ... they were setting alight to a granary when soldiers caught them."

Aedan peered at the figures, and when his gaze alighted on the bloated purple face of one of them, his breathing caught.

Lucon.

He recognized the other warrior as well. He couldn't recall his name, yet he too had been part of Maccus's band.

The backs of Aedan's arms prickled.

It hadn't occurred to him earlier, even after his encounter with Maccus, that the leader of the outlaws might have led this attack. Yet it did now.

Of course, that supply convoy had yielded much—and he'd used his newfound riches to gather an army.

Aedan's brow furrowed.

Did Maccus honestly think he could take one of the Wall forts? He'd been clever, sending Lucon and his companion in to set fire to the vicus—for it had created confusion and chaos, and the distraction they needed. But the garrison at Onnum was five hundred men strong, and Severus Juventus was a skilled military commander.

Maccus had miscalculated, and it had cost him, and most of his men, their lives.

Aedan's mouth soured. *What a waste.* The stench of death hung heavily in the air, and Aedan felt no joy in knowing that the warriors he'd once lived amongst were dead.

His chest tightened then. He understood what had driven Maccus; the brutalization of his wife at Roman hands had set him upon this path.

He had every right to seek reckoning—yet, in the end, it had consumed him. It was a warning to Aedan, one that he would heed.

Colombia watched her father walk into the courtyard.

Blood-spattered—his once gleaming lorica smeared with ash and gore, his fine red cloak tattered—Severus Juventus limped slightly.

Nonetheless, he still managed to carry himself proudly.

Moira stifled a gasp at the sight of him, while Colombia stepped forward. The rain had eased, yet the air stank of smoke. "*Pater*," she said softly. "Are you hurt?"

Her father stopped in front of her before shaking his head.

"But your leg?" Colombia glanced down at the blood that slicked his left knee.

"A shallow cut."

"Shall I call for a medic?"

"No need ... Moira can deal with it."

Colombia nodded. Her gaze then searched her father's face. He wore an odd expression—severe yet wary. "What happened out there?"

"A large warband of Brigante laid siege to our walls," he replied. "But not before two of them ... who were already inside the fort, set fire to the vicus."

Colombia swallowed. "They're defeated?"

"Yes."

Silence swelled between father and daughter then, and awkwardness rose within Colombia.

Curse it, after her father had made her a prisoner inside the praetorium and informed her he was sending her back to Italia, she'd told herself she hated him—but that was all nonsense. She'd spent the long night pacing the portico around the courtyard, listening to the blood-curdling sounds of battle, and imagining the worst.

The truth was, despite his stubbornness, and his hypocrisy, she adored her father. She had no siblings, and her mother was dead. Apart from an uncle and aunt who'd never liked her, he was all she had in the world.

"I'm glad to see you safe, *pater*," she murmured, dipping her head. "I shall leave Moira to tend your leg."

She turned away, yet he forestalled her. "Colombia ... wait."

Raising her gaze, she found him watching her. "What is it?"

The commander glanced at Moira, his mouth lifting at the corners. "Fetch your healing basket and some clean bandages, and I shall see you in my quarters shortly."

Moira nodded, her gaze flicking between them. "Yes, *dominus*." She then walked off.

Alone in the courtyard, as a pale dawn crept over the fort, father and daughter eyed each other cautiously.

"Moira tells me you know about us?" he said after a pause.

Tension coiled within Colombia. She was surprised he'd bring that up, especially now. Warily, she nodded. "I thought you had no time for the people of this land?" She couldn't help it; resentment welled up within her. "But I suppose you made an exception for your pretty Brigante slave."

A nerve jumped in his cheek. "Colombia ... I—"

"Yes, I know" —she cut him off with a wave of her hand— "You're a man ... and men have needs."

Severus raked a hand through his damp hair before murmuring an oath under his breath. "I don't admit when I'm wrong easily," he ground out, "but I must do so now."

Colombia stilled. What was this? Was her proud father about to deliver an apology?

"Too long have I held ... inflexible views," he continued. "Yet no longer. People can indeed surprise you."

Colombia took a step forward. His words confused her. "*Pater* ... what happened?"

"Your man fought alongside us upon the walls."

Colombia's brow furrowed. *Your man?*

For a moment, she wondered whom he was referring to before realization dawned. "Aedan? He fought with you?"

Her father's mouth quirked. "He saved my life."

Colombia's breathing hitched. "He did?" She paused then. "Is he hurt?"

Severus shook his head. "He's tough ... as are you, daughter. I must admit the pair of you are well suited."

Colombia stared at him, her lips parting.

"I haven't thanked you properly for what you did the other evening." His voice lowered. "Your mother would have been proud ... as am I."

Colombia swallowed. "Thank you," she whispered. "That means a lot to me."

Her father cocked a dark eyebrow. "I know you think me harsh ... but I'm not completely heartless. I can see you and Aedan are devoted to each other."

"We are," she whispered.

Her father's features softened further, and then he gestured toward the atrium. There were no guards there now; the exit was clear. "If Aedan is whom you want, I'll no longer bar your way ... go to him."

XXXIV. IN THIS LIFE AND BEYOND

COLOMBIA MADE HER way out of the compound, glancing up at the grisly spectacle as she passed under the gate into the vicus.

Her father had warned her the two Brigantes who'd set fire to the fort had been strung up there.

Nonetheless, the sight of the two bodies, swinging above her, made bile sting the back of her throat.

She was no stranger to violence and death—not anymore—yet it sickened her. She never wanted to witness it again.

Hurrying on, she cut across the soot-covered square.

Now her father had given her leave to go, she couldn't reach Aedan fast enough. Even so, it was impossible not to stare at the devastation the blaze had left in its wake. The buildings lining the square, including the magistrate's residence, were nothing but blackened, smoking shells. Ash fluttered down over the vicus like snow.

The acrid tang of burning caught in the back of her throat, and she coughed.

Gods, she hoped Keir's workshop had been spared.

She quickened her step, circling past the crowd of citizens who now camped out in the heart of the market square, and headed to the street that would take her to Aedan.

However, up ahead, she spied a familiar figure.

A tall man with wavy light-auburn hair walked toward her.

Like her father, Aedan was blood spattered. Yet he walked with a warrior's loose-limbed stride.

Colombia's heart leaped, and she broke into a run. "Aedan!"

He saw her then, his sea-blue eyes widening. He halted and opened his arms, letting her fly into them.

She clung to him as he swung her around. Her arms linked around his neck, and she turned her face up to his, even as her vision swam with tears.

"Colombia," he gasped. "What are you doing out here?"

She hiccoughed a laugh. "*Pater* has given us his blessing. He told me to go to you."

His breathing hitched. "He did?"

Colombia smiled up at him, even as tears trickled down her cheeks. "We can be together now. No one will try to stop us."

Aedan stared down at her, swallowing hard.

An instant later, he bent his head and claimed her mouth in a bruising kiss that stole her breath away.

Colombia arched into him, not caring that he was filthy and covered in blood and gore, not caring that they would be drawing stares from those around them.

All that mattered was that she was in Aedan's arms. She was home.

When they eventually drew apart, both panting, Aedan's eyes glittered. "Colombia," he breathed. "My heart is yours, little dove."

Reaching up, she cupped his cheek. "And mine is yours, Aedan," she replied huskily. "My brave warrior."

Watching as the druid held out his hand, a smooth stone upon his palm, Colombia's pulse fluttered.

This was happening.

She and Aedan were getting married.

It wasn't the ceremony she'd always envisaged though—one where she'd wear a white dress, holding hands with her husband-to-be in a temple, before a priest. Instead, she and Aedan stood outdoors, a few miles south of the fort—at the edge of an ancient oakwood, on the banks of a burn. The day was clear and bright, yet cold. Even so, they were both barefoot, as was the druid.

Instead of the traditional white Roman wedding dress, she wore a simple pale-yellow tunic, trimmed with gold. And around her neck, she wore a gleaming bronze torc—a gift from Keir for their wedding. It had belonged to his wife. Aedan wore bracae made of soft leather and a cream-colored tunic. His light-auburn hair fell in waves around his face.

He'd never looked so handsome, and she'd never felt so proud.

Wordlessly, Colombia and Aedan placed their hands upon the 'oathing stone', hers under his.

The elderly druid named Ultan—clad in black robes, his face tattooed in blue swirls—finished tying their hands together. His intense gaze swept over their faces then, and he murmured a few words.

Before the ceremony, Aedan had told her the druid would speak a blessing—and that they would repeat the words of their vows after him.

Colombia did her best, although she was sure she stumbled through the vows.

Even so, Aedan had explained to her what the words meant.

You are blood of my blood, bone of my bone. I give you my body, that we might be one.

The vows were beautiful, and Colombia's skin prickled as she listened to Aedan reciting his. Ultan murmured something then, and Aedan removed his hand from the stone, nodding to Colombia to do the same.

Aedan produced a ring. It was silver and decorated with knots, like the interlinking roots of the great oaks they stood under.

Smiling, he slid it onto the ring finger of her left hand. "I swear to love you, Colombia," he said huskily, switching to Latin. "Completely and without restraint, in sickness and in health, in plenty and in poverty. In this life and beyond."

Colombia swallowed to ease the tightness in her throat. "And I swear the same to you, my love."

The druid cleared his throat then and said a few more words.

"He's calling on the Gods to bless us," Aedan translated. "The Mother, The Maiden, The Warrior, and The Crone … may our lives together be long, and may you bear me many sons." He winked at her then. "I'll settle for daughters too though."

Colombia smiled—of course he would.

Five days had passed since the attack on the fort. Aedan had wanted to wed immediately, but with Onnum's vicus half-destroyed, and the outer perimeter in need of repairs, they'd waited.

Keir had gone off to find them a druid—a search that wasn't easy these days, for the mystics preferred to dwell far from the Wall.

However, the carpenter's search had been successful; Ultan had been willing to conduct the ceremony between Briton and Roman.

"Is it done then?" she asked, glancing at the druid's gaunt face. The man was watching them intently.

"Yes," Aedan replied. "Except for one thing." Taking her hands in his, he stepped close and lowered his head, kissing her.

Colombia's eyes fluttered closed, and she leaned into the embrace, forgetting where they were, or that they had an audience. The kiss drew out before a cough intruded, breaking the spell.

Pulling back, her cheeks warming, Colombia glanced over at the small group who'd witnessed the ceremony.

Apart from Ultan, there were two others present here on the edge of the oakwood: Keir and Severus Juventus.

Colombia's gaze met her father's, warmth suffusing her chest. When she'd approached him to ask if he'd attend her wedding, she'd braced herself for his refusal.

But to her surprise, he hadn't.

Next to him, Keir was grinning widely. "Time to get back to the fort and break open a barrel of ale," he announced in Latin. "A wedding deserves celebration."

Colombia smiled back. Over the past days, she'd learned that Keir had suffered much tragedy. Nonetheless, the man was still able to find joy in life. She noted how fond he was of Aedan, and how relieved he was that they'd agreed to stay on in Onnum.

Aedan was extending the lean-to, to provide a bigger space for them to live in, and he would continue to work as the carpenter's apprentice. One day, Aedan hoped to run his own workshop, yet for the time being, he wished to improve his craft at Keir's side.

"A day such as this does indeed need to be marked," Severus announced then. "And that being the case, I've asked my cook to prepare a special supper." His gaze shifted from Colombia to Aedan. "After you've enjoyed a cup of ale, will you join me ... and Moira ... in the praetorium?" He glanced then at Keir. "*All* of you."

A shocked silence followed the invitation.

In the days following the attack on the fort, Colombia had seen little of her father.

He'd been busy, of course, taken up with overseeing repairs on the defenses. And just two days before, a pay wagon had arrived from Eboracum—nearly a month earlier than anticipated and welcome indeed. As soon as the sacks of coin had been deposited in the strongroom, Severus had paid his men.

Their successful defense of Onnum, and the arrival of their wages, had sweetened the soldiers' moods considerably. There were no longer any rumblings of discontent within the fort.

But Colombia had also been nervous about approaching her father—and didn't want to ask too much of him.

Yet, here he was, inviting them into his home.

He was also acknowledging Moira. Her father did indeed care for the woman he'd taken to his bed.

"We would be honored, Commander," Aedan spoke up then, breaking the silence. Glancing his way, Colombia noted his smile and the warmth in his blue eyes. The tension that had been building in her chest unraveled.

Severus held Aedan's gaze for a moment before his lips lifted at the corners. "Good," he murmured.

They walked back to the fort over rolling hills. The sky was still clear, although the shadows were lengthening now. They were marching ever closer to the shortest day and longest night of the year, and the breeze that stirred their hair and snagged at their clothing had a sharp bite to it.

A group of soldiers waited for the wedding party a few furlongs from the oakwood and escorted them back to Onnum.

The attack had made the commander wary—and he hadn't wanted his daughter venturing beyond the walls this afternoon without protection.

Severus stalked ahead, while Keir and Ultan followed. Colombia and Aedan brought up the rear of the small group.

Walking hand in hand with her husband, Colombia didn't mind the cold or the damp grass underfoot. Instead, happiness swelled inside her, the sensation so strong that it made her chest ache.

"I never thought to see your father attend our wedding," Aedan admitted then.

"Me neither," Colombia's gaze shifted forward to the tall figure in the distance. As always, a fine scarlet cloak rippled behind Severus. He'd donned his crested helmet and full lorica for the ceremony too. "I never thought he'd fall for his slave either … but my father is full of surprises."

"He's not bad," Aedan admitted then, "for a Roman."

Colombia cut her husband a sidelong glance, to see he wore a teasing smile. She'd once believed he'd never let go of his resentment toward her people, yet she'd noticed a change in him over the past couple of days—a softening. He appeared happy to make a life with her at the fort, although she would have departed with him if he'd asked.

A gust of cold wind buffeted them, and Colombia shivered, moving in close to Aedan. He put his arm around her shoulders, drawing her against him as they crested another hill.

"Jupiter," she murmured. "The wind this far north has teeth."

He huffed a laugh. "It does … but just wait … it gets much colder than this."

Colombia muttered an oath, and Aedan gave her shoulder a gentle squeeze. Then, after a moment, he asked, "Do you miss Italia?"

Colombia glanced up at him to see his expression was serious now.

"No," she said after considering his question. "I don't."

"Why not?"

"Asculum offered me a comfortable life," she replied, favoring him with a smile. "But I never fitted in there. I was always too outspoken, too independent. My aunt and uncle were happy to be rid of me, I think." She paused then, her smile widening. "The ways of your people suit me better … the strength of your women is celebrated. Moira tells me that she can wield a sword and fight like a man … for a Roman woman to learn such a skill is rare."

Her voice must have sounded wistful, for Aedan made a sound at the back of his throat and gave her shoulder another squeeze. "Well, that can be remedied. I can show you how to handle yourself with a blade, if you like?"

Colombia cut him a sharp look, sure he was teasing her. However, his gaze was steady, and there was no trace of humor upon his face. "You're in earnest?"

"I am."

A smile flowered across her face. "When can we begin our training?"

"In the evenings, after I finish up in the workshop ... and before we sit down to supper." He paused then. "A woman should be able to defend herself."

Colombia couldn't have agreed more.

"I also need to master your tongue," she said then. "Moira taught me a few phrases, but I feel like a halfwit whenever I try to speak it."

His mouth curved. "And I'll be happy to teach you that too," he assured her, his blue eyes crinkling at the corners. "I've already discovered you're a quick study."

The intimacy of his tone made warmth rise to her cheeks.

She knew what he was referring to.

They'd spent every night together over the past days, but both had gotten little sleep. Instead, they stayed up late exploring each other's bodies. Aedan had taught her how to give and receive pleasure, and Colombia was greedy to learn more. He was a wickedly sensual lover— and whenever Colombia thought of the things he'd whispered in her ear as he'd taken her, her body flushed hot.

As it did now.

"You're blushing," he observed, his smile widening.

Colombia gave a snort, an answering smile tugging at her lips. "If I am, it's your fault."

EPILOGUE. NO REGRETS

Two and a half years later ...

AEDAN WAS WALKING toward Onnum, towing an empty handcart behind him, when the ground started to tremble. He'd just delivered a row of shelving to a Roman farmer whose villa lay outside the fort, and had taken Dere Street home.

Turning, he caught sight of a plume of dust rising to the west. And as he looked on, pilums and standards appeared, bristling against the pale-blue summer's sky. The outlines of riders at the front of the column appeared then, followed by neat ranks of soldiers marching in rows behind.

The sight of newcomers didn't surprise Aedan. A month earlier, the Wall just outside Onnum had been damaged after a Caledonii raid. Repairs were taking longer than expected, and Commander Juventus had no doubt contacted one of the surrounding forts for assistance.

Moving off the road, Aedan watched the column approach.

A tall man, silver lorica and helmet gleaming in the noon sun, rode at the head of the column upon a spirited black horse.

And as the rider drew closer, Aedan stiffened, recognition dawning.

He knew that face.

It had been nearly four years since he'd last seen Justinian Aquila. However, the man hadn't changed much.

Standing by the side of the road, Aedan set his cart down and waited for him to pass by. He wondered if Aquila, who commanded Vindolanda, would glance his way. And even if he did, he'd likely not even recognize him.

When Aedan had served him, his hair had been cropped short in the Roman fashion. Yet now it was shaggy and bleached by the sun.

The ground shook, the rattle of armor and creak of leather drifting toward him.

The first riders were almost past Aedan when a deep voice rumbled across the road. "Aedan?"

Aquila raised his hand, bringing the column to a rattling standstill behind him. He then drew his horse to a halt. The beast tossed its head, pawing the ground impatiently, yet the commander held it easily in check.

Aedan also recognized the man riding next to Aquila—Marcus Camillus, his second-in-command.

Marcus grinned at him, and Aedan found himself stepping forward, a wide smile splitting his face. He'd always liked Marcus.

He shifted his gaze back to Aquila. The man's distinctive golden gaze was just as intense as he remembered. Aedan's mouth quirked once more. "Good day, Aquila … Camillus."

Aedan and Aquila locked gazes then, for a few moments, before the commander spoke once more. "It's good to see you."

"And you."

Aquila studied him. "Do you live at Onnum?"

"I have for nearly three years now."

"I thought you would have returned to your kin?"

"I tried that … but then discovered there are some rivers you can't cross twice. There was no place for me there."

Aquila's gaze shadowed before he nodded.

"I have no regrets now though," Aedan assured him. "I have a good life in Onnum and a trade. I'm a carpenter and run my own workshop ... two streets back from the southern gates."

A smile warmed Aquila's face. "And have you found yourself a wife?"

"I have ... I'm wed to a Roman woman."

The commander's head cocked at this admission. His smile then widened. "You've found your place in the world then?"

Aedan nodded.

"I'm glad."

Their gazes held for a long moment, a silent understanding passing between them. They'd once been enemies, and then slave and master, before Aquila granted him his freedom. But now, years later, they were just two men, and in another life, they could have been friends.

"How fares Fenella?" Aedan's gaze flicked to Marcus then, remembering that the centurion had wed a woman who'd also been Justin Aquila's slave. "And Kahina?"

"They're both well," Aquila replied. "We have a son ... Leo."

"Kahina has just given birth to our second daughter," Marcus added, pride lacing his voice.

Aedan smiled once more at this news. Fenella and Kahina had been good to him, and he'd shared a kinship of sorts with them both.

"I shall bring Fenella with me on my next visit to Onnum," Aquila said then, white teeth flashing against the deep tan of his face. "She will want to see you again too."

"And I will welcome you both," Aedan assured him, "although our home is a humble one."

Aquila snorted, making it clear he cared little about such things. He then nodded to Aedan. "Until the next time we meet then."

The column lurched forward once more, and Aedan watched it go. The company from Vindolanda marched toward the walls of Onnum, crossing the vallum to the haunting cry of a horn.

Once the dust had settled, Aedan picked up his cart and followed them into the fort.

Aquila would be heading to the compound, to meet with Juventus and discuss the repair work on the Wall. However, Aedan didn't travel in the same direction; instead, he cut through the backstreets toward his workshop.

And these days, it did belong to him.

Keir had died six months earlier. The carpenter passed away in his sleep; Colombia had found him the following morning when he didn't join them at dawn for bread and broth as he usually did.

His end had been peaceful, yet they'd both grieved him deeply. Taking ownership of the workshop had been bittersweet, and it had felt empty ever since. Aedan missed chatting with Keir as he worked, and the light-hearted banter between them. The three of them had been a family. Colombia had wept for days after they'd buried him.

Aedan and Colombia had eventually moved from the lean-to into the dwelling that had once belonged to Keir. Six months on, it was starting to feel like their home.

Nonetheless, whenever Aedan approached the workshop, he half-expected to see Keir bent over his workbench, sawing, sanding, or hammering.

Instead, today, a woman stood in the doorway. Across her front, she carried a baby in a sling.

Their daughter, Julia, was nearly four months old now. She had his auburn hair and her mother's smoke-grey eyes.

Colombia watched him approach. Like his, her hair had lightened over the hot summer. She'd pulled the front of it back from her face, but the rest of her tawny mane flowed down her back. Aedan liked her hair loose, and the simple blue tunic girded at the waist also suited her.

His wife's beauty shone like newly polished amber in the noon sun. She needed no adornment.

"I just crossed paths with Justinian Aquila," he greeted her. "I didn't think he'd recognize me, but he did."

Colombia grinned. "Was he pleased to see you?"

"I think so." Aedan lowered his cart to the ground and crossed to her, bending to bestow a kiss upon Colombia's soft lips. At the same time, he stroked the downy red-brown hair on his daughter's crown. "And it was good to see him again too." He smiled as he straightened up and met his wife's eye. "He was surprised to find me here."

Colombia inclined her head. "Where did he think you'd be?"

"He likely imagined I'd be in Moedin, sitting in my father's chair, ordering slaves about, and drinking mead with my warriors."

Their gazes held for a moment before Colombia's expression sobered. "I know you love me and Julia," she murmured, "but do you sometimes wish that had been your fate?"

"No," Aedan replied without a moment's hesitation. He lifted his hand then, stroking Colombia's smooth cheek. "Not for an instant. I told Aquila, and I shall you too. I have no regrets about the road the Gods laid out before me ... for it brought it for you."

And he meant it. Before he met Colombia Juventus, he'd been lost, searching for meaning and purpose. He'd been full of bitterness too—but that man seemed to belong to another life. He walked lighter, and taller, these days. The sight of a Roman pilum piercing the sky, the flutter of a crimson cloak in the wind, didn't make his gut clench as it once had. Instead, those were familiar and welcome sights.

Colombia's lovely face broke into a smile. "I have no regrets either," she assured him. "I'm so happy, Aedan. Sometimes I wish I could stop time. Just you, me, and Julia ... like this forever."

Their life was simple, yet full of joy. He worked hard, but his wife and daughter were with him for most of the day. As he toiled in the workshop, he'd smell the delicious aromas of the noon meal or supper wafting through. Colombia would often come through to sweep the sawdust from the workshop floor, and he'd take the opportunity to catch her by the waist and steal a kiss.

Aye, it wasn't the life he thought he'd have, but he didn't envy his brother any longer. He hadn't for years now. If Aedan were any happier, his heart would burst.

"I know what you mean," he said softly. "If only we could."

⤿⤾

The End

FROM THE AUTHOR

When I embarked on TAMING THE EAGLE (the first book in this duology), it was meant to be a standalone.

However, readers thought otherwise!

Justin and Fenella's story was so popular, and I had so many requests for a sequel, that I decided to tell Aedan's story as well.

Ancient World Romance will always have a special place in my heart, and so it's never a chore to return to 2nd century AD, and to immerse myself in the culture clash between the Romans and the people they ruled.

Aedan starts off embittered by the hand life has dealt him. He's restless, searching for a purpose. Meeting Colombia gives his life the meaning he was looking for. Likewise, Colombia begins the story a little lost. She's a determined woman, yet all her energy is going in the wrong direction as she chases after a man who doesn't want her.

Fortunately, that chase leads her straight into Aedan's arms! The phrase 'love conquers all' was made for these two. I hope you enjoyed their story!

Jayne x

HISTORICAL NOTES

As with TAMING THE EAGLE, I did a lot of research for ENSNARING THE DOVE.

To make things a little easier to reference, I've provided a glossary (in the next section), which covers some of the terms you encountered during the novel. However, in this section, I wanted to do some historical 'scene setting' for you.

Like Book One in this duology, ENSNARING THE DOVE contains slavery—something that was commonplace in the 2nd Century. Both the Picts and the Romans had slaves, and how they were treated depended on the owner. Although the idea of owning a slave seems alien and repellent to us now, it was part of life in ancient times. That doesn't mean that slaves were happy with their lot, or that some didn't try to escape the bonds of servitude. The title 'domina' (feminine) or 'dominus' (masculine) was used by slaves when addressing their mistresses or masters.

While posted on the frontier, many Roman soldiers took Briton lovers—and some of them got married. Roman soldiers weren't technically permitted to marry during their service to the empire, but far from Rome, things were a little lax! I'm not sure how many Briton men took Roman women as lovers, and wives—likely not many. In some cases, Roman women were taken as spoils of war. However, since I wrote about that in BARBARIAN SLAVE, I wanted a different kind of story for ENSNARING THE DOVE.

It was fascinating writing about a Roman heroine off the back of a feisty Pict woman (Fenella). The two cultures treated women differently, and despite that our heroine, Colombia, is a noblewoman, I wanted to depict her role with realism. Even high-born Roman women didn't have voting rights, nor could they become politicians. Their fathers and husbands had absolute dominion over them. As in most ancient cultures, Roman women were valued more as wives and mothers—and unlike some Pict or Briton women, they never fought alongside the men.

As a side note, I also mention Roman wedding dresses. Our modern tradition of the bride wearing white comes from Victorian times, but Roman brides also wore white. It was usually a simple dress with a white sash tied in a knot around her waist, usually fastened by the bride's mother. The groom would then unknot the sash on their wedding night.

Most of our tale centers around the Roman fort of Onnum on Hadrian's Wall. Onnum (also known as Hunnum), or Halton Chesters today, was a real location. The fort was originally 4.37 acres in size, later to be extended in the 3rd century AD to 4.87 acres, making it the only L-shaped fort on the wall. This was probably done to accommodate the cavalry unit. The original garrison was likely a mixed infantry and cavalry unit.

The fifth fort along the wall, Onnum guarded Dere Street, and crosses Hadrian's Wall through the valley immediately to the west of it. The original fort was built between 122 AD and 126 AD. It was oblong-shaped with four main gates, with double portals and guard chambers. Onnum would have been an impressive fort. There were towers at each corner, and also on either side of the main gates.

Like all Roman forts, Onnum was intersected by two streets: Via Praetoria and Via Principalis. At the point where these streets crossed sat the commander's residence (the praetorium) and the headquarters (the principia). The fort would have had barracks, storehouses, granaries, and a hospital. A civilian settlement, a vicus, existed outside the walls.

In this story, I write about a mutiny at the fort. Indeed, these were commonplace throughout the Roman empire—especially in the later years. Outposts like Hadrian's Wall were difficult to command at times, and if there was a delay in the arrival of pay wagons, the troops became restless. As I mention in the book, most of the legionaries weren't Italian. Instead, they were from the empire's many colonies, and signing up to the Roman army wasn't about furthering the glory of Rome, but getting a regular wage. As such, it didn't take much for resentment to take root and grow.

Hadrian's Wall itself is one of history's most impressive engineering works. Emperor Hadrian began work on his wall in 122 AD, completing it in 128 AD. Today, the wall stretches 73 miles (117.5 kilometers) across northern England.

Our hero is one of the Brigante—a tribe of Ancient Britons who, in pre-Roman times, controlled the largest section of what would become Northern England. Their territory, often referred to as Brigantia, was centered in what was later known as Yorkshire. The fort Aedan hails from, 'Moedin' (later called Maiden Castle), was an actual iron-age fort located above the River Wear near what is now Durham.

Although there are no written records of the Brigantes before the Roman conquest of Britain, there was some mention of them during the occupation. The Brigantian queen, Cartimandua, was a Roman ally, although there appears to have been a rebellion in the north sometime in the early reign of Hadrian. Details are unclear—which allowed me to take some creative license and imagine that perhaps Maccus and his men were behind it!

I hope you found my notes helpful and insightful. I write Historical Romance, but I adore history and like my novels to be rich in detail. I want to truly take you back to another time and place!

GLOSSARY

Pict and Latin words (alphabetical order)
atrium: entrance hall
carpentum: a four-wheel car (on four pilentum), used by wealthy Romans.
Caesars: the Ancient Romans
Caledonia: the Roman name for what is today Scotland
caenum!: filth
cena: midday meal (Latin)
Cruthini: the name the Picts gave themselves
cubiculum: bedroom
Futuo!: Fuck! (Latin – vulgar)
Futue te ipsum! Go fuck yourself! (Latin – vulgar)
ientaculum: breakfast (Latin)
Latrunculi: Roman chess
lorica: plate armor worn by Roman soldiers
malum: jerk (Latin – vulgar)
mentula: dick (Latin – vulgar)
Picti: the name the Romans gave the Picts (literally: 'the painted ones')
praetorium: fort commander's residence
primus pilus: the senior centurion of the first cohort in a Roman legion
principia: fort headquarters
Saturnalia: Roman mid-winter festival
stulte: fool (Latin)
stultissime: a complete idiot (Latin)
tablinum: living room
vesperna: supper (Latin)
vicus: a civilian village outside a Roman fort

Place names (in alphabetical order)
Asculum: a town in northeastern Italia, today called Ascoli Piceno
Brigantia: the name for the Brigante territory
Coria: Corbridge (a Roman fort 2 ½ miles south of Hadrian's Wall)

Dere Street: a Roman road that traveled north from Eboracum, traveling to Onnum on Hadrian's Wall and then up into Caledonia.
Eboracum: York
Onnum: Halton Chesters
Londinium: London
Moedin: the ancient name for 'Maiden' an iron age fort near present-day Durham.
Rhaetia: a province of the Roman empire, present-day Austria
The River Tin: The River Tyne

Briton Gods and Goddesses*
The Mother: Goddess of enlightenment and feminine energy—the bringer of change
The Warrior: God of battle, life, and growth, of summer
The Maiden: Young Goddess of nature and fertility
The Hag: Goddess of the dark—sleep, dreams, death, winter, and the earth
The Reaper: God of death

Briton festivities*
Earth Fire: Salute to new life and the first signs of spring (February 1)
Bealtunn: Spring Equinox
Mid-Summer Fire: Summer Equinox
Harvest Fire: Festival to salute the harvest (Aug 1)
Gateway: Passage from summer to winter (October 31/November 1)
Mid-Winter Fire: Winter Equinox

* Author's note: I have taken 'artistic license' when it comes to the names of Briton festivities, and gods and goddesses. The historical evidence is very scant, making it a challenge for me to get an accurate picture of gods and festivities in 2nd Century Britain. The Brigante were an enigmatic people, and we only have their ruins and symbols to cast light on how they lived and whom they worshipped. To make my setting as authentic as possible, I have studied the rituals and religions of the

ancient peoples of Scotland, Ireland, and Wales of a similar period and have created a culture I feel could have existed.

ABOUT THE AUTHOR

Multi-award-winning author Jayne Castel writes epic Historical and Fantasy Romance. Her vibrant characters, richly researched historical settings, and action-packed adventure romance transport readers to forgotten times and imaginary worlds.

Jayne is the author of a number of best-selling series. In love with all things Scottish, she writes romances set in both Dark Ages and Medieval Scotland.

When she's not writing, Jayne is reading (and re-reading) her favorite authors, cooking Italian feasts, and going on long walks with her husband. She lives in New Zealand's beautiful South Island.

Connect with Jayne online:
www.jaynecastel.com
www.facebook.com/JayneCastelRomance
https://www.instagram.com/jaynecastelauthor/
Email: contact@jaynecastel.com

www.ingramcontent.com/pod-product-compliance
Lightning Source LLC
Chambersburg PA
CBHW051141190726
48290CB00006B/1937